D0873459

Praise for Cooper Davis
Taking You Home

"...a well written and deeply romantic novel."

~ *Well Read*

"Cooper Davis writes with such tenderness and emotion that I couldn't put it down."

~ *The Long and Short of It*

"This book is all about love, commitment, family...and above all being true to yourself. I thought that Cooper Davis had written a terrific story when she penned *Boys of Summer*, but *Taking You Home* is the first book on my Top 10 Books for 2011, it's that great."

~ *Reviews by Jessewave*

"There are many great scenes in this story...and some wonderful secondary characters, all of which help make this a wonderful story and will bring the author many new fans."

~ *Literary Nymph Reviews*

"*Taking You Home* is heavy on the sweet but it has some spice too."

~ *Well Read*

Look for these titles by
Cooper Davis

Now Available:

Boys of Summer
Taking You Home

Forces of Nature
Bound by Nature

Taking You Home

Cooper Davis

SAMHAIN
PUBLISHING

Samhain Publishing, Ltd.
11821 Mason Montgomery Road, 4B
Cincinnati, OH 45249
www.samhainpublishing.com

Taking You Home
Copyright © 2011 by Cooper Davis
Print ISBN: 978-1-60928-343-8
Digital ISBN: 978-1-60928-321-6

Editing by Tera Kleinfelter
Cover by Natalie Winters

This book is a work of fiction. The names, characters, places, and incidents are products of the writer's imagination or have been used fictitiously and are not to be construed as real. Any resemblance to persons, living or dead, actual events, locale or organizations is entirely coincidental.

All Rights Are Reserved. No part of this book may be used or reproduced in any manner whatsoever without written permission, except in the case of brief quotations embodied in critical articles and reviews.

First Samhain Publishing, Ltd. electronic publication: January 2011
First Samhain Publishing, Ltd. print publication: December 2011

Dedication

To Tera Kleinfelter, for all you've done to support me. You are a real gift in my life.

Prologue

This is a wedding story. Well, it's my wedding story at least, which definitely takes a different parade route than what's on TLC every weekday. No, my fairy tale is more like that show on serious drugs, with maybe a little dash of Trading Spaces thrown in for good measure. Except instead of Paige perfectly rearranging Max's apartment, you'd have Max perfectly rearranging my life.

Even better—I can see our best friends, Veronica and Louisa, taking over the show for our episode. Those two could definitely do a damned good job of the transformation showcase. I can hear it now:

Meet Hunter Willis. Until Max, he was floundering on that last outpost of his heterosexuality. Floundering, sputtering and gasping for air. Wait! That was after he met Max. Beforehand he was doing a pretty good imitation of a mid-western jock with a Harley, riding that manly bike to his construction job every day, where he might even throw back a few beers with the boys. And in the evenings, Hunter had a penchant for hockey and baseball, in that particular order.

Yes, sir, Hunter's Guy Town passport was stamped and in universally good working order.

Now, thanks to our guidance and expertise, Hunter has been completely transformed. Not only do he and Max enjoy riding the Harley together on weekends, they share a cozy bed seven nights a week. They've definitely swung all the way out of their closet, thank you very much.

And you should see the rings!

But then I step in, karate-chopping my hands together and shouting. "Wait! Cut!"

It's enough that this is my life, although I wouldn't exchange a moment of the past year. No trading places through the time space continuum or anything. I've got Max and that's all I want, honest.

Well, that and the next sixty or so minutes of my life, I think, as I gaze out the windowpane at the flower-draped gazebo in the garden below. Our friends have already filled the seats and music floats upward, something classical and romantic.

I could even swear that some kind of pinkish petals shower down from the trees in the orchard. Cherry blossoms? Can't possibly be.

And if I squint my eyes just so, the scene actually melts to slow motion Technicolor, all hazy, like something from my daydreams.

Especially because I just got my first look at Maxwell all day, and I'm not sure my heart can stand the damage that Armani tux is going to do.

Yeah, this is a wedding story all right.

Mine and Maxwell's...and you're cordially invited to attend, too.

Chapter One

It can't always be this hot in Winchester. I mean, not if people actually live in this sleepy outpost of a town. We live in Los Angeles, for God's sake. I thought Virginia would be temperate and pleasant by comparison.

I fumble with the air conditioning vents, directing one on to Maxwell, especially when I see the thin sheen of perspiration that has formed on his forehead and upper lip.

"Hot as hell here," I grumble, but really, I'm just worried about him.

"Always has been this time of year."

He turns to stare out the window, at the mountains and rolling highway. I've manned the steering wheel ever since leaving Dulles Airport, just trying to get him to relax, but so far I can't say it's done much good. He keeps fiddling with the CDs, so silent I have to fight the urge to shake him just to get some kind of reaction.

I remember how he calmed me on the plane last month on the way back from the beach. I'd agreed that I was ready to come out to all our friends about being gay, about loving him, but that didn't mean the decision was easy. He held me together on that plane and when Louisa met us at the airport.

"It's going to be fine," I encourage, even though I have some pretty serious doubts myself.

For a moment, we hold hands and ride in silence, the radio blaring some cheesy disco song. I almost miss the sign that promises Winchester, dead ahead. There are pictures of caves and roadside tourist stands, and someone's selling boiled peanuts along the roadside. Max's hometown is the weirdest thing about him; no wonder being gay was so damned easy.

Until today. Until facing his past and his twin sister, Leah. Until taking me home to meet his parents for the very first time. Damn, I want it to feel good for him because I'm really comfortable now. I'm gay and that's cool. It's like I've felt about Maxwell from the start, just this raw, blazing pride about being with him. And who wouldn't? I mean, he's handsome and sexy, smart as hell and has great taste in just about everything. Like me, I think with a wicked little grin, and am about to say so, but my laughter dies on my lips.

"She won't accept you." He stares straight ahead, expressionless.

It's like he's speaking to me from another lifetime.

"Leah?"

"She hates that I'm gay, Hunter," he explains in a thick voice. "Hates this part of me."

"Why?" I'm treading as gently as I can, not pushing, just following his lead. These are the things he wouldn't say back in L.A. Maybe it took excavating his past to get him to open up.

Max shakes his head, doesn't answer as he stares out the window.

"Tell me why." So I guess I am pushing after all. I love him too much to let it go.

"It's disgusting." He cuts his eyes at me. "That's what she told me when she realized."

"Well, fuck her." How dare she hurt him, how dare she make him feel ugly and ashamed about this? About us.

"Hunter, please," he whispers, raking a hand through his hair.

"She should love you! She's your goddamned sister."

He fires right back: "She should love *you*, because I do."

Not much I can say to that, as he turns toward me. "That's what hurts, Hunter. Don't you get it?"

That it matters to him at all perplexes me, but I just nod my head. I know families are complex and byzantine. I know it even though I've barely ever had one. Maybe that's the reason why I *do* understand.

Funny, but the thing I notice in that moment is the engagement band glinting on his finger, and I can't suppress a swell of pride, knowing it's a promise of what will happen between us in the spring.

Knowing he's marked as mine, just by the wearing of it.

Almost as if he reads my mind, he fiddles with the band, turning it on his finger absently. Maybe he regrets not leaving it in his leather jewelry box back in L.A.

"You can take it off," I suggest. "I'd understand."

"I won't walk in that door without it."

"Max, maybe it's better to just...I don't know." I shrug. "Maybe to work up to that, you know? With your family."

"They know we're together, and I'm not going to lie. I love this ring." He gestures with his hand, and for a moment, I flash back to the night I slipped it on his finger. "I love you and I'm walking in the door wearing it." The familiar temper has kicked in now, and I'm actually glad, because so long as he's fighting, I can handle anything with his family. It's his morose, nervous mood that's left me feeling uneasy all morning.

His hand rests in his lap, the gold band contrasting with his tanned skin, and I trace the outline of it with my fingertip.

There are three small diamonds set into the ring—one symbolizing each of us, and then a center stone for the union that's yet to come. That diamond is the largest of the three; perfect because it represents the biggest freaking change that my life will ever know.

It's definitely an engagement ring, although it looks plenty damn masculine, being a thick gold band and all. Max claims he's had a few curious looks down at the office from the crew who I now jokingly refer to as "the gaytraders".

Then again, while it may be a guy kind of ring, it's still an engagement band, and Max has no shame about wearing it right on his ring finger. So it's no time for me to regret that it might draw attention; I made my choice the day I walked into the jewelry store and selected it. If I'd wanted subtlety, then that was my moment, right then and there.

But I didn't want subtlety. I'd finally embraced the truth of who I was, how much I love Maxwell, and I wanted something a little bit obvious. I *wanted* people to notice.

And frankly I was anticipating this day, and I wanted his family to notice, too.

So far, they have no idea what we've planned. In fact, although they've figured out that we're together, Max has never openly admitted that we're a couple, even after I moved into his place three weeks ago. I've answered the phone a few times when his mom has called, and she's been polite, distant. Kind of acted like I was the maintenance man who just happened to be grabbing her son's phone.

Max's parents definitely know about me, but that's a far cry from accepting that I'm the one who's swept their baby boy right off his feet.

I have a hard time picturing them at our wedding no matter how many ways I rearrange that family portrait, just like I can't imagine Max explaining his engagement ring to them.

No wonder he's so damned nervous.

"Why are we here?" he asked that night two weeks ago as I guided the Harley over onto the edge of Mulholland. He had to shout a little to be heard over the bike's thundering engine, and I killed the motor as we pulled off at the overlook.

The night wrapped around us like a cloak, even as his strong hands held on to my waist. I love nothing more than taking Max out on my bike, feeling him behind me, holding me like a lover. I didn't even mind that several times on the drive down Sunset motorists had glanced at us curiously. You know, two men on a motorcycle together. A little bit suspect, obviously.

They had to know we're a couple, especially with Maxwell clinging to me like some skittish girlfriend—he adores my bike, but he's always a little anxious too. His hands fold around me just a bit desperately, and it makes my heart hammer like the wind.

"Wanted to show you this." I roll the motorcycle onto the soft gravel shoulder. My boots skid on the loose dirt, and his hands grasp at my T-shirt. "You're okay," I promise, as the bike shudders to a stop.

He just laughs in denial. "I'm not nervous." But my shirt is still bunched within his hands, held fast.

"Yeah, right, man." I pry his fingers loose, twining them together with mine. We sit on my bike like that, staring down into the twinkling lights all below. I'm aware of his legs open to me, of how the tight muscles of his thighs form around my own. His body is thin and wiry, but I find it absolutely sexy as hell.

I unfasten my helmet and loop it over the handlebar, then reach and take his. That one just rests between my knees, as we drink in the humming City of Angels all below us.

"You know how much I love this view." He leans against me, and I think of our first date, of his client's house and how we watched the sun dip low into this same valley together.

"Yeah." A boyish grin spreads across my face because that's exactly why I brought him up here. "I remember." I reach into my jacket pocket with my free hand and feel the contour of the velvet box with my fingertip as he sighs against my back.

"Summer's over," he says on a whisper, and I urge the box open without looking.

"Not quite. Another couple of days left."

The band is poised between my fingertips, and gingerly I reach for his ring finger and slide it onto the tip.

"Wh-what?" He jolts against me in sudden surprise. "Hunter, what is this?"

Our fingers remain twined together, and I swing my leg over the bike, turning on the seat to face him. "You can still say no."

He gazes down at his hand, the golden band glittering in the moonlight; the diamonds sparkling even in the dark. "God, Hunter, is this...this..." He's sputtering, and I beam at how pleased he is, how flustered and beautiful.

"I'm asking you again." My voice is so thick it surprises me. I've got his hand in mine, just kind of working the band all the way onto his finger. "I'm asking you if you'll wear this ring."

His mouth opens and shuts as he stares down in surprise. I see how he blushes, even here in the near darkness. For a moment I laugh that he's so shocked; I mean, hell, I did already ask him to marry me. Maybe it's the ring that's caught him off guard, I'm not really sure.

"I know you-you asked," he finally stammers. "I mean, me to marry..."

I just roll my eyes at him in exasperation. "Maxwell, I'm giving you a ring and asking you to spend your life with me, okay?" There. Maybe it's a bit blunt, but hell I love him, and this is what I want.

"We can't really do that, can we? Get married, I mean?" His voice is a little melancholy, yet edged with an innocent hopefulness too. He just stares up into my eyes, waiting. Waiting to know if I'm fucking with him or if this is a genuine possibility.

"Yeah, baby, we can. Not here, but in Vermont."

"Vermont." He repeats the word, but his eyes are darting wildly, and I see how fast his quicksilver mind is working.

"It would carry over here. But...well, we'd get married there," I explain, and I surprise myself with how shy I feel about this all of a sudden. Hell, we talked about it before, but letting him know how much I've really looked into the logistics makes me feel oddly embarrassed.

Until I see that perfect, lovely smile of his. Until I see how it spreads across his face, lighting him from the inside out.

"I thought you were just...I don't know." He brushes at his bangs with a shy little gesture. "Talking about a commitment ceremony or something." Then he looks up at me in apparent alarm. "Not that I didn't think that was great. I mean, that would have been wonderful, too," he blurts, and I get that he's afraid he might have somehow said the wrong thing.

"Baby," I laugh. "I understand, okay?" I take his hand in mine, and draw it up to my lips for a tender kiss. For a long moment my mouth lingers against his palm. "I want it all," I say at last, "because you said you'd give me that."

Oh, holy shit. Now where did that come from? I've become

unrecognizable, even to myself, just some kind of lovesick imbecile, but that's beside the point. Maxwell worked his mojo on me a good four months ago, so nothing should shock me now.

"I know I did."

"And you did say yes, you know," I remind him, grinning smugly. A little thrill shoots right through my heart. He's mine. We're heading to Vermont; we're calling Aunt Edna.

"I meant it too." That voice is whisper soft, just wrapping around the words like the gentlest of pledges. I shiver and wonder if our vows will sound that way when they pass his lips.

"Then you'll wear this ring?"

He reaches to touch my face and strokes my jaw for a long moment. "I don't know why this surprises me so much." His touch is unbelievably tender, the way he caresses my cheek beneath his fingertips.

"Because you think I'm a big unromantic idiot."

He laughs and shakes his head, staring at the ring on his hand. "Not at all. I just never thought you'd be this...well, this out, quite frankly."

I narrow my eyes predatorily, glancing at him through my lashes; it's meant to be a smoldering gaze, to undress him with a mere glance. "Well that's your fault, and you know it."

He cocks a coy eyebrow and gets all flirty right back with me. "That kiss again?" he purrs silkily, and I get a hard-on just hearing him.

Oh, yeah, the kiss felt round the world. No doubt.

"You. It's all you," I murmur and cup his face. I draw his mouth to mine and it's not about hunger this time, it's a confession.

Slowly, his tongue darts and wars with mine, and I feel his

hands working at my T-shirt. Down the hill, the engine of a distant car thunders, but I can't let go. Not yet, even though I know it's risky to keep at him this way. My palms are splayed on his strong thighs, drawing him closer. God, I just need all of him, right here and now.

Through the corner of my eye I glimpse the arc of headlight cresting upward onto the hill, and reluctantly I drop my hands and turn away. As out as I am, some things are just between Max and me. My feelings are far too personal, too real, for the world to see. At least tonight.

But he won't let go; his hands are still around my waist, grasping at my soft shirt. The car guns past, as I stare into the valley below.

"That a yes?" I ask without looking back at him.

Warm fingers move beneath faded cotton, pressing close against my abdomen. No one has ever touched me like he does, not even with a simple gesture like this one.

"You know it is."

"How soon?" I ask, and I'm a little desperate, my mind already working at the details, hammering on things I refused to even contemplate before I had his answer.

Strong, muscled arms wrap around me, pulling me close against him. "As soon as you want. Tomorrow. Next week. The spring."

Aunt Edna would definitely smile on a spring wedding between young lovers.

"Why spring?" I manage, suddenly aware that my breathing is frantic, uneven.

There's just silence for a moment, only the rushing sounds from the hills below us, until he says, "Because it would be beautiful."

"I want the spring," I agree with a nod. His hands stroke my chest, roam like wildfire beneath my shirt and jacket. "I want you," I manage. It's a growl, a prayer, and he only laughs in my ear.

"Take me home and do something about it then." Just that quickly, something changes in his demeanor, and I know what all his clients must hear on the phone each day. That velvet voice becomes pure male in its throaty timbre, and I take comfort in the fact that he's all mine.

I nod as his fingers press down within my pants, wandering dangerously along the waistband of my jeans. "Stop it," I caution with mock gruffness. He knows I love what he's up to; I'm instantly taut and pushing hard within the confines of the denim, and it's an aching sensation.

"No way." Yeah, well he's pretty damn pleased with himself, especially when he runs his fingertips along the bulge in my jeans. "What's this, Willis?" he teases, stroking my painful erection.

"You're gonna pay, Daniels," I warn, handing his helmet to him, and swinging my leg back over the bike.

"I hope so." He squeezes his thighs tight around me, and I realize he's pretty damn aroused himself.

"Then hold on." With a shudder, I snap my helmet strap, as his sweet hands fold around my waist again. I swear I can nearly feel that golden band press into my side as I gun the engine and roll the bike out onto the road again.

Everything felt easy that night as we followed the back roads home to his apartment in West Hollywood. Our apartment. Maxwell was behind me and we were going to take on the world. Our families and friends would bless our union, the champagne would flow; our future was golden.

Not so easy now, standing on the front step of his childhood home. Especially since there's something about the way Phillip Daniels looms there in the doorway. It's in how he sizes me up—it instantly makes me regret that I'm not a more impressive man. Like, if I weren't just a glorified construction worker, I might be able to promise a decent life to his amazing son. A weekend home in Palm Springs, or a little cottage in Brentwood, that kind of thing. Instead, I know it seems I'm just the kept man in this affair.

But it's not just about the money, because even for a half a moment, I wish I were better looking, someone more on a par with Max's intense beauty.

And most of all, Phillip Daniels's disapproving scrutiny makes me wish like hell that I weren't gay. I could be Max's best friend again, because then he wouldn't be examining me in this way that every father has scrutinized would-be suitors throughout the ages. It's that look of keen disapproval that suggests a shotgun might be hidden just behind the man's door.

I recognize that look all right, the withering glare of a protective dad, and I know he thinks I've deflowered his son. Well, he's not all wrong on that point, but I could explain a few things about precisely who led whom astray in this relationship.

But instead, with the steely bravado of a seventeen-year-old on a first date, I extend my hand and boldly say, "Nice to meet you, sir."

A firm grip shows you can be trusted. That's what Aunt Edna always said. I want Phillip Daniels to know that, if nothing else, he can trust me to love and protect his son.

Instead, I get the distinct feeling that he considers me the closest thing to anathema to ever grace his doorstep.

"Hunter." He pronounces my name like it's something bitter and distasteful he's suddenly found in his mouth.

There's a terribly awkward moment, a piercing silence reverberating like a gong, as we're left outside without an invitation to enter. Finally, Max coughs, and asks, "Can we come inside, Dad?"

My heart clenches at the quiet pain I hear in my lover's voice.

Phillip nods, opening the door wider. "Of course, come on in, Max."

I don't miss that *I'm* not included in that invitation, but I follow right on in with a wary smile. I've never responded well to intimidation tactics, and a counter-plan is already forming in my head.

Chapter Two

We're led into the living room, with me tagging along behind Max like some wayward puppy. Of course, it's hard not to feel lost after the big brush-off his dad's just given me.

But all my plans for some counter-attack fade once I meet Max's mother, Diane, who really is a very sweet lady. A little clueless, I can tell, but she's all right. Might even remind me a bit of Aunt Edna, especially the way she pats my hand reassuringly as she takes it.

"Nice to meet you, Hunter." She gives me an uncertain smile, and I'm pretty sure this whole scene makes her uncomfortable.

Then next thing I know, she's offering us sodas and little tea sandwiches, the kind without the crusts. That's when Leah and her husband appear from a back hallway, and the temperature in the room drops by a few crucial degrees upon impact.

Max's sister is even more stunning than Max led me to believe, but it's as if all his natural warmth and gentleness were drained right out of her. Instead, Leah takes that room like steel, unbending and icy smooth in her demeanor. I'm the very first person she looks at. Not Max, and I stand a little too quickly, bumping the tray of sandwiches like the oaf that I naturally am.

Max starts to introduce us. "Leah, this is—"

"Hunter Willis." She cuts Max off, sailing straight to me. She extends her hand, pure ivory goddess. "Max has told us so much about you." She smiles, and the words are friendly, but they're hollow all the same.

Then she embraces Max, pulling him close. Uncertainty shadows his eyes as he folds those strong arms around her. I watch them both together, and the only thought drumming through my head is that she better not fucking hurt him. My stomach knots with my need to protect him, and that's when I realize that somewhere along the line, I've become his partner already.

I'm thinking all these thoughts while pumping her husband, John's, strong hand, plastering a smile across my face. But he's an easy guy, much more relaxed than everyone else who has taken battle positions within the room. That, and he's the only Hispanic in our midst, so he's undoubtedly used to that outsider vibe around this crew.

So we settle on the sofa and pass the polite little sandwiches around. It should be a pleasant scene, meeting his family. Instead, the tension is palpable, particularly with Leah and their father, both of whom have chosen to ignore my presence.

At least John is a pretty friendly guy. He asks me about the trip out from L.A., and we wind up talking about Harleys, since he aspires to be a weekend rider. This garners a huge frown of disapproval from Leah, the only time during the visit when she genuinely looks my way. Her scowl intensifies when Max says, "Oh, Hunter's Harley is just gorgeous. We go out on it all the time."

"Together?" she asks.

"Yeah, Leah, together," he explains wearily.

Yeah, sweetheart, you should see us, I want to shout right in her face. I can only imagine her reaction to the way Max clings tight to me.

"How long have you been riding?" John perseveres and I wonder if he's clueless, or just a natural born peacemaker.

"Since I was a kid. Back in Iowa."

"That where you from?" he continues, and for a moment I see Max's dad glance in my direction. *Yes, sir! Your son's boyfriend is a corn-fed Iowa kid. Solid red, white and blue!*

"Yeah, mostly." I decide to leave out the details of my parents' death, Aunt Edna and all that.

"Probably great for riding." John nods in approval. "Lots of open roads."

"It taught me to be safe." I meet Phillip's tentative glance. I want him to know I'm careful with Max, that I'd never put his son in danger, not even for a moment. "To respect the road."

"Respect is a good thing." Phillip's gaze grows keen and penetrating as he continues staring in my direction.

For some reason I bob my head and smile, feeling like an idiot. I have no idea what he's up to, or even what he means. But I'm desperate to make a good impression, want him to know that I'm here to stay.

"So you go riding together?" Leah asks again. "Around L.A.?"

"Sure." I shrug. "All the time."

She gives me a mildly horrified look. "Isn't that a little *weird?*"

"Why?" I meet her gaze, head to head. I can play this game as well as she can. "I'll take John if you guys come out to L.A."

Immediately her fair cheeks stain pink, and I wonder if she assumes I'm insinuating something a lot more than I am. "Or you. Anybody is welcome, so long as they wear a helmet."

"It's really great out on the coast," Max adds, smiling a little uncertainly at me. "Especially around Long Beach."

"I bet," John agrees with a hearty nod, and suddenly I think I love this guy. He's really all right, because he's got to know this is a standoff of sorts.

"Yeah, sometimes we take the coastal highway, then we stop off for seafood at sunset, right when it's getting a little cool," Max explains with a genuine smile, and then he just chatters happily about our life together. I settle back into the sofa and let him share, and somehow it seems maybe the tension has let up a little. At least for now.

But as he gestures and talks, I wonder if his family gets the most important detail of all his vignettes about our life—I wonder if they see how happy he is.

Dinner is a little strained. Well, not the dinner itself, which is an old-fashioned family kind of experience, complete with lazy Susan and all that. Ironically, growing up, Max had the family I was mostly denied, and yet I think I had a whole lot more love from Aunt Edna than he ever got here. Funny how the cards play out; the kid who gets the tough break and winds up an orphan is the one who feels most doted on and accepted.

No wonder Max melts in my arms every time I hold him. No wonder he laps up my affection and just glows beneath all the love I give him. Damn, I only want to love him more, seeing how his family holds him at such a stiff-armed distance.

So dinner is okay, but it's afterward, when Leah spies Max's ring that everything goes straight to hell. She stares at it pointedly all through coffee. Doesn't ask, mind you, just looks at it, her eyes wide and disbelieving. She thought us riding on my motorcycle together was a shock!

I'm proud of Max when he doesn't say a word: If she can't even ask, then he shouldn't explain.

But then Phillip's gaze trains right on that band, and I see how his jaw begins to tick until Max bows his head and folds his hands in his lap.

I want to cry at how he literally crumples with shame right before me. This is the man who has been bold and confident about being gay everywhere he's gone—except right here in the bosom of his own freaking family.

Beneath the table, where no one else can see, I take his hand in mine and hold it tight all through coffee. I'll be damned if they'll make us back down from this.

But then his mother smiles and says something about how she's made up the guest bed, and Max can sleep there while I take his room. For a moment, I'm confused because we put both our bags in his room, and his mother knows that. I mean, we'll share a bedroom, like we always do. Like we would if they weren't worried about which way our sexual pendulum swings.

"Max, your bedroom is the nicest, so you don't mind if Hunter takes it, do you?" she asks again with an awkward smile.

Max hesitates a moment, and I see a little glance pass between his mother and father. I get the feeling she might have been put up to this.

"Sure, Mom, you're right," he finally agrees, and I can only stare in disbelief at his quiet acquiescence. "I'll take the guest room."

"Good." She smiles much more easily this time; her relief is palpable as she rises from the table. "I'll go get some extra pillows from the hall closet."

27

Damn, that's when it hits me.

With as much as we've come out in the past month, they've just managed to shove us kicking and screaming right back into the closet.

There's no way I can sleep, not without him—not when his family has separated us this way. So I toss and turn in his childhood bed until the cool sheets are tangled all around me. It's almost like his scent is still in this room, even after all these years. Of course, he didn't wear cologne back then, and there's a little musty odor in here too. Like the room has been closed up for a really long time, which of course it has been.

His past is all around me, winking at me through the darkness. There are old posters and books with crackled spines, an empty aquarium in the corner. Somehow, all these youthful artifacts only make me long for him more intensely.

I prop my head on my elbows and stare at the stars etched onto the ceiling. Or maybe they're stickers? I'm not sure, but they twinkle above me like some artificial mountainside canopy. Max has always insisted that I've never really seen the stars, not until he's taken me out into the mountains at night.

I want to see this world through his eyes.

For some reason, I think of Max's Rolex and Tiffany tastes, how he loves Cuban cigars, the way a fine suit fits his body. Then I picture him here amidst his family, so awkward and uncomfortable and ashamed of what we are. Who we are together.

For a moment, I feel rage, and something tightens right in my middle as I think of his sister. The way she looked between us both, how her lip curled slightly, as if she might be ill when she glanced down at his ring. Fuck her. Absolutely, fuck her.

She's breaking his heart, and she doesn't even get that?

What is wrong with these people?

I blow out a frustrated breath, when I hear his bedroom door creak open. I startle, sitting right up in bed, but then Max fills the frame, standing there in just his boxers and a sleeveless undershirt. "Hunter?" He steps tentatively into the room.

"I'm awake." I sigh, biting my lip to quell the anger.

Carefully, he closes the door behind him, and then I hear the soft shuffling sound of his bare feet against the carpeting.

"They're asleep," he explains.

"I'm not."

"Hunter, look, I'm really sorry." He settles on the edge of the bed. I move to the side, making room for him, but he only sits on the mattress edge. I want him in bed *with* me, not miles away like this, so I reach for him, pulling at his waist. He stills my hand, and now I'm just really pissed off.

"You realize what you've done?" I hiss into the darkness, the full rage suddenly making its way to the surface. He blinks at me, mouth open.

"You let them closet us completely." My hands have begun to shake. "That's what. With just one moment, you let your damned family force us into hiding about this."

"Hunter, it's not that simple," he tries, but I won't hear it.

"Baby, you don't get it? They have you sneaking down the hall to me like a teenager just to fucking talk about it."

"I didn't know what to say." He sounds so defeated as he buries his head in his hands.

"How about that I'm your boyfriend?"

"They already know that."

"Yeah, right. Only by implication." I roll away with a weary sigh. Suddenly I wish that I'd never left L.A., that I'd stayed there among the safe cadre of our friends. But then I feel his gentle fingers stroking my hair, his lithe body curling against mine as he lies down beside me.

"It's not that I don't love you," he whispers in my ear, caressing my arm, my shoulder, warm hands roaming around my stomach.

"Feels weird, that's all."

The soft hairs of his thighs tickle my legs, and as the stroking intensifies, his hands wander down the length of my legs. He palms my hips and I'm getting aroused as hell, but I'm determined to ignore it.

"Weird how?" he whispers into the darkness.

"Like you're shutting me out. Like...you're ashamed." For a moment, I think of all the months that he ached to tell our friends about us, and how freaked I was, but I shove that thought aside.

"Never. Never, ashamed." He's folded his body right behind mine, holding me so tight that I struggle to breathe with the warm sensation of him loving me this way. If he were really ashamed, would he be in bed with me like this, risking being found together?

His hips shift behind me, and then suddenly I feel the ridge of his arousal press right into my backside. My eyes water as he begins stroking the hardened length of me, right through the front of my cotton boxers, and I wonder what he wants right now.

"Relax," he murmurs in my ear, kissing my neck, my cheek. His scratchy face brushes against mine, and the scent of him intoxicates me. God, I want him enough to take him right here, to hell with his family.

"But I thought..."

"I just didn't know how to handle it. Don't you get that? I'll stay the night in here if it will make you feel better."

I have no idea how to answer that. So instead, I arch back into his arms, allowing his touch to truly pleasure me. My eyes press shut, and then his other hand wanders right down into my boxers, stroking and coaxing me a whole lot further.

Not sure when, but we've begun rocking together, moving as one and I stifle the cries of pleasure that find their way to my lips. I feel his legs opening behind me, and he thrusts a knee between my thighs, parting them.

"Not here," I manage thickly, as he lowers my boxers off of my hips. "Can't...here."

I roll to face him, and in a sudden motion, pin him against the mattress. His dusky eyes grow wide, filled with desire and shock at how I've gotten him beneath me so fast.

"Why not? If we're quiet?"

I've pulled his T-shirt up, until now it's bunched around his shoulders and I begin kissing his muscled chest, especially lingering over the one nipple I love best. That mole right beside it just drives me half crazy, and I kiss it every chance I get. He laughs huskily in my ear, stroking my hair.

"When are we ever quiet?" I murmur against his chest, slipping one palm beneath him and raising his hips.

"Make love to me." He's not going to let me demure on this, and I lift up onto my elbows until our eyes meet in the darkness. The golden gaze doesn't leave my face and I really get that he means it. He wants to have me, right here in his parents' house.

"I-I don't...have..."

"I do." Just like that he pushes me off of him and is across the room, rummaging through his suitcase. Zippers open and close, and there's a muffled sound before he comes back to bed, stripping off his shirt and boxers along the way. I'm not sure which way it's going to go, until he presses the small tube into

31

the palm of my hand and rolls onto his back, staring up at me in absolute invitation as his legs part a bit.

"Oh." I smile, just nodding. Then slowly, deliberately, I begin to caress him in just the way that drives him most wild. The small hips begin to squirm and lift in a heated little motion, and then I don't waste a moment about what I want.

Max Daniels is my addiction; that's what a month of making love to him has taught me, and right now I need all of him. I push and strain, determined to get all the way inside his tight walls without stopping.

Beneath me he trembles, clinging to my shoulders in desperation. And then the soft pleading begins as he urges and begs me to move. I love these first sounds he makes almost as much as I love being deep inside him, so I smile languidly, kissing his jaw and his mouth, but I don't move just yet. Even though it nearly kills me, I savor the tightness of him, wrapped all around me, the feel of his narrow hips pressed flush against mine.

"Please," he moans on a sigh. "Please, Hunter...you know what I want."

As our lips crush together, I begin shifting my hips against his, a tender rhythm that I know won't hurt. That I know will cause him to tense beneath me and writhe and quiver. A rhythm I know will take him straight to paradise.

The familiar talking starts then, his sweet stream of words and cries, but I'm lost in him. We're so different, and we even make love that way, but I adore how he responds to me.

"I-I...oh, yes, baby," he moans tightly. At least he knows how to be quiet, I think, as our movements intensify and I feel his loving hands roam all across my hips and lower back. He touches me everywhere, and it's all I can do not to buck like a madman within him.

That's when I hear the muffled sound from the hallway, and we grow still, gazing at one another in intense alarm. There won't be any way to explain what we're doing; the truth will be painfully evident. I'm making love to Maxwell, end of story. He's curled beneath me like a goddamn prom queen.

For an eternal moment, we grow still, and stare into one another's eyes. Our breaths are burning and furious, and I'm scared I'm going to lose it. Gently, he strokes my chest beneath his fingertips as we just listen.

He's helpless beneath me, and I'm helpless pushed this hard inside of him.

But there's only silence from the hallway.

He sucks in sharp gulps of air, watching me in wide-eyed expectation, as I slowly shower him with sweet kisses. His forehead, his cheek, his nose, anywhere I can find. Anywhere I can be as silent as I need to be.

"Please," he finally whimpers, his eyes fluttering closed. "There's no one...there," he gasps, pleading quietly in my ear, and I'm relatively sure he's right. "Hunter, please."

At that one word I arch my back, thrust my hips and take him all the way. I feel the warmth of him explode all between our bodies, causing us to slip and ache all the more, as I bury my face against his neck.

Then I feel my own warm seed release all inside of him as I collapse against him, gasping for the life of me.

His family doesn't understand this is what he does to me, how much he loves me. They don't understand that I've never known anything this sweet in all my life, because if they did, they would give us their blessing.

They'd plan the damned wedding for us, if they even halfway knew.

Please, baby. Please tell them about me, I want to cry, as everything grows soft and muted between us.

Please just tell them what that ring really means.

Chapter Three

"Oh. My. God!"

I hear the shriek, and weave it into my dream for a half-moment, but when Max bolts upright beside me, the sleep fades away. Then it's all happening so quickly, I don't have time to process a damn thing.

Leah's standing in the middle of his bedroom, and the sheet has fallen away from his body, revealing him in all his naked glory. And then there's just me, bare, right beside him.

A couple of gay lovers found tangled up together in the sack.

Leah's brown eyes are wide as hell, and she just works her jaw. "In our house?" she finally manages, staring at Max. "You brought this into our childhood home?"

"Leah, please." Max clasps the sheet, drawing it up over his chest protectively, and I just rake a hand over my sleep-filled eyes. Morning sunlight filters through his windows and it's apparent that we've definitely overslept. And slept together, for that matter.

"Oh, there's not even anything to say about this!" She stomps toward the door. "About you and this...this person." She emphasizes the last word with such disdain that her face literally scrunches up, and that just pisses the living hell out of me.

"Yeah, you know, actually there is," I announce really calmly, sitting up in bed. If she had any doubts about my own nakedness, well, they've all faded away now. Thank God for Maxwell's weight room.

"And that would be?" she asks tartly.

For a long moment I stare her down, and her gaze does waver a bit before I say, "I'm Max's boyfriend, okay? So get that much straight."

I feel Max tense beside me, hear a soft little hiss of breath. Then, she just shakes her head in apparent revulsion and spins on her heel.

"Straight?" she laughs from the doorway. "Well, the one thing I've got straight is that Max sure as hell *isn't.*"

Then she disappears into the hallway, and there's the sound of a door slamming a moment later. It's so loud that the wall behind us reverberates as I reach for Max.

But he shrugs me off angrily, and I know it's not about me as he shimmies into his boxers with a scowl. Down the hall, I hear raised voices and arguing and I realize it's only a matter of time until Max's parents have been dragged into this scene.

Deliberately, I climb from the bed and begin dressing; I don't have a damned thing to hide from these people. Let them come charging in here, asking questions about what we are to one another.

Lovers, damn it, that's what I'll tell them.

We're lovers, and come spring, they're cordially invited to stand right alongside Aunt Edna when we speak our vows.

Max darts into the hallway once he's got his boxers and T-shirt on, but I figure it's best for me to dress completely. I listen to the murmured cries and shrill voices from the end of the hallway and take my time as I tug my jeans and T-shirt on.

When I reach the kitchen though, everything's already at a fever pitch and Diane is leading Leah away from Max. Then there's just Max, standing there half-clad in the middle of the kitchen, facing his father. He suddenly seems incredibly muscular and strong, even though his father towers over him.

Phillip glances at me, scowling. "I want to talk to Max alone."

"No, he stays," Max disagrees, sounding a little breathless. "He's part of this."

Phillip folds his arms over his chest, setting his jaw. "Fine, then the three of us will discuss this problem."

"There's no problem." Max's voice rises, becoming sharp and defiant. "Leah came in there on purpose. To set me up."

"You're sounding paranoid, son."

"Yeah, well I wonder why I'd feel that way!" Max rakes a hand through his tousled hair, pacing the linoleum. "From the moment Hunter and I got here, you've all been treating us like we're...we're..." Max hesitates, glancing at me, though I'm not sure what he needs. I take a little step closer. "Like you're ashamed of me," he finally finishes.

"No, Max, never." His father shakes his head in sharp disagreement.

Max suddenly extends his hand toward his father. "Then why did you look at my ring that way last night?" he asks in a voice laced with undeniable pain. "You saw it. I *saw* you looking at it."

Phillip closes his eyes with a weary expression. "I was surprised."

"You know Hunter and I are together! You know I'm gay, Dad. You've known it for months now."

"No, we haven't. Not for sure." His father drops heavily into one of the chairs around the kitchen table. "You never told us a word."

"I tried, Dad! I told you that Hunter meant a lot to me," Max explains, and I notice his hands are trembling as he gestures. "That's what I said, don't you remember? Those were my exact words. That he meant a lot to me and I wanted you to meet him."

"But you never told us the exact nature of the relationship." His father can't quite meet Max's gaze as he lies. I'm Max's boyfriend—what the hell else would he think?

"How could I?" Max's voice becomes a plaintive whisper. "Look how you've reacted now that I've finally brought him home."

Silence falls between them as Max takes the seat across from his father. I can't shake the feeling I should say something—do something—but I just don't know what it is. So I lean against the doorframe, keeping my own silence. I can tell that Phillip wishes I'd leave them, and his gaze keeps wavering in my direction, so I fold my arms across my chest in what I hope makes a resolute gesture, just staring back at him.

"We weren't expecting the ring," his father finally says again. "We weren't even sure about...well, you, Max. We just weren't."

"Leah was sure. We discussed it, Dad."

Phillip nods, absently arranging sugar packets on the table. Apparently anything is better than looking at his gay son—or his gay son's lover.

"Didn't Leah tell you?" Max leans into his father's line of vision. That one gesture, his undeniable need to simply be seen by his father, tears at my heart.

"Yes, son, she told us what she suspected."

"Then why the hell should my ring shock you so much?" Max shouts, slamming an open palm on the table in a furious explosion of temper.

For a moment Phillip stares at him like he's been slapped soundly across the face, until quietly he says, "You didn't used to talk that way. Guess that's a new lifestyle change, too."

"Yeah? Think so?" Max throws his shoulders back. "Well, try this on, then. I'm marrying Hunter in the spring. How's that for a lifestyle change?"

With those words, Max stands so quickly from the table that the chair spills backward with a loud crash. He pushes past me without a word, and I'm left staring right into the furious gaze of Phillip Daniels.

And in that moment, I know one very important fact: Max Daniels is all grown up now, and by his father's calculation, I can see that it's my damn fault.

Late in the afternoon, once I'm dressed for dinner, Max's father ushers me into his study, a masculine room lined with leather-bound volumes and smelling of fine cigars. The kind of space that might have intimidated me a while ago. But after hanging with Max all these years, I know that these are just the trappings of power, so I drop into the plush armchair across from Phillip Daniels's desk without a second thought.

Well, I am having second thoughts, but they have nothing to do with intimidation tactics and everything to do with impressing Max's family.

He pours me a small glass of scotch, then fills his own and takes the seat across from me.

The whisky burns going down my throat, even with just a small sip. Expensive, single malt for sure. Maybe this is where Max's caviar tastes come from.

"Nice," I observe, and Phillip smiles in agreement. "Salty," I add, wanting him to know that this Iowa boy has his moments of refinement.

"A discerning palate." He smiles genuinely and I realize that I've hit a bulls-eye quite by accident. "Balblair."

I have no clue what that means, but I give the glass an appreciative sniff for good measure. "Like it," I say, nodding in admiration. He's definitely served some good stuff, so it's not like I have to fake my reaction.

I swirl the liquid within my glass and we fall into an awkward silence. He's sizing me up again, and I tilt my chin boldly to meet his gaze. Finally, after what seems an eternity, the man speaks.

"I want you to know that I plan to prevent this civil union from going forward," he announces, his hands forming a little temple just beneath the bridge of his nose. I suppose he thinks it represents his legal mantle or something like that.

"Marriage," I correct, meeting his cool gaze as I take another sip of my scotch.

"No, Hunter, the Vermont ruling only provides for a civil union." His voice is calm, quiet even, but there's a fiery resolve in his expression that unsettles me.

"Call it whatever you want, sir, but come April twenty-eighth, I'm standing with your son and making this legal."

"This?"

"Our relationship. We're getting married, sir. That's what we're doing."

He shakes his head in apparent disagreement. "I work with the law for a living, son, and a civil union is not a marriage."

"And I suppose that makes all the difference to you?"

"No, I don't support a union between you and Max, no

matter what it's called."

"Didn't think so, seeing as how you began this conversation saying you'd do anything in your power to stop it."

"I don't want this coming back on Max in a few years. He's worked too hard to build a successful career, reputation, to have the legal entanglements of a dissolution like that on his hands."

I'm not about to back down, and I lean forward in my chair to make my point. "We're not separating. Not ever. This is what we want, sir."

"Right now, Hunter. It's what you want right *now*."

"I love Max. Maybe you just don't get that."

For a moment, his expression softens, becomes surprisingly kind. "No, I think I do get that."

I lean back into the chair, leveling him with a hard gaze. "Then I don't see why you should have a problem with this."

"Because two men do not belong together, not in the way that you and Max are. Certainly not in marriage, which is a sacred institution between a man and woman."

"Oh, so *that's* it," I huff. "You're just down on the fact that Vermont basically made it legal for Max and me."

"I'm concerned that my son will come out of this getting hurt. Or far worse."

"I guess this means we won't be seeing you at the wedding?"

His father considers my question, taking a long sip of whiskey before he speaks. "You can have a ceremony in California."

"Not a legally binding one."

"That's true," he admits with a small nod of his head. "But at least it wouldn't involve all the potential entanglements."

"Would you come? If it were only a commitment ceremony or whatever?" I'm unable to suppress the hope I feel growing deep inside. I mean, it's not what we want, but if it would get Max's parents there, it might be worth a compromise.

But all those shiny hopes are instantly dashed.

"No." It's all he says, but at least he seems regretful. For what, I'm not precisely sure.

"Then we'll stick with Vermont, sir." I rise from my seat making sure my body language communicates everything I'm feeling: This discussion is over, and there won't be any negotiation about what's to come in April.

He says nothing, as I open his study door, though I hear an oddly weary sound from him, a kind of defeated sigh that catches me off guard.

Yeah, well he is defeated, so good thing he seems to know it.

Chapter Four

By the time we head out to the swanky little French restaurant where Max has booked dinner reservations, he's pressed no less than two martinis into my hand. While he doesn't know about my conversation with his father, he must see how tense I am, the way I keep pacing around their living room, picking up his childhood pictures.

It's strange to see all these framed images of him as a little boy, especially the pictures of him with Leah. A sleeping bag with Max's dark head and Leah's golden one poking out; the two of them running on the beach. Later, what must have been high school, and Leah's in a cheerleading outfit and Max is holding her pompoms and laughing. They were obviously very close at one time, and I wonder again what went wrong along the way. When this icy distance settled between the two of them, dividing them like an unbridgeable chasm.

That thought causes me to toss back the rest of the martini, and I sink onto the Daniels' sofa while I wait for everyone else to appear in the living room. Late afternoon sunlight tracks across their carpeting and I squint at the patterns of light and shadow. I'm a little tipsy, I gather, from the way those patterns fascinate me, but I don't think I'm dangerous quite yet.

In fact, in the giddy haze of olives and tinkling glass, I've already come to think of my conversation with Max's dad as the Drawing Room Contretemps. Definitely fodder from Aunt Edna's historical romance novels. She used to leave them on the back of the toilet, and I'd read them for a good laugh.

I'm not laughing now, although I have managed to amuse myself by redefining what happened between Phillip and me. I've recast myself as the naughty, ne'er do well aristocrat, the one who gambled his fortune away and now just trades on his tarnished reputation. That's me in this affair. And Max? Well, he'd be the innocent duke's daughter who I somehow managed to ruin. Kissed him in the rose garden late one afternoon without a chaperone. Or *her*, since we're talking duke's daughter here, not Max precisely.

I guess that makes this the morning after and everyone here in the Daniels home is just trying to sort through all the shame and moral perfidy. Only one difference—nobody wants me to marry the daughter. Not by a long shot. They just want me bribed and sent out on a rail.

Well, I'll be damned if I'm not getting my fairy tale now. Not after working my way out of the closet, not after owning up to being totally gay. Hell no, baby.

About the moment I sniff indignantly at the thought, my stunning groom-to-be appears in the doorway and I have to swallow hard at the sight of him. How is it Max always looks so ridiculously hot in those expensive suits?

"Look nice," I pronounce with what I know must be a slightly drunken, besotted grin, and my timing just sucks because Leah appears behind her brother at that precise moment. Her eyes widen, but I really don't give a shit, though I sure don't miss the way Max's face reddens. He smiles uncertainly, and I wonder if he regrets my openness, especially when I see the way the tips of his ears turn bright red. That never happens, so I get sheepish and just stare down into my drink.

"Freshen you up?" John offers, all relaxed and friendly as he steps into the living room.

"Nah, probably had enough," I mumble.

I just don't get how the rules are changing now that we're back here in Winchester. Max has wanted us all the way out. He's been proud as hell of who he is and loving me. Now all of a sudden I'm supposed to hide what's going on between us, even when they all know.

"Is that what you're wearing?" Leah asks, her voice pure innocence, and I stare up in surprise when I realize that she's talking to me. I finger my jacket uncertainly. It's a suit, so what's the problem?

"Leah, please," Max snaps as I stare down at my tie. It's the one I bought for my first date with him.

"Max, it's a nice restaurant," she explains with forced patience.

"Yeah, and it's a nice suit, Leah." Max glares at her, jaw tight as a wire.

For a moment, I have to count to ten, because otherwise I'm out the door. Seriously. Max must realize this because he drops beside me onto the sofa, still staring at his twin sister.

"Everyone ready?" Diane chimes as she appears in the living room, followed by Phillip. Max leans close and whispers in my ear, "You look amazing. You always do."

"Take me shopping when we get home." For a moment, I imagine a spree on Rodeo Drive, kind of a gay version of *Pretty Woman*, with Max cast as my very own Richard Gere.

The film clip is rolling in my mind when he leans close again, and says sweetly, "You know you take my breath away."

I believe him, but still, sitting there and fingering my tie, an avalanche of inadequacy descends in the space of moment.

Max is rich and handsome and could obviously have anyone he desires, male or female. On the other hand, I'm just a construction worker from Iowa, moderately handsome on a good day. And now to top it all off, it turns out my best suit apparently sucked without me ever knowing it.

Dinner begins as the miserable failure I feared it would be, riddled with awkward silences and unvoiced questions. The restaurant is one of those overly quiet places, so the tension is punctuated by the clattering of silver against china.

But I have to hand it to Max—he's as refined and classy as ever, even under these tense circumstances. In fact, he's commanding the entire event, as bottles of rare wine and dainty hors d'oeuvres are brought to our table in a procession worthy of the best L.A. restaurants.

In particular, Max's mother seems to really be responding to his overtures, and as the dinner progresses, I get the idea that she might even like me. Hell, maybe victory is still within our grasp.

Then there's John, and he's just a real standup guy, asking loads of easy questions, particularly when he turns the full spotlight onto me.

"What kind of work you do, Hunter?" he asks, right about the time a bottle of champagne appears at our table.

"I'm a carpenter."

"Construction," Phillip clarifies, but it's a correction, an effort to make me look blue-collar here beside his decidedly white-collar son.

But Max won't have a moment of that. "Hunter is a finish carpenter at Universal," he beams. "He's in set construction." He really is proud of me, and something about that causes me to blush unexpectedly.

"Really?" His mother asks, all breathless and excited as she leans across the table toward me. This was my trump card, and it feels good to have finally played it, as she nearly sings, "You work in the movies?"

My gaze wanders toward Phillip, and I'm a little smug. "Yeah, but it's more just the pre-production side of things."

"Oh, but that's so interesting." His mother draws out the last word for an indefinite period of time.

"I enjoy it." I shrug like it's just a casual thing, glancing at Max with a soft smile. He's got his hands folded elegantly in front of him, just watching me, and my heart absolutely swells with love for him. That look in his eyes betrays how much he worships me, and while I don't always understand it, I can't help but lap it up right now.

"Ever see anyone famous?" John asks.

"Sure, most every day."

I sense Max lean a little closer toward me. "Tell them about Julia Roberts."

"Oh, Max." I laugh with a dismissive little wave, and then laugh again at how much like his wife I just managed to sound.

"No, we really do want to know," Diane encourages.

And so I launch into my Julia Roberts story, making sure to include all the pretty details I know his mother will enjoy. But Leah's listening, too, I see it in the way her dark eyes study me while I share. She's silent, but tracking with this whole discussion.

I wonder why Max never told them about where I work. It wouldn't have changed the blue-collar facts, but it would have at least sounded sexier. Maybe he was being as strategic as he is in his job every day, saving the winning details until he closed in for the kill. Or moved in for the close, in our particular case, since it's us he's hoping to sell his family on.

I'm still glamorizing my very basic job when the maître d interrupts, asking Max to taste the champagne he's just delivered to our table. Max sips, and then nods approvingly, and I find his sureness more than a tad arousing. He's pure male, surveying the menu and restaurant like a wily general. And I'll be damned if he hasn't already conquered a few of the civilians with gracious ease. In fact, they don't even seem to realize it themselves.

As glasses are poured around the table, his mother continues to ask me about the specific movies that I've worked on. Her focused attention alternately pleases and rattles me.

Once all of our glasses are filled, Leah interrupts me, looking to Max. "A toast?" she asks.

Max nods thoughtfully, staring down at his hands for a long moment without speaking. The silence of the restaurant comes rushing inward then, deafening in its freight train roar as it closes around us.

Finally Max takes his glass in hand, clearing his throat, and when he speaks, his voice is more quiet than usual. I lean a little closer just to hear him.

"Well, you've all seen my ring," he finally says, his gaze fixed on Leah. "And I know there are, well, a lot of questions. But I wanted to take this time to tell you officially that Hunter and I are...are..."

Oh, God. He's just stalled out, and he can't seem to actually say it aloud. So, I take a fortifying breath, raising my glass. "We wanted to ask all of you to toast to our union ceremony in the spring," I finish for him.

Beside me, I sense Max nod in agreement, as he rushes to fill the void, stammering quietly. "We're having a ceremony in

Vermont, actually, where it's legal," he hesitates then adds, "For us. Where it's legal for us. So here's to Hunter Willis, the newest member of our family."

He raises his glass a little higher, squeezing my hand, and then the most horrible thing happens.

Silence. A rushing, gaping canyon of pure silence. That, and both our glasses extended like an unanswered question, as his family just stares at us, shocked.

Well, except for Phillip. He knows exactly what's going down in the spring, of course. And Diane surely does, too, though her face is a freeze-frame of unexpected surprise.

After a moment, it becomes painfully clear that no one is going to share Max's generous-hearted, hopeful toast, so I clink my glass against his.

"Here, here." I have to fight the tears that burn my eyes. They're not for me, mind you; my heart's just breaking for the love of my life.

"To Hunter Willis," he repeats hoarsely.

But then my faith in this family gives a little gasp of life when John Ramirez slowly lifts his own champagne flute with a smile.

"To true commitments," he pronounces slowly, as if he's choosing his words as he speaks. "And a lifetime together." Then he clinks his glass against Max's and mine with a reinforcing nod, suggesting he really believes what he's just said.

Okay, so he's my new best friend, and I'll make no apologies for that fact. Especially since Leah turns to him aghast and he doesn't even pay her a moment's notice.

But my shock value increases triple-fold when Diane lifts a tentative glass, clearly gathering her thoughts.

My heart hammers, because whatever comes next will establish the tone of my relationship with this family for years to come.

Tight breaths burn within my lungs as she slowly says, "Here's to my son, whose heart has always been so incredibly true."

Maybe that's it. Maybe she won't mention me. And I'm okay with that, I really am, because she's given us a strange blessing of sorts. But then she finally finishes her toast with a nervous smile. "And to Hunter, who has obviously managed to capture that heart."

"Here, here," John chimes, and then all four of our glasses clink together.

I glance sideways, and the most charming smile has spread right across Max's face. He's visibly relaxing, finally, because we've turned some critical corner of this whole visit home.

"When's the big day?" John asks, settling back into his chair with the glass of champagne, and I've got to hand it to this guy, he's got balls of pure steel.

"April twenty-eighth. At a country inn, and if the weather's good, the ceremony will be in the garden."

Max continues sharing the details with his mother and I choke back a roll of laughter when he mentions that we're hiring a wedding planner. I think it's the way Leah's eyes nearly bug right out of her head at that one that's nearly my undoing.

"For a gay wedding?" she asks incredulously. "Who would do that?"

I pipe in for this one, because it's worth it to see her reaction. "A gay wedding planner. There's loads of them, all over the country."

"I see," she coughs, covering her mouth with a prim hand.

And all this time, Phillip Daniels is silent as the grave. But he's listening—and watching too, because I glance at him periodically, hoping to gauge his reaction.

For a brief moment, I think he even seems interested in the events we're describing. Maybe because from the moment the tension let up, Max started bubbling away about everything, his golden eyes dancing with unabashed joy. Anybody could see it, particularly anybody who loved him.

So maybe his dad gets the picture a little more clearly now. Not only do I adore his son, but I'm here to stay, kind of like the old marriage saying, "two become one".

That's really what we're talking about, and it should be evident from the way Max has opened up about this. He's talking flowers and rings and happily ever after. Not something furtive and hidden, not something easily annulled two months later.

What Phillip needs to get is that Max is talking about the rest of our lives.

Chapter Five

Once we're all in for the night, Max heads for the shower and I decide to snag one of his Cuban cigars for a backyard smoke. We agreed privately to take separate rooms tonight, knowing it would be the most political move. So once I rummage through his bags for the cigar, I give him a quick kiss goodnight.

He just stands there, wearing nothing but his suit pants and undershirt, looking sexy as hell. "Smoking without me?" he asks, sounding slightly peeved. God, he turns me on when he's sulky like that.

I shrug, kissing him again. This time my mouth lingers against his, tasting the sweet champagne on his lips. "My consolation prize."

"Oh, really now?" he purrs as I run my fingers through his silky hair. A quick glance confirms that his bedroom door is closed, and I draw him close against me.

"For a night without you," I whisper against his cheek, "I need a lot of consolation, baby."

Then, our kiss deepens into something amazing. With all that we've shared, with as intimate as we've become, he can still just break me with one gentle kiss. Those sure hands wrap around my neck, urging me closer, and I feel his heart hammer against my chest. He's all sinew and strength, yet a little delicate at the same time. I'm definitely a bigger guy and I've always loved the way he feels within my arms—that he's masculine and hard, yet edged with a strange softness that makes me half-crazy.

Like now, the way I have to lean down a little to steal this kiss, and how I hold his narrow hips right within the palms of my hands. God, I'm even a little giddy from the way the strawberries and champagne taste on his luscious lips.

Maybe that's why I turn into a romantic fool, as I trace my fingers tenderly over his lips, savoring the feel of them. "Oh, you're just so sweet," I whisper, closing my eyes. "Sweetest thing I know, I swear."

For a moment, he kisses me again, but then he steps backward. His gaze drops and an odd look passes over his face, kind of like a storm cloud shadowing the sun.

I scratch my eyebrow, confused. Maybe it was a weird thing for me to say, but I don't really understand what the problem is.

Then he speaks, his voice heavy and intense. "I was always gay, Hunter."

With the back of my hand, I wipe my mouth, still wet from his deep kisses. "What do you mean?" I ask, willing my heart to slow its insane tempo.

"Sweet," he says, raising his eyebrows for emphasis. "That was always me."

"Maxwell, look, I was just being—"

"Romantic, I know. But that's not my point." His voice is anguished, and in turn, that anguishes me.

I don't want him hurting, and I sure as hell don't want the way this visit is starting to tear us apart.

"Tell me then," I urge as gently as I can, reaching for him. But he shrugs me off with an angry wave, and that one gesture nearly kills me.

"It wasn't just Bruno. Or Brian," he cries, his hand clutching at his heart. "Don't you get it, Hunter? It wasn't my little gaytrading venture or anything like that." His voice becomes suddenly whisper-soft, like loving velvet. "And it wasn't even falling in love with you."

"Okay." I nod, feeling a little light-headed as I stand there, listening.

"This is what I am, that's what my family doesn't understand. They think I've made some kind of choice just to be rebellious or something." He turns away from me and stares into the full-length mirror on the back of the door. Almost like he's expecting to find something in his reflection, something that wasn't there before. Until finally he faces me again, tears filling his dark eyes.

"They don't get that I fought this for years, Hunter." He stares at me, intense and focused, wiping at his eyes. "For years. That it goes back to college, earlier even. And once I started down this path, I couldn't stop myself anymore."

This is more than he's ever told me about his sexuality or his desires, so I'm not sure what to say. I mean, one minute I was getting a raging hard-on, and now it's suddenly confession time.

But he's not finished, at least not quite yet. "I know they don't understand that once I found you, I'd found my destiny," he whispers fiercely. "You're not a choice anymore, Hunter, you're just my life."

His words are so heartfelt and unexpected as he stands there in the middle of the room, looking up at me with tears shining in his eyes, that for a moment my throat tightens sharply.

I'm no idiot; I know what I say next has to be good. It has

to somehow convey how much I love him, but more than that, how much I accept him. And like a gift sent from above, I remember what he said about Bruno and that very first kiss they shared, how it felt for him.

"Until you really accepted this," I begin, choosing my words carefully. "Well, accepted this about yourself, you were kind of shut off. You couldn't really be the guy you're supposed to be, Maxwell. But when you stopped fighting, it was like you opened up inside."

"Yes, that's it." His eyes widen in amazement that I really do understand what he feels, that I can put it into words for him.

And I feel damned good that these mysteries his family can't seem to fathom aren't remotely lost on me.

"Like Bruno's kiss," I add softly. "The way it was for you."

Then he smiles, such a perfect thing, and he's just beautiful to me. "You remembered."

"Yeah, course I did, Maxwell," I say, inexplicably shy all of a sudden. "Because that's how I felt the first time you kissed me." I brush at my hair, just kind of stealing glances at him for a moment.

He steps close again, a look of innocent wonder on his face. "It doesn't bother you or make you feel weird? Knowing that I was into guys for a long time?" I guess he's thinking of my own very recent conversion, and that he's the one who brought me over to his side of things.

"Maxwell, just get over it, man." I roll my eyes in exasperation. "You're queer as hell, so why am I going to start holding that against you now?"

For a moment, he looks shocked and his golden cheeks turn deep crimson. But then he bursts into a gentle roll of laughter, his eyes dancing. "Good point. Seeing as how I'm wearing your ring and all."

"No shit. Besides I've gone all pink triangle now, too. Thanks to you, babylove."

"Babylove?" He coughs as I grab the cigar off the bed. "Sorry, but that one doesn't make the cut, Willis."

"How about jailbait?" I kiss him full on the mouth. "You naughty little seductress. Should be illegal, the way you look at me."

"Excuse me, but my recollection is that you stole my virginity."

"Stole it, my ass," I growl, cupping his bottom for good measure as I tease him. "That was a giveaway, thank you very much."

He gives me a little shove toward the door. "Go smoke your cigar."

"Go take your shower."

And with that, we part ways for the night.

Opening the door to their backyard, I step onto the dew-soaked lawn, and I'm all slouchy in my jeans and T-shirt. The first thing I notice is that I'm not alone; someone else is smoking out here, too, and it sure as hell isn't a cigar.

The arc of light from the kitchen falls over the yard, illuminating the lawn and the glider, and I see Leah quickly stamping out what looks to be a cigarette.

So we're not the only ones who've been keeping our share of secrets in this family. Interesting.

"Don't mean to interrupt." I step across the lawn toward the long glider that she sits on.

"You're not." She stares away from me, into the yard, as she folds her arms across her chest. Like me, she's taken off the formal wear, and as I settle beside her, I see the words "West Winchester High" on her shorts. Looks to be old gym clothes, even after all this time. She follows my gaze and fingers the hem with a soft laugh, "They were in my bedroom drawer. Can you believe it?"

"Hey, you're probably just lucky they still fit."

She glances up at me in surprise. Maybe because I can laugh with her, I'm not really sure. "Actually, you're right."

I withdraw Max's Zippo lighter from my jeans pocket and tap it against my open palm for a moment. "You mind?" I indicate the cigar, and again she laughs.

"You probably don't realize that John has a terrible cigar habit," she explains. "He'd be out here with you if he knew you were smoking."

I nod toward the ground, where she stamped out her own smoke. "He know about the cigarettes?"

She looks suddenly self-conscious. "He thinks I've totally quit, but I still sneak one now and then."

We fall silent for a while as I light the cigar and give it several long drags.

After a few quiet moments, she turns to me. "You make him happy. That much is obvious."

I hesitate, not sure how to talk to her. "I'm glad you can see that." Seems like a safe choice for now.

"Oh, Max is definitely happy with you." She doesn't smile at all.

"But you're not happy with Max."

"I think he's making a terrible choice with his life." Max's words from just moments earlier ring in my ears, and I cringe at how right he really was.

"There's no choice about it." I fold my arms over my chest.

"He's gay, Leah, and that's the way it is."

"But he's choosing this lifestyle, this thing of being with you. Whatever." She waves her hand in the air for emphasis and turns her mouth up in distaste.

"You're wrong."

"No, I don't think so."

"I suppose just talking to Max would be too much, huh? Letting him tell you how it feels to him?"

"Listen, I've known Max a lot longer than you have—"

"Yeah, and you've hurt him a hell of a lot more than I ever have, too."

For a moment, she just blinks, a little stunned. "He told you that? That I hurt him?"

"He doesn't have to tell me a freaking thing. I can see it every time you're together, every time you give him a goddamned phone call."

"Oh." She kind of crumples right before me, and I actually regret that I've been so hard on her. I mean, in a strange way, she's a part of Max, even looks a little like him when the light hits the right way.

"It's not just this thing with Max and me," I ask gently. "It's deeper than that, isn't it?"

She nods, and I take a long drag on my cigar while I wait for her to speak.

"It's all my fault," she finally says, her voice edged with pain.

"What is?"

"That he's gay."

"What?" What the hell is this chick even talking about? I have to suppress a spasm of coughing behind my hand; it's partly the cigar, but partly the insanity of her remark.

"It's because he spent too much time with me. Because I couldn't approve of his relationship with Louisa," she begins in a rush of words that barely make any sense to me at all. "If I hadn't smothered him all through school, if I'd just encouraged him when he and Louisa got together, instead of fighting that...if, if I'd just let him make the male friends he needed without always being around..."

I raise my hand, making a time out sign. "Leah, wait."

"I mean, obviously he loved Louisa," she continues, and that's when I realize that she's not really talking to me. She's talking, in some strange, twisted way, to her twin brother. Even though he's in the house, in the shower, without a clue about what's going down in the backyard.

"And he should have married her. It's Louisa he should be marrying, not you." Then, she does seem to notice me again, because she turns to me, making a little scrunching expression with her nose. "I mean he shouldn't be marrying another man, for crying out loud!"

I ignore her jab, and instead go for the hard truth. "What did you tell him about Louisa?"

Silence falls over us for a moment, and she chews on her lip thoughtfully. That is, until it begins to tremble and tears well within her large eyes. "That marrying Louisa would be like marrying his sister."

Oh, holy shit. Now we're on to something here.

"I see."

She glances at me, wiping at her eyes. "Yeah, so he broke up with her about two weeks after that. He told me later that I saved him years of heartache, of trying to understand what wasn't working with her. That he finally understood himself then."

That's when it all comes rushing home for me—his big

revelation of gayness came out of his conversation with Leah. I can't believe it. No wonder she's freaking out. No wonder she thinks it's all her goddamned fault.

But what she doesn't know is all that he just told me. That he spent his whole life trying to be something other than what he really is. A beautiful, proud gay man. The one I want to marry in just a few more months.

"Leah," I begin as gingerly as possible. "Max is finally happy. If you did anything, well, you freed him up."

"No, no I didn't," she disagrees firmly, brushing at her neat ponytail. She hesitates a moment, then quietly says, "And then there was Eric."

With that one name, a name I've never heard before, the ugly jealousy rears its head once again. "Eric?" I manage, but my heart begins to thunder like a wild fucker.

"His college roommate. Didn't he tell you?"

I shake my head, swallowing hard, and finally manage a thin, "No."

"Oh, he and Eric were just," she hesitates, reaching for my cigar. I pass it to her mindlessly. "Inseparable. It was so incredibly...weird. I knew something was wrong even way back then."

I'm spiraling into a category five panic. Eric? He's never told me about Eric. Who the hell is Eric?

"What happened?" I manage in a thick voice.

"They did everything together," she explains, dragging on the cigar. I guess she and John have shared a few secret habits. Come to think of it, secrets seem to wind their way all through this family that I'm marrying into. "Until senior year, and then..." She sighs heavily, staring into the darkness.

"And then what?" I growl possessively, not even trying to

restrain my wild jealousy anymore. Hell, maybe Bruno wasn't even the first kiss.

"Until Eric got a girlfriend, and then something seemed to really just separate them."

"I see."

"I tried asking Max, because that's when I first suspected something was wrong with him. Something with his, you know, sexuality."

That's it. I'm just done here. Eric isn't a threat, never was. The only threat comes from right within our own camp, Maxwell's own beloved family.

"Look, Leah, nothing is fucking wrong with your brother," I bark, my voice furious in its pitch. "This is what he is. He's gay. He's gay and he's with me, and if you want to really lose him, then keep at this shit."

With those words I rise, and I'm just shaking all over. Except, while she may be cool and calculating, Leah is still somehow her brother's twin.

"Hunter, wait," she calls after me, her voice much softer than a moment before.

"Look, let's just do this later." I storm toward the door with an angry stride.

"No, I want to talk to you, Hunter. Tonight."

I stop in my tracks, surprised to find the cigar has broken within my angry grasp. So I let it fall to the ground, and grind it beneath the heel of my hiking boot, kicking at it for good measure.

I stand right where I am, my back to her. "Okay."

"Come back," she urges, and I rake my hands through my hair. Everything is so damned fuzzy. The martinis and whiskey, the cigar...it's all left me in something of a bleary fog, and I'm a little unsure of what she's after. I was certain of what I wanted to say, but not so confident now in how it's all playing out.

I slink back to the glider and settle onto it with a decided scowl. Hell, this was her idea, to keep talking.

"You make him happy," she says again, only this time around, her voice breaks like fine china.

I nod wordlessly and tears fill my own eyes, burning and unbidden.

"You make him happy." She draws in an audible breath. "And...I think I want to understand that."

Despite myself, at her simple confession I begin to cry like some lost, wandering child. And the weird thing is, she knows that I do, but I feel okay with that.

I feel okay, because she's crying like a lost child, too. We're crying together, and as we just rock there on the glider, I finally have hope that I'm going to find my place in this family.

And I finally have hope that Max is going to find his peace here in Winchester, Virginia.

That he's going to find his place in this family too.

Chapter Six

"So, have you always been this gay?" Leah asks and I try not to flinch at her bluntness. Our tears have stopped, and it feels a little awkward between us, but at least we're talking honestly now.

"You know..." I cough, wishing I still had that cigar to hide behind. "It's not really a thing of how gay I am or not."

"Well, you're pretty sold out, thinking about marriage and all."

"Not thinking about. It's what we're doing." Why do I feel I've had this conversation a dozen or so times here in Winchester? It's like some kind of bad fever dream, where I find myself repeating the same three phrases over and over to weird natives who don't speak my language.

"Okay, so you're marrying Max," she agrees, rolling her eyes. "I understand that. But what I mean is whether you were always a homosexual."

God, you know I hate the sound of that word in the hands of a raging homophobe, how it just gets kind of injected with paranoia and shame. I never would have felt that way six months ago, but things have definitely changed for me.

Yet her question hangs out there, a skydiving, adrenaline-rushing question on steroids. Got to answer it, but not sure exactly how just yet.

"Well, were you?" she persists.

"I'm gonna take a pass on that right now." I just can't go there yet. I don't trust her enough, and I'm still feeling things out with her along the way. Besides, I'm not positive I hold the answer within my hands, even after all these months of loving her brother.

So, I'm surprised, and not a little bit grateful, when we grow silent and just kind of rock on the glider, listening to the midnight sounds of the Daniels' backyard. Fall is supposedly here, but it sure doesn't seem like it based on the sultry heat that threatens to choke the life out of everything around us.

"He was a groomsman in my wedding, you know," she says suddenly, her voice kind of hushed. "Max was, I mean."

"Yeah, I know. There's a picture at our apartment."

"Really?"

"A couple of them, sure." I don't tell her that they're the only pictures of her that he displays, or that he has loads of his closest friends, Louisa and Veronica and Ben, all around his place. Even a few of me he managed to collect long before we got together.

"Oh, he was so handsome too. All my bridesmaids were just going nuts over him." Her expression becomes melancholy as she remembers. "But he never seemed to notice any of them."

"Clue number ten about your boy hero," I offer helpfully, but she doesn't laugh.

"We'd already begun to drift apart by then." It doesn't take much for me to do the math on that one—that would have been after the now ubiquitous Eric.

"Was Louisa at your wedding?"

She looks a little ashamed. "I didn't ask her. They weren't dating yet."

"Yeah, but she was his best friend," I remind her, wondering why she had so obviously turned her back on the one girl he ever spent real time with over the years.

Leah's expression sours like day-old milk. "But they weren't involved or anything. And that's just it. He never dated. Only Louisa, maybe a couple of other random girls in high school."

I'm still thinking about the wedding blow off when I say, "He loves Louisa, still does, even now."

"Not like a man should love a woman, though."

I decide to ignore her jab, and focus on the critical stuff. "Nope, you called that one right."

"But why?" she cries, looking at me with incredible sadness. "Louisa wasn't the right choice, obviously. They were just friends, but why not find a girl he could really love? Instead of..."

"Hold up." I silence her with my hand. "He didn't need to find a girl because he was always gay, Leah."

This shuts her down completely for a moment. Maybe she's just trying to square my comment with the Max she's loved her whole life. I mean, I've just explained a lot of things for her, but whether she's willing to believe me is another matter.

"You know, I always pictured us raising our kids together," she says, her voice getting kind of hushed. "Our families spending holidays with each other, maybe renting a big beach house every summer...growing old together, while our kids played in the sand. That's what I wanted."

It's a bittersweet image, the thought of their children growing up that way, and I understand why it causes her voice to hitch when she says, "I'm never going to have that dream now, Hunter."

"That's not necessarily true. Max and I might adopt," I offer, but even as I do, I think of all the stories I've heard, how tough it still is—even now—for gay couples to adopt.

She nails me with a hard, pain-filled gaze. "Might. It won't be easy, you know?"

And with that, well, I have to agree. For a moment, I imagine the beautiful dark-haired children Max might have fathered, and I get a clear image of them playing with Leah's golden-skinned toddlers. And yeah, I get exactly why it hurts her, and maybe even why she's fought this thing in him so damn hard.

I get it because knowing that it might not happen for them, and even that Max and I could miss out on that dream ourselves, kind of kills me too.

"It breaks my heart, that our lives are taking these different paths," she admits. "That I might never be an aunt. That Max and I won't have the picket fence life...with predictable families, boringly normal ones."

"But you and Max can still be close. Like you used to be," I offer.

She nods. "I want that. I really do, but I'm not sure how to reach him anymore."

"All he wants is your acceptance, Leah. He's been this way a long damn time."

"But what about you?" she asks again, really pushing at me. "You were with Veronica when he met you. I remember that very distinctly."

Maybe she needs to understand my own journey in order to get a handle on her brother's sexuality. I'm not really sure, but for some reason I can't even understand, my face burns at her probing questions. I feel incredibly queer, a little like I'm coming out all over again, with her asking about precisely when I joined the rainbow coalition. Or maybe it's that I was straight for so long, and she seems to suspect that.

"I'm not like Max."

"You're not gay?"

The heat creeps further down into my neck. "No, I'm definitely gay."

"But you were with Veronica," she presses, a strange expression of curiosity forming on her face. Her blonde eyebrows kind of arch, and I get that she's not trying to shame me or anything.

I shrug by way of explanation. "And Max was with Louisa."

"But you said Max was always gay, so are you saying that you weren't?"

"You're not gonna let me off easy here, are you?"

"I'm trying to understand all this, Hunter."

I sigh heavily and stare her straight in the eye. I've got to stay as bold as I've been with his family, as strong as I was with Phillip, even here beneath the microscope of the Gestapo Princess.

"I was always straight. I had plenty of girlfriends over the years, slept with my share of women, and I won't lie and say I didn't enjoy it. But when I met your brother..." I hesitate, trying to figure out how to explain it. "He changed me. Suddenly something that I'd never thought about just had me in its grip. Maybe it had always been just below the surface, I don't really know."

She stares at me, her jaw actually dropping. Mine is dropping, too, because I seriously can't believe I just opened up to her like that. Then those big brown eyes get a little wider, and she says, "Oh my god. You fell in love with him, didn't you?"

"Well, no shit."

"No, no, I mean, that's why you turned gay, wasn't it? Until

Max, you'd never been with a guy."

My face burns even more painfully at her honest assessment. "I never wanted to."

"So Max was just *the one*, wasn't he?" She's gotten oddly breathless, as if some crazy jigsaw piece is finally tiling into place. "That's why you changed."

For a long moment I debate what comes next, whether or not I have the guts to say what I feel. But then I realize that I have to lay it out now, because she's his sister, and she's got to understand.

"He's the love of my life, Leah."

She says nothing, just looks at me, until finally she says, "He is wonderful, isn't he?"

"Damned amazing." And she actually laughs, kind of sweetly, really.

"So you fell in love with him, and took this, well, a path you'd never thought about before."

"The night I met him everything changed. Just took me four years to know the score."

"The night we met? Well that's good to know." His sexy, quiet voice chimes from right behind me, and Leah and I both jump with a start.

"Man, you shouldn't sneak up on people like that," I scold him as he steps around the glider to where we're sitting.

"No sneaking, you two just didn't hear me."

"Well, yeah, so maybe you could've..." I hesitate, as he gives my arm a tender squeeze, "coughed or something."

"Hunter and I are getting to know one another," Leah explains softly, drawing her feet up beneath her. She makes a point of not seeing him touch me, and Max wins kudos for being out enough to do it.

There's a lounge chair right beside me, and Max drapes himself in it lazily. He's wearing nothing but a tank undershirt, the kind that really emphasizes his chiseled biceps, and a pair of khakis. They're faded and soft, and my first thought is that he can be my sailorboy any time he wants.

"You were telling Leah about the night we met," Max prompts and I toss him what's meant to be a playful glare. All I get in exchange is a gentle smile that sets my heart beating like mad. I can tell he's over the moon that I've made this kind of headway with her, and he doesn't even know the half of what he's missed. He can't know that things have altered forever with his family tonight, that this icy distance between the two of them has begun to thaw.

"You tell her," I urge. "About how we met."

Max hesitates a moment, then says, "It was at this trendy little bar down on Sunset. Some place that Veronica was in to at the time."

"I was *in to* Veronica at the time," I add, and he grins at me.

"And I was with Louisa," he agrees. "But then came Hunter through those doors. Tall, handsome, totally arresting." He actually gives a dreamy little sigh as he remembers the night.

"Arresting?" My chest puffs outward and I have the urge to thump it with pride.

"I know there was music in that place, that there were loads of people, that it was really loud," he reflects. "But when I remember the first moment I saw him, it's perfectly silent. There's nothing but Hunter Willis taking that room two steps at a time, heading straight toward me."

"Wow." Leah just stares at her brother, a kind of wonder in her eyes. "It was love at first sight, then."

She's getting this, and I can't honestly believe it. She's getting how hard we fell, how intense our attraction was from the very first moment, that this couldn't possibly be a choice.

Max glances at me and I realize that I've twisted the hem of my T-shirt in my hands.

"I had a crush on Hunter for years," he admits and I'm so proud of him I want to give him a sloppy, full-mouthed kiss of appreciation. He's telling her the truth, admitting openly how long he wanted me. It's one step away from what he confessed to me in his bedroom earlier tonight.

"Tell her about our first date," I suggest, and Max's expression darkens unexpectedly.

"She already knows about that." Max looks at her. "Leah knows all about you, Hunter. How I asked you out, about our beach trip, you moving in with me, all that."

Now, this is a surprise, and I glance between the two of them, confused. "I thought, well, that you'd never really discussed our relationship much."

"We haven't. Not much," she agrees, and her gaze is trained right back on her brother.

"I sent her a letter," Max finally says, but he's not looking at me. He's still staring at his twin sister. "Before we came home. Telling her that I wanted the two of you to be friends. To be close."

"Max, I should have answered," she says, that lower lip trembling again.

There's something here that I'm missing. Maybe it's one of those spooky twin things, the way they're staring at one another so intently.

"But you didn't, Leah." He glances at me, almost like he's trying to change the discussion. "What happened to the cigar?"

"All gone."

"I know I didn't," Leah continues, ignoring our little

interchange. "I didn't know what to say. I was so overwhelmed by...this."

"*This*," Max repeats, his voice rising. Warning bells sound in my head and I know Leah had better tread carefully.

"By Hunter," she clarifies, her voice remaining quiet and even.

"Okay, so you were overwhelmed. Why not call me and tell me that?"

"Because I didn't know how to respond."

"How about by telling me that you wanted to meet my boyfriend, huh?" he snaps. "Not by ambushing us once we got here, by rushing into our bedroom when you know for a fact that we're lovers. What did you think? That by outing us, it would change things?"

"That maybe, I don't know, this whole silence about it would be broken," she admits in a small voice. "That you'd go back to being who you were before."

"There's no before, Leah. There's only what I've always been. The problem is that I was never who you wanted me to be."

She hangs her head at that one, and even though he's right, it's not the right time to say it.

"I love you, Max," she suddenly whispers with a loud sniffle. "I love you and I don't want to hurt you any more than I already have."

He just stares at her, dumbfounded I think, by the change in her outlook, the sincerity of her words. I mean, he knew we were connecting, that we all were, but I doubt he was ready for this much of a change.

His expression softens as he leans forward in his chair, looking only at her. "You hurt me by turning your back on what

I am."

"I know that." She's crying again now, wiping at the tears as she nods her head. "But I want to understand now. About your being gay, about what you feel for...for, well for Hunter."

"What about our marriage?" he asks, and I know he's bracing for rejection. I see it in his eyes, on his face, and I just hope he can handle it when it comes.

She says nothing, just rocks a little as she hugs herself. "I want to be there. I want to be part of it, because it means so much to you."

"You'll come?" The way his voice breaks over the words causes my chest to tighten with emotion.

"Yes, I'd like to be there."

"I-I can't believe that you would."

"Well, actually, I can't either." She laughs, wiping at her eyes. "But how can I not come? You're my brother and I love you."

"Okay." He just kind of nods his head, dazed. "Wonderful."

"Yeah, that's cool. Now we have like six people instead of four," I laugh, but she doesn't smile.

"What are you talking about?" she asks, turning to me in dismay.

"Well, it's not like we're going to have a bunch of guests there, Leah," Max explains, and his voice is edged with sadness. "I mean, you know we can't share this with that many people. It's why I wanted my family to be there."

"But only six?" she asks again, her eyes wide in disbelief. "It's a wedding. You have to have more than that."

"Okay, so like ten, maybe fifteen," I admit honestly. "But it's not a big group, I'll tell you that." What I don't say is that we can't even come out to most of the people we know, so we sure as hell can't invite them to our nuptials.

"You need serious help with this," she announces, clasping her hands neatly together. "You need my help."

Oh, no. Not sure I wanted this much acceptance. "We're hiring a planner," I interrupt before she gets any bright ideas.

"No, don't do that," she insists with a little wave of her hand. "I'm great with these kinds of things, really. Just ask Max."

I don't ask Max because he's staring at her in such shock that I'm not sure he'd be able to answer me. I give the arm of his chair a little tap with my fingertips, and he stares down at my hand.

"Max?" she finally prompts. "Tell him that I'm great at planning events."

"Uh huh." Okay, it's definite now; Max has gone into catatonic shock or something.

"Well, maybe you don't want that, though," she says, sounding insecure. "I mean, maybe you'd rather work with someone who's gay and all. Really, I'd understand."

She glances between us, her brown eyes still shining with tears, and thankfully, Max manages to recover his composure. He glances at me for approval and I nod, still wondering how the hell I'm going to handle working with Leah on all this.

Well, that part's on Max's shoulders now, since after all, he's the one who's been taping Wedding Story episodes off of TLC like there's no tomorrow. Good place for ideas, my ass.

"No, no, that would be fantastic," he agrees, bobbing his head. "We'd love it if you helped."

But he still looks like he's been caught in the headlights of an oncoming truck. And as we agree to discuss the plans further in the morning, once we've all had some sleep, I have to admit I feel a little blindsided by this turn of events myself.

Blindsided, but hopeful. And you know, I'm getting kind of used to that feeling, because it's not all that different from falling in love.

Chapter Seven

So it's finally time to go home, and I have to admit that I'm pretty happy to be blowing this town. Not sure I could have handled staying in Winchester much longer, especially not under the same roof as Maxwell's family. An idiotic grin must be flash-frozen across my face after these past few days of working so hard to impress them all.

No wonder I'm so damned relieved to be going, I think, as I spread my suitcase across Max's bed. The sooner I'm packed, the sooner we'll be hitting the road for L.A.

And, of course, the sooner Maxwell will be back in my arms, with that beautiful bare body pressed hard against my own.

Okay, now that thought is enough to inspire some seriously fast packing, so I begin folding my T-shirts double-time, right as I launch into a daydream that includes me dragging Max to the sofa the moment we enter our apartment.

I'm to the part where I'm tugging off his T-shirt, touching him in places that his parents should never think about, when suddenly his velvet voice interrupts my little reverie.

"Do you have room for these in your suitcase?"

I blink, confused by the discordant image of him appearing in the bedroom, especially since what I'm really picturing is tearing those blue jeans right off his sinewy little body.

Instead, he's walking toward me, balancing a precarious tower of bridal magazines in his arms. No wonder I can't suppress my laughter.

"Oh, please," I snort, shaking my head at him. There's just something wrong with the image of Maxwell Daniels cradling stacks of *Bride Beautiful* against his chest.

"What's so funny?" He chews his lip, and I kind of wish I hadn't given him shit about it.

"Ah, hell." I take half the copies out of his hands helpfully. "Makes perfect sense to me. Blushing bride, and all that."

"Oh." He glances down at the magazines a little self-consciously. "They're Leah's. She thought we might get some good ideas from them."

"Uh, huh." I toss a dubious glance at the glossy stack. Somehow, I have no problem imagining Max curled up beside me in bed every night, insisting that I look at foldouts of tuxedos and flower arrangements.

The rest of the magazines slide out of his arms, as he bends low over the bed.

Keeping Your Dream Guy Relaxed on the Big Day! Choosing a Honeymoon Destination to Last a Lifetime!

For a moment I can't help imagining the gay version of this spread. *Bride or Groom? Which One is He Really?* Or maybe, *When His Folks Learn You're Both Queer as Folk!*

"And look at this." He sounds a little breathless as he pulls a CD out of one of the magazines. "It's a computer program that tracks your wedding expenses."

Oh, no. Nuptials combined with financial software? It's certain now—my baby's headed straight for a massive hard-on.

"Cool." I nod, rubbing the sleep from my eyes. I'm in serious need of some coffee, especially with how late we all stayed up last night.

Max steps a little closer to me, so that his lips brush close against my cheek. "Looking forward to getting back home," he breathes, and I catch the faint aroma of his aftershave. "Well, not home, exactly. Just you, Hunter."

Uh, oh. Now I'm the one headed for the major hard-on.

I gulp, feeling helpless beneath his moody gaze. "Can't wait either," I manage with a slight nod of my head.

"I love you," he murmurs against my cheek, stepping away. He pauses in the doorway for a moment and grins, kind of fluttering his eyes for emphasis.

He's practiced that maneuver, I'm sure of it, because every time he works it on me, I kind of come apart at the seams. He's a goddamned eye fluttering genius, that's what he is, and he's going to pay for it later. I'll be exacting my tax right between the sheets.

"Love you too," I mumble, ruing the way my jeans have begun tightening across the front.

That lovely smile spreads across his face, and then he makes a point of allowing his glance to wander slowly down my front, until it stops right on the bulge in my pants.

"Stop that." I turn from him in a huff, tugging my T-shirt lower.

"I'm not doing anything." Pure innocence, that's my baby. Angel all the way. "Let's get packed so we can hit the road, though," he says, becoming businesslike in his demeanor. "We've got a long way to go before we're home."

Yeah, I know what business is on his mind. Same business that's on mine; I need to get seriously lucky after these few days apart from him.

And after this interchange with him? I need it pretty

freaking bad, that's for sure.

"Thank you for Visiting Winchester", the sign declares, and by the time we pass it, I can finally breathe again. Funny, but I didn't realize I'd spent the past few days quite that on edge.

But I feel good now, really good, and I think Maxwell does too. He's riding beside me, flipping through a couple of the bridal magazines, and the contrast with the morose guy I brought into this town is just amazing.

He's glowing, literally, and that makes this farm boy glow all over, too.

Of course, I already had a pretty good buzz from our big driveway send off. Max's mother even hugged me, patting my cheek with her hand. Talk about an Aunt Edna maneuver—I'm beginning to think those two might share a DNA pool. But we won't go there, because that thought's just weird.

Leah had totally thawed out too, and while I expected it after last night, it still blew my mind when she pulled me into her arms for a quick embrace. And I mean a real embrace, not something stiff and forced.

But it was the way she held on to Max that practically brought tears to my eyes—for a moment, I honestly didn't think she'd ever let him go. Meanwhile, John pumped my hand warmly, congratulating me again on our upcoming wedding, telling me he looked forward to attending.

All of this, incidentally, under the chilly scrutiny of his father-in-law—it's those balls of steel in action yet again. No wonder John's my new best friend. After all, I have great taste in guys, don't you know?

But Phillip was another matter altogether, and I guess he's simply our last holdout. He shook Max's hand, formal and cool in his demeanor, and it makes me wonder if he's always been that reserved with his son. He barely shook my hand at all, but at least it's not just me. I glance sideways at Max, wondering if he's okay, if he noticed the major brush-off I received.

But from the sweet look on his face, I know he's happy, and that's all I care about for now.

We're both totally beat as we drop our suitcases inside the apartment door. Max walks to the kitchen table, thumbing through the mail Louisa brought in for us earlier today, and I head straight for the shower.

The warm water pelts me, soaking my hair, and I come alive again. Just in time to hear a rustling sound beyond the shower curtain. I squint, wiping soapy water from my eyes, when suddenly cool air hits my body as Maxwell steps inside. He must have stripped out of his clothes in the space of a heartbeat, because he's gorgeous and naked and right in the shower with me.

"God, I missed this," I murmur, slipping my wet arms around his waist and drawing him flush against my hips.

He lifts his hands and brushes at my wet hair, stroking it away from my eyes. The warm water rolls down his cheeks, his back, and he's like some shimmering sculpture. He's perfect and lovely, as I run my palms over his hips, his abdomen, staring at him in deep appreciation. And who wouldn't, because the man's just gorgeous.

Truth is, he never looks quite so beautiful as when I glimpse him like this, glistening and hard.

My whole body has tightened because of his proximity, I realize as I reach for the soap. In one quick motion, I'm behind him, sliding the bar over his chest. God, it's so smooth, not a hair on it; just the way I like it best. I work the soap over his nipples, then lovingly over the cordons of muscle on his abdomen, his thighs.

He arches backward into my arms at the slick sensation, gasping in pleasure as he reaches one hand over his shoulder to caress my cheek. His fingertips stroke my scratchy face, and I meet his lips with my own for a searing kiss; a slow, burning brand of a kiss, the kind that only deep lovers share. And we're nothing if not deep lovers now.

"Missed feeling you like this." I breathe again, and he nods as slowly I work that lather between his legs, stroking his erection with my fingertips. He actually shivers when my hand touches him there, his whole frame giving a little shudder within my arms.

I drop the soap and take him within my hand, slippery and wonderful as I caress the length of him.

"Oh, God," he manages, stiffening hard within my arms. I brace my forearm across his chest, pinning him against me, but he reaches out to steady himself against the shower wall. His hands splay against the tiles, and I follow him, covering his body with my own.

My mouth trails over his shoulders, down his strong arms, and all the while my hips are moving gently against his, my fingers exploring the silky warmth between his thighs.

For a long moment, he leans his forehead against the wet tiles as we rock together, and I can't stop. God help me, but I can't. I know we can't do what I want, not here, but I keep pretending that we can—and with the way he's moving against me, I know he is too.

"Hunter," he moans tightly, as I cover his hands with my own. "Please."

"Please what?" I murmur in his ear, nipping at it with my teeth. "Tell me what you want."

"I want you," he cries out as he manages to turn within my

arms. His back is pressed flush against the tiles, and he stares up at me, panting and wide-eyed. He drapes his arms around my neck, pulling me down toward him.

My growl is my answer, little more than an urgent rumble as I take his mouth wildly with my own.

Our kiss is fevered, our tongues warring and twining together, and I'm not sure how, but suddenly we're slipping to the floor of the shower. We're nothing but a tangle of desire and heat, and thank God it's a garden tub. We collapse together, the water beating against our bodies as the kiss keeps growing deeper. He's easing me onto my back, although there's nothing graceful about this. It's all about our hunger and our burning need to reconnect.

He's got me beneath him, all wet and slippery, his cock pushing hard between my legs, as I clasp him from behind, urging our bodies together.

My shin bumps hard against the water faucet, but hell if I care, as our hips begin bucking together.

"Oh, baby, sweet baby," I moan, raking my hands through his mess of wet hair. He kisses my chest, dipping his head low as he draws one of my nipples into his mouth. I arch and hiss at the sensation, as I work my fingers between his thighs from behind.

He makes a harsh little sound at the intimate contact, his head lifting straight up. "What's wrong?" I ask, stroking his back as he rises upward.

"This." He looks at me with a hooded, sensual gaze. "I can't take it anymore. I want to make love."

"We already are." I brush a kiss against his jaw. I don't want to move, no way in hell, not with him on top of me like this.

"No, I mean really." Those feline eyes growing wide and

urgent. "Right now."

I swallow hard, as he lifts off of me, and then the shower water hits me hard in the face because he's not there to block it anymore. He's already moved out of the tub and into our bedroom, and I wonder how fast I can possibly follow.

He's already sprawled on his back, waiting for me, and there's something in his demeanor that catches me off guard, something forceful that I'm not quite expecting.

It doesn't take long for me to figure out why he seems so assertive, once he draws me down onto that bed with him. He's totally ready to take me, slippery and slick as we roll within one another's arms. The thought of it makes me half-wild, and I moan right in his ear as we tumble together.

Then, in one graceful motion, he pins me on my back, and my heart begins hammering like crazy because I know for sure what he wants. I see it dancing in his golden gaze.

I blink, as he spreads his palm on my upper thigh, urging my legs wide open to him.

Maxwell's only made love to me once, ever. And it sure as hell wasn't while staring straight into my eyes. No way. As much as I wanted him then, I just wasn't ready for that, and I'm not sure I'm ready now.

Don't get me wrong, I trust him with my life, but this much intimacy just scares the shit out of me.

"Max, I, I don't know...about this," I stammer as he pushes between my legs, kissing me full on the mouth.

"About what?" he murmurs, coaxing my thighs open even wider.

"This, uh, having you on top," I explain breathlessly, shoving my palms against his chest in an effort to slow him down. *"This."*

He leans up, stroking my wet hair away from my eyes. "I've made love to you before," he says quietly. He's so loving and gentle, but I can't stop shaking, not even as he rubs my chest in an effort to soothe me.

"Not like this," I cry, squirming beneath his weight, but he won't budge. Never mind that I make love to him practically every damned day.

Thankfully, he doesn't say that, but instead ignores my desperate pleas and pulls my legs right around his hips. I grow still, kind of staring up helplessly into his eyes.

"You'll love it," he reassures me, kissing my forehead. "Okay?" He doesn't move or push, because he's waiting. Even though he knows what he wants, he's not going to force things, either.

After a moment, I close my eyes, nodding as I wrap my arms around his strong shoulders.

"I won't hurt you, I promise." The words are like velvet, whispered right in my ear.

"You wouldn't," I say, my voice suddenly thick, as I cling to him. "I'm just, just..."

"Scared," he finishes for me. "But it's me, Hunter. You're safe in my arms."

And you know, he's right. What am I so damned worried about? I feel him slowly push inside of me, hard and insistent.

Maybe I'm just scared of him seeing me, really seeing into me. Hell, I don't know, but I keep my eyes shut tight, as suddenly I'm just full with him. It does hurt some, but I don't say that, instead I kind of groan at how deep I'm taking him. I clasp his hips, trying to stop him a moment, but he keeps working his way into me, and that only makes me howl with unbelievable pleasure.

"Baby!" I cry out. God, there's just so much of him. So damned much, like last time, only...different.

"Look at me," he urges. All I can think is that nothing should feel so freaking amazing as having him inside me.

I suck in frantic gulps of air, anything to still my body's insane reaction to what he's doing to me. My eyes are still closed, and I feel him cup my cheek within his palm. "Hunter," he murmurs, and I get that he's not going to move until I can look right at him.

Slowly, my eyes flutter open and I find myself gazing up into the loveliest eyes I've ever known; my lover's eyes.

We're perfectly silent, perfectly still, just breathing one another in, and I swear it's almost like our souls kind of touch.

That one moment tells me all I'll ever need to know about myself; there's nowhere to hide when you're completely bare to the one you love.

And the thing of it is, I don't want to hide anymore. Not from him, not ever again.

Max has collapsed on top of me, his face nuzzled sweetly over my heart. Damn, when we're like this, just sweaty and satisfied, curled up in one another's arms, I wonder if anyone in the world knows how good I've got it. I never felt this way with any woman, not once in all my life.

That he can sleep atop me so innocently, after nearly ravaging me in an explosion of need, well it speaks volumes about the depth of what we are to one another.

Hell, I know our relationship is complex, and I won't even begin to analyze it. We're lovers, best friends...brothers, even. So what? It works and that's all that matters to me, as I take in the delicious scent of him.

It might be weird that I consider him family these days. But then again, isn't that what marriage is all about? Two become one, a mystery that transcends physical dimensions.

The thing is, apart from Aunt Edna, I haven't really known what it is to have family since I was five. Not until now, with him.

That thought causes me to press my eyes shut and remember my father, a simple man with a simple factory job. And as tempting as it is, I refuse to wonder what he'd have thought of all this, me turning out gay.

One thing I've always known was that my daddy loved me, and I have to believe that he'd have been able to deal with Max. I mean, isn't that what love really is after all, acceptance?

I'm thinking about family and how I'd even define it, especially after our visit to Maxwell's hometown, and that's when it hits me, causing an answer of adrenaline right through my whole body.

I still haven't told Aunt Edna about Max, not one damned thing.

Holy shit, talk about a revelation. And lucky me, it's all mine to give her.

Chapter Eight

It pisses the hell out of Maxwell, but I kind of drag my feet on sharing our big news with Aunt Edna. Not like she'll have a problem with it, and I try explaining that to him, but every time I do, he just gets all hurt with me.

Not until Louisa and Veronica begin planning an engagement party for us do I finally gather my nerve. I mean, Edna has to get an invitation, and I really do want her to meet Max long before the wedding.

So late October, a couple of weeks before the party, I come home from work, open a beer and dial the phone. I make sure Maxwell's working late, because I just can't handle that conversation with him sitting right beside me. Maybe that's a double standard after everything we tackled back in his hometown, but it's all I can do to make the call in the first place.

The phone seems to ring forever as I chug half the beer without blinking. I'm about to hang up when I hear Edna's warm, musical voice on the other end of the line. For a moment, I nearly lose my nerve, but then she says, "Hunter?" Shit, she's obviously discovered caller ID.

"Hey, Ed," I say, coughing into my hand. I can do this, I coach myself. I can definitely do this.

"Hi, sweetheart." Her voice is as reassuring as ever. "I've

been thinking about you."

"Sorry it's been a while." I'm already feeling a little guilty right off the bat.

"You've been busy, I know that." She's gracious, and it's funny, but I kind of relax as we shoot the breeze a little. Right up until I remember that I need to tell her what's going down in the spring.

"Well, I've got some news," I say, trying to sound hyper-casual even though my heart nearly beats its way out of my chest.

"Oh?"

"Yeah, uh, well," I kind of stall around a bit. "Well, I met someone. Someone amazing."

Her voice actually pitches upward with breathless excitement, as she says. "Really? Tell me!"

"Um, yeah, well I think we're getting married. I think. In the spring."

"Married?" she squeals, just like I imagined she would. "Hunter, you don't mean it? That's wonderful news!"

"Yeah, yeah it is," I mumble. "Isn't it?" Hell, my question is a lot more uncertain than it should be, but I can't seem to stop myself.

There's a quiet pause on her end, and then she says. "Of course it's wonderful, if you love her." Her. Her. Shit, her.

"I do."

"Well, then tell me all about her, how you met. Everything!" The excitement on her end is undeniable.

"I've known...uh, her, for a while."

"Is it that Veronica DeLuca?"

"No, no, not her. Listen, it's gonna take a little bit of explaining, actually."

"Hunter, what aren't you telling me?" she asks, suddenly as pointed as a laser beam. "There's something you're hiding, and I want to know what it is." Mothers. Their x-ray vision is downright spooky sometimes.

I sigh heavily, taking another long swig of beer, anything to fortify me for this conversation. "I fell in love. That's all. No secret about it, that's why I'm calling you now."

"But who, Hunter?"

I hesitate, closing my eyes for a moment. Just then, the beer kind of hits my system, and I feel a little fuzzy as I say, "Max Daniels. That's his name."

And she says nothing. Absolutely nothing for what feels like a whole damn minute, and I think I'm going to jump right out of my skin at that silence. Until she coughs softly, and asks, "Max Daniels? You've known him for a while, haven't you?"

"Yeah, like four years."

"So then you didn't just meet him." Her voice is gentle, calm. Hell, I feel calmed just by how she's talking to me about it. "You've been good friends for a long time."

"Best friends, yeah."

"It's much better not to rush things," she reflects, invoking all the wisdom of her sixty years. "To really get to know one another first, before starting something."

"Probably so, yeah," I admit, thinking of the long dance of infatuation that Maxwell and I engaged in for all those years.

"Especially if it's a different kind of relationship, don't you think? Because then the love has to be even stronger."

I just mumble something unintelligible in agreement, because I feel like I'm seeing myself from the end of a long tunnel, almost like the moment's an out of body encounter.

"And he makes you happy?"

Tears sting my eyes, because this is classic Aunt Edna. She breezes right past the shocked accusations, the thundering question of why. Instead, she goes right for the hard truth, whether or not Max will treat me right.

"Oh, yeah," I agree on a sigh. "I'm...really happy, Edna. Like I never thought I'd be."

"Good. Then I'm happy, too."

And I begin the whole, strange story of how I fell in love with another man.

My man, the one I plan to spend the rest of my life with.

The afternoon of our engagement party, things are hectic down at the studio. There's some situation with a Jackie Chan movie I'm working on, something related to the stunt people and a wall that has to give way pretty easily when Jackie kicks it.

So I'm rushing around, trying to coordinate things, but finally I have to give up on meeting Edna at the airport. Max is the perfect fiancé, willing to reschedule his entire workday just to go pick her up for me.

But my heart aches when I'm talking to him from one of the sound stages, actually trying to balance the cell phone against my shoulder while working a Skil saw, and he says, "I'm still hoping my folks might show up tonight." He added them to our guest list in a burst of optimism, despite my gentle suggestion that he leave them off.

"Maxwell, I wouldn't plan on that." I turn off the saw, squatting there amidst shavings and noise all around. Juan Valdez, at least that's what I jokingly call him, grabs the saw from my hand, and I try to hear what Max says over the din.

"They might come. There's still a chance."

"By whose odds?" I wonder if he's talked to Leah, who already told me there's no chance in hell his old man's going to show tonight. Even Leah and John had to stay home because of work commitments, so nobody's going to be representing his tribe.

"I mean, it's last minute, but they could still show up," he says, sounding kind of small. I rake my hand through my hair, wishing I weren't surrounded by so much damn testosterone in every direction. Especially when I spy Jackie Chan walking right toward me.

I start hurrying him off the phone. "Gotta go, Maxwell. Thanks for getting Ed."

"No problem." Oh, no. He's pissed; I can hear it in the tight way he talks to me.

"I want to talk, I just can't right now."

"Talk to you later, then." The phone goes dead, and I sigh, rubbing a hand over my tired eyes as Jackie booms one of his friendly greetings.

Hell, I just wish the day were over, party included at the moment.

The shindig actually comes together, there in Louisa's backyard. By the time I make it, especially after all the last minute Jackie Chan problems, well the party is already hitting its stride.

I figured Maxwell would be really pissed off by then, but he gives me one of the sweetest kisses imaginable, and my heart just leaps.

"Thought you were mad," I say, glancing around Louisa's

dark backyard. It's after nine, and I really am very late.

"I can't ever stay mad at you." He's shaking his head, looking toward Edna, who I spy laughing with Veronica and Louisa. "Never could."

"Good thing, because I was afraid the wedding might be off."

"What?" He waves a hand at me with a kind of exaggerated gesture. That's when I realize he's already been hitting the champagne, and pretty damn hard.

"Where is it?" I ask with a devilish grin.

"What?" I smell the good stuff on his breath, and I know by the besotted little grin he gives me that I'm not wrong.

"Whatever happy sauce it is you've been helping yourself to."

"It's a celebration, don't you know?" He laughs way too loudly. Uh oh. He's more than happy, and perhaps moving toward sublime.

"Yeah, I know." I glance around, and wonder if his ecstasy is a good thing or not. Louisa catches my eye right as Edna looks my way, and there's a painfully knowing look between us. "I'll be back in a jiff, babe," I promise him, moving out of his drunken grasp.

Louisa covers the distance separating us as fast as I do. "What's going on with Maxwell?" My voice is urgent, but low.

"He couldn't let go of the idea that his parents were going to come," she tells me, holding me by the arm. "And when they didn't, well..." She looks pointedly at Max, who has managed to lay his hands on another flute of champagne. "He went a little wild."

"How's Aunt Edna?" I ask, watching her slow progression in my direction. She's laughing with Veronica, just nodding her head knowingly about something. That long, gray braid is bobbing up and down the length of her back.

"She's having a blast. Apparently she and Max shared wonderful bonding time. He took her to lunch on Rodeo."

"I'm in love." I breathe a sigh of relief, and Louisa laughs, giving me a sudden hug.

"He's fine. You're both fine, so just relax, okay? Edna adores him."

"He's drunker than a skunk."

"Yeah, well, so what? His parents aren't coming and his heart's breaking in two."

"Why are they hurting him like this?" My voice kind of cracks harshly over the words. "They could've come, for crying out loud." Louisa says nothing, just reaches her hand to Edna as she joins us.

"Is this my wayward nephew?" Aunt Edna asks, smiling up at me. I always forget what a small woman she really is, but it stands out to me because she and Louisa are shoulder to shoulder, nearly the same height. "Couldn't even get away from Hollywood for your own engagement party?"

She reaches her small, weathered hands to my face, cupping it. "You're looking like a young man in love."

We embrace then, and her scent is so familiar. It's that face cream she always uses, I guess. She kisses my cheek and says, "He's a wonderful young man."

Okay, I'm a grinning fool now, given her approval of Maxwell. "Yeah, you think?" I brush at my hair and don't give a crap that I sound like a total dope.

She just shakes her head, smiling broadly. What a beautiful woman, all natural and so genuine. "Hunter Willis, you know what you've found. Max is a very fine person."

"I know," I admit, folding my arms across my chest. My gaze wanders toward the love of my life, at how loudly he's laughing with...whom? A really gorgeous guy, strapping and tall, and there's just something in the way they're relating that I instantly dislike.

"Do you know that he bought me a scarf at Hermes?" she asks excitedly. "I think it might have cost hundreds of dollars! But he didn't care at all, wanted to buy me something special on Rodeo Drive. Probably because I talked about Pretty Woman for much too long over our lunch."

I laugh, nodding. "He loves shopping."

"I saw that, and loves cooking too, he tells me. Wants to leave stock trading to become a chef. Did you know that?"

No, not actually, but I'm not concerned with that fact at the moment. I'm watching Maxwell and Mr. Six Foot Tall Guy laugh it up—and stand really close to one another.

"He mentioned that," I lie, still staring at Max from across the yard.

"Really?" she asks, beaming up at me. "Because he said he hadn't told you yet."

"No, not really," I mumble with an absent frown.

"Hunter, what's wrong?" The sweet smile fades from Edna's lips. She tracks with my gaze, and then informs me, "That's Max's friend, Brian. From his office. He's a trader too."

"Thanks, Edna." I plaster a winning smile across my face. "I better go say hello."

Friend, my ass. They're flirting it up so big at my own damn engagement party that I'm about ready to take somebody outside. Wait, we already are outside, I think, when I breeze my way right up to them, hearing the word "smitten" ring through my head. Smitten, smitten, smitten.

"Hello," I say, sounding as cool as I want to be. Brian's entire demeanor changes, and he extends a hand my way.

"Hunter, great to meet you. And congratulations." He flashes what looks to be a genuine smile. "I'm Brian Edwards. I work with Max."

"Yeah, I know who you are," I snap, feeling sulky as hell. And Max is just no help at all, happy as he is off the champagne.

"Brian's coming to Vermont, can you believe it?" he asks giddily.

"Guess that makes ten people now," I grumble.

"You'll have more than that," Brian says, sounding way too sunny for my grumpy mood. "For sure. Look how many people made it tonight." Yeah, so there are about thirty people here, by my speedy calculations.

"Tons, obviously." Who cares if I sound irritable, because he's way too interested in my fiancé. I'll just bet he's coming to the wedding, so he can be the guy who objects at the last moment.

But Brian's not concerned about me; his gaze wanders right across that backyard, and his expression changes instantly. "Peter's here," he smiles, giving a little wave. "My partner."

Huh, funny, but he's not looking at Peter the way I was pretty damned convinced he was staring at Maxwell. He's smiling like an idiot, and only seems to have eyes for the nice looking guy striding right across Louisa's backyard.

I know that look, I really do, and it has everything to do with how I feel about Max—and nothing to do with Brian.

Okay, I'm jealous, guilty as charged, but Maxwell doesn't even seem to care, he just whispers in my ear, "I love you. It doesn't matter about my folks, because I'll always have you."

"That's true, baby," I agree, feeling guilty I was ready to send heads rolling a moment before.

"Let's go look at the presents," he laughs, placing his hand in the small of my back, a strangely intimate gesture in the middle of the party. "There's bunches of them. Leah and John sent something in a Williams Sonoma box."

He beams at me, and I'm not sure if it's at the thought of more cooking gadgets, or simply because Leah sent something really nice in honor of our event.

The fact that she took the trouble isn't lost on me, especially since all the invitations indicated that no gifts were expected. Hell, we haven't even registered anyplace yet.

But Leah definitely knows her twin brother, and fact is Maxwell doesn't love anything so much as a present, all wrapped up in ribbons and paper. I remember that now, watching the way his dark eyes kind of dance as we approach the gift table.

Hell, I wish I'd remembered before now, and gotten him something really special for tonight. But there's always Christmas, I tell myself as he picks that first gift up, giving it a little jostle right by his ear.

Yeah, Christmas is coming, and I still have time to get it just right.

The morning after the party, Max makes a killer breakfast for everybody, cooking up these omelets I could definitely devote the rest of my life to understanding. I breeze past him in the kitchen, feeling kind of hung over, but happy as hell.

"Hey, there," I whisper in his ear, patting him on the ass when nobody's looking. "How you feeling?"

"Kind of bad," he admits with such a sheepish little expression that I can hardly be angry.

"Well, you should feel bad, man," I say. "You and that champagne had become best friends before I even got to the party."

I pour a couple of glasses of orange juice, one for me and one for him. "Hair of the dog," I advise. "Not really, but it'll help."

"Thanks," he agrees, turning back to the stove.

"So you want to leave trading?" I ask gently. "That's what Ed told me."

He turns to me, the lovely eyes wide with slight panic. "Hunter, I don't have to do that, I'm happy in finance. Your aunt told me she wasn't going to say anything."

"Famous last words, baby doll."

"I don't want to make a change tomorrow."

"Well..." I snag a slice of cheese off of his cutting board. "I'm cool with it. Just so you know."

"Yeah?"

"Maxwell, I don't want your money. I want you. Hell, you ought to know that by now."

He just nods, chewing on his lower lip as he works his omelet magic. "I do, I really do."

"Be happy, that's all I ask, okay?" I kiss him for everyone to see before I turn to leave the kitchen. But Aunt Edna's busy gabbing it up with Louisa and Veronica, and laidback Ben is listening to them while lazily sipping an orange juice that probably has a little spike to it.

I sail into the living room and Edna smiles up at me, patting the place beside her on the sofa. "Nephew?" she says with a sweet smile. "Join us?"

"Sure." I drop onto the sofa beside her.

"You mention the chef thing to him?" she whispers in my ear. Oh, she's quick, I tell you. Listening when I thought nobody was.

"Yes, Ed. We talked about it."

"Good, because he's sick of trading stocks."

"I kind of got that idea."

"He was afraid you'd be mad..."

And on it goes, advice from one who barely knows him. But she knows *me* really damn well, and that means she knows how to guide me with the love of my life.

Valuable input, I tell you, and I'm not above listening to it, as she makes sure I realize that he's picked out a culinary school in the L.A. vicinity.

"Did you know he's a millionaire?" she asks sweetly, patting my arm. "He can do this, and you'll both be just fine."

Yeah, I did know about the bank accounts, and frankly? I didn't give a shit at all. I only care if he's happy, and so long as he is, well then I am, too.

"So you like him?" I ask, turning toward her.

She doesn't hesitate for a moment. "Immensely. He's a very fine young man. And he loves you, which is all that I wanted to be sure of."

I could have promised her that, but I know it wouldn't have been enough; sometimes, you've just got to see these things for yourself.

"You'll come to Vermont?"

"Oh, Hunter, I wouldn't miss it for a moment. You know that!"

I do, but it's just great hearing it, as she leans up to kiss me in a sweet, motherly way. "I love you, son," she says, patting

97

my cheek, and I close my eyes, just imagining that she really is my mother.

And for a moment, smelling her face cream, and feeling her unconditional acceptance, it's easy to believe that the daydream is real. That time has kind of stopped, or moved backward, and my parents understand what I'm doing with Max. They understand and somehow, magically, they approve of it all.

What a dream I weave, but it's a happy one.

Chapter Nine

Over the next month, we start double-dating with Brian and Peter, and it's weirdly refreshing to be with another couple like us. It never would have occurred to me that we needed that, but it turns out I really like hanging with other gay people. Makes me feel a little less hidden away, and now that I'm out of the closet, that's where I like to be.

Then, after Thanksgiving I agree to something I told Max I'd never willingly do—go with them to a gay dance club. The whole scene just kind of blows my mind, the way we don't roll out of our parking lot until about one a.m. That it's a huge cruise scene worthy of the wildest episodes of "Queer As Folk". I always thought that show was just exaggerating things. Well, now that I've been there, apparently not.

What surprises me the most, though, is how Max dressed the very first time we went. I was rummaging through his side of the closet, looking at some of his shirts—incidentally, one cool thing about being queer is that you can trade off clothes with your boyfriend. Only problem, though, is that Max is pretty slightly built, so most of his stuff doesn't fit me. It's that whole size differential thing again, which I like when it comes to lovemaking, but it throws a wrench in the wardrobe switch-hitting.

But Max does have a handful of polo shirts that work, and

for that first visit to the dance club, I felt like shaking things up a little.

So, I was standing there in front of the mirror, holding up two different shirts to my chest, just kind of trying to pick, when Max entered that room dressed to kill. Hate to say it, but it was the first time I've ever looked at him and thought he really looked gay.

Frankly, the skin-tight T-shirt just surprised me, and I couldn't help but gawk some. I mean, he had on what I'd think of as a gay uniform; the clingy shirt that rippled over his arms and chest, the sleek, low-slung jeans. He looked hot as hell, but definitely like he was playing a certain role for the night. I'd have pegged his sexual orientation anywhere, just based on the outfit he'd chosen.

"You don't like it." It was a statement, definitely not a question.

I folded his shirts over my arm, and shook my head emphatically. "No, that's not true."

He ran his hands over his short sleeves a little self-consciously, glancing in the mirror. "It's how they dress there, at the club."

"I'm sure it is. You look great." I nodded with vigorous emphasis, but he looked at me a little warily.

"You think I look gay, don't you?"

"Uh, because...you are gay. We both are."

"I'm serious, Hunter. Does it make you feel weird? Me being this obvious?"

"You look great. Go for it."

Still, the uncertainty didn't fade and it started to make me feel a little worn out. It was Friday night, end of the workweek, and I just wasn't up for one of Max's girlfriend moments.

"I like looking gay," he admitted softly. "At the club." That's when I remembered that he's been part of this lifestyle for a hell of a lot longer than I have, and it explains a lot. About the little uniform he's put on, about whatever this is he's trying to say to me.

"Okay," I encourage, and I have the feeling there's still something more.

"I want to go back next week, okay? To the club."

"Sure."

"It's something...well that I'm excited about." He folds his muscular arms over his chest. Yeah, baby, I love that tight T-shirt. It's my other new best friend, right alongside John Ramirez.

"You're excited about the club?"

"No, next week at the club. Um, it's, it's..." he hesitates, scratching his ear in this really sheepish, sexy way. "Well it's drag night."

"Drag night?" I manage to choke out through a spasm of coughs.

"Well, yeah, and I want to go." He's blushing. Furiously blushing, and I can't stop thinking that there's no way in hell I'm putting on a dress.

"No. Fucking. Way." I shake my head, stepping past him toward the closet, anything rather than to look at him while we have this humiliating discussion. Max has lost his mind.

"Not you. Me." I can barely hear him, he's so quiet, and I actually lean a little closer. "I want to go in drag. With you."

Oh, God. Now he's starting to make sense, and so is this awkward moment. How uncertain he seems, how shy and uncomfortable, and it's right about then that I notice his jeans. There's a definite bulge in front, because apparently just talking about it has given him a raging hard-on. I can only imagine what actually dressing that way's going to do for him.

That's when it hits me with full-impact force; he wants to play a little role with me. Like what he's saying about looking gay tonight. This all turns him on somehow. Fine by me, because standing there, looking at him in the slinky T-shirt, I'm getting a hard-on too.

"I see. So that's when? Next week?" I ask in my hyper-casual way, as I turn back to the closet, and act like this is just no big deal between us at all. Like Max isn't saying he wants to dress up like a woman for me next week.

"Next Friday." He steps a little closer, right up behind me. "But I don't want to freak you out, and if the idea of that...that does, well maybe it's too soon, or too weird," he says in a rush of nervous words that cause my heart to ache. I never want him to feel ashamed of this, of what he wants. Not after all that he told me back in Winchester, about his desires and all. So I turn to him, placing my fingers over his lips.

"Max, I'm cool with it. I'm always cool with you, you know that."

He just nods, gazing at the floor in silence, even though I know there's a load more he wants to say about it. Maybe it's how close we are now, but instinct tells me he's fantasized about doing this for a long time.

"In fact," I add huskily, stroking his hair. "I'm kinda turned on by the whole idea."

His lovely eyes widen, and I know I've hit a bull's eye. "Yeah?"

I run my hands over the tight material of his shirt, just feeling his chest appreciatively. "I mean, look what tonight's visit to clubland is doing for me?" I breathe, stroking him down to his waist. "I can only imagine you all decked out in something of Louisa's."

"Veronica's, actually," he clarifies with a gentle smile. "A better fit."

Yeah, come to think of it, they are about the same size. Veronica is long and tall, much more so than petite Louisa.

And that's the only part of this set up that's just flat weird. My boyfriend is going to dress up in my ex-girlfriend's clothes? I'm living an alternative lifestyle now for real. Check.

"Or something brand new," I suggest as sweetly as I can. "I'm down with whatever." For a moment, I flash on Rodeo Drive again. Pretty Woman gains a whole new meaning in this context.

He cups my face within his palms, and draws my mouth down for the sweetest kiss. "I love you," he whispers. "I love you so much, Hunter."

Ah, love. It's got me right by the balls, doesn't it?

That next Friday night finds me tossing back beers while the wedding nazi grills me about unresolved issues on the phone. This, all while I'm trying to ignore the fact that Max and Louisa are behind closed doors, transforming him into a mass of slinky sequins and spiky heels. I know, because I saw the goods when Louisa brought them over earlier tonight.

"Hunter, can't you just get Max over to Williams Sonoma?" Leah asks with a weary sigh. I know that planning our wedding must be a tiring affair, because what's worse than trying to get one's own groom to fall in line? The answer is two grooms you can't seem to wrangle into place. Poor girl.

"Leah, he's been working late every night," I explain, staring at the closed door that leads to our bedroom. I'm out on the sofa, just wondering what the hell Louisa is doing to my boyfriend in there. "Honest, we're not ignoring you, okay?"

"What about tomorrow? It's a Saturday, you can go then," she prompts. "You guys have friends who won't make it to Vermont, and they'll want to get a nice gift."

I grin like a schoolboy, knowing I'm going to push her buttons as I say, "Yes, Herr Daniels."

"What did you just call me?" she snaps tartly.

"The Wedding Nazi, actually. That's my new name for you, Leah." I slip into Max's pet nickname for her without even meaning to, and while I hear a little intake of breath at my somewhat derogatory joke, I think she probably liked the familiarity.

"Oh, please," she finally says. "I'm not that bad."

I hear the bedroom door opening, and say, "Oh, Leah, gotta go. Talk to you later," and before she's even finished I've hung up the phone.

But it's Louisa who appears in the doorway, not Max, and her face is drawn into something of a worried scowl. "What's wrong?" I demand.

"Oh, nothing. Nothing's wrong," she says with a sigh, closing the door behind her. Then she walks to me, taking me by the arm and quietly says into my ear, "He looks unbelievable, Hunter. So unbelievable, that it's freaking him out a little."

"What do you mean?"

She hesitates a moment, not looking at me, then whispers. "He looks convincing, Hunter. Very convincing, that's what I mean. And I think he's afraid of how you'll react to that."

Convincing? Now why the hell doesn't that surprise me one bit?

"I think he needs a little reassurance from you, you know?" she explains.

"Sure thing." I nod, but my heart is beating like a fucking traitor. I'm not an idiot; I know that if he looks as beautiful as I imagine he would, that this is going to play holy havoc with his sexual identity, and might even awaken some of his hometown demons. Maybe this idea was terrible, after all. Then again, if I can back him up here, if I can give him what he needs, this might heal a lot of things that still haunt him.

I follow Louisa, feeling incredibly nervous as we enter the bedroom.

And then I see him. The love of my life, kind of standing there in the dressing area that leads to our bathroom. Mirrors line the closet doors and I see the convincing evidence in every direction.

He's a goddamned gorgeous woman. Breathtaking, absolutely. It certainly doesn't take a college degree to get why this has him so freaked out.

Louisa steps behind him, just kind of rubbing his back with gentle reassurance, and I step close in kind.

"Wow, baby," I say, ignoring the crazy tempo of my heart. Ignoring how much this terrifies me, seeing him all decked out this way.

He won't even look at me, just keeps staring at the ground, so I haven't really seen the makeup. All I've seen is the long-sleeved, black sequined dress, kind of a Christmas cocktail outfit. Which makes sense because it's the first week of December. Hell, got to hand it to my boy, he's not only dressed to the nines, he's dressed for the season.

The outfit clings to his body, to his narrow little hips and to Veronica's aqua bra. Convincing doesn't cover this, no fucking way. Especially not when he finally gives me an uncertain glance, and I see the truth.

The golden eyes have become girlish and cat-like now that they're lined in dark green, and highlighted by a similar shade of eye shadow. But it's the luscious mouth that's utterly kissable, all dark pink with lipstick that Louisa has obviously applied with great care.

Or maybe it's the way Louisa has fastened his hair on both sides, so that it curls perfectly within tiny black sequined combs. She must have used rollers, because his naturally wavy hair is just a mass of sexy curls.

Louisa hugs him from behind. "I think you look awesome, Max," she says again. "What do you think Hunter?"

"That I can't breathe." I don't even think before I say that, and he blushes wildly.

"I wasn't expecting to look so..." He hesitates, glancing back at Louisa. "Well, so, so feminine."

"What'd you expect then?" I ask, serious. I mean, he wanted this, didn't he? "You're in drag. That's the whole point."

"I don't want to scare you off."

"Does it look like I'm scared?"

Slowly, he smiles, and that's when he really takes my last breath away. "Not actually, no." His voice has changed, that's the weirdest part. It's pitching a little higher, a little more breathy in its timbre and I know he's not even doing it on purpose. I shiver a little, and half expect to hear a good version of "Happy Birthday, Mr. President".

Louisa drops to the ground, touching his legs. They're the only part that gives the whole act away. "You know, Max, you should shave. Really. Not just your legs, but your arms, too."

She runs her hands over his calf for emphasis, and it's funny because it would be a sexual gesture if it were between

Max and me. But Louisa seems more like she's a seamstress or something, kneeling there beside him in the dressing room.

He looks to me and I nod encouragingly. "Go for it, Maxine." I pat him on the ass with a flirty little wink and walk right out of that room.

In fact, I walk right out of the room, straight to the fridge, grab two more beers and guzzle them without taking a breath.

I'm on my third beer, clicking between basketball games, when Max steps into the living room, holding Louisa's hand.

Now, with the legs all shaved, and teetering in two inch sequined pumps, he's finally done me in. I can't think of a goddamned thing to say, except that he looks fantastic.

I'm glad the lights are low, because it allows the illusion to really take hold of me, as I just kind of stare up at him, squinting. There's something going on with Louisa, though, because they're way into the whole silent communication thing. I'm confused by it, especially when he turns to her, and does something I'm definitely not expecting.

Max cups her small face within his hands, just like he always does mine, and leans down and kisses her full on the mouth. There he is, dressed all like a woman, and I swear he's kissing his best girlfriend. And it's not a friend kiss, either. What I watch play out there in the middle of our living room is deep and passionate, and my blood goes wild with jealousy.

Until finally it breaks, and then he just strokes her hair, their foreheads bent together. She's crying, as he says, "Thank you, Louisa. So much." That's when I get that there's no point to my possessive thing at all. Still, I'm definitely curious.

She just nods, wiping at her eyes. "You gave me the most amazing gift any friend could ever give," he says. "You helped me find myself, you know that, don't you?"

Again, she nods and then he kisses her on the forehead, whispering, "I love you."

"I love you too," she says, smiling through the tears. "Here, you smudged the lipstick a little," she says, rubbing at his mouth and they laugh together.

The beers make everything a little fuzzy, but I think I understand it now. This whole cross-dressing affair has brought out something between them tonight. While I wasn't privy to the actual conversation, I gather that they've talked about him figuring out his sexual identity when they were together. It never occurred to me, but it had to have hurt her, that he went to play for the opposing team like he did while dating her.

And that makes it even more meaningful that she's the one who dressed him tonight. She's been his handmaiden in this whole gay thing, the one who helped him understand himself.

But what that kiss just did was show her that she's a beautiful, sexy woman, and that his change had nothing to do with her. No wonder he chose a moment when he was dressed as a woman to lay one on her like that.

"Meet Maxine Daniels," Louisa introduces with a flourish, and I give a low whistle.

Max has the nerve to turn to me then, and look unbelievably shy, just kind of fluttering his lashes and staring at me with those ultra-sexy eyes. Tonight, they're girl's eyes and it's going to make me half-mad before we make it home again.

Then he licks his lips and moves toward me, and I think Louisa must have coached him on this. Because he's not moving like a man; I'll be damned if he's not walking with the grace of a freaking debutante.

Oh, just luscious.

"You like it?" he asks, the voice soft and breathy.

"Louisa, you gotta go, babe," I tease, winking at her. "I need to get this girl out on the town."

She laughs, and then does something that surprises the hell out of me. She leans low and kisses me on the forehead. "I love you, Hunter," she says. "You're an amazing person."

"Uh, thanks?"

"Yes, that would be the appropriate answer." She laughs, her eyes still shimmering with tears as she opens the door to leave.

"Have fun, you two."

Oh, we'll definitely be having fun, I think with a wicked grin. Because now it's just Maxine and me, at least until Brian comes knocking on our door.

At the club is when the whole role-playing thing really hits its stride. I spend very little time with Max, mostly just watching him move around the club. He's at the bar, drinking a Kir Royale, or he's standing at the railing alone, taking in the scene. He doesn't want to be with me precisely, he just wants to be watched by me. I can be down with that, because he's damned amazing to look at.

The funny thing is, it kind of falls to Brian and me to do that watching. Peter is in drag too, so Brian and I are playing the macho roles tonight. Too bad for Brian, but *Petunia* over there just doesn't make nearly the lovely woman that my Maxine does. Hell, looking around the club, there's nobody that looks as sexy as my love.

That does make me feel territorial, because I see all the guys checking Max out. "She's beautiful," Brian breathes appreciatively, and I'm caught off guard.

"Who?" I look around for a woman at this mostly all-guy club.

"Maxine." He nods toward the bar where Max is sidled up with another Kir Royale, holding the glass just like a girl.

Okay, this is getting weird. He just called Max "she".

"Max?" I ask, trying to get a handle on all that's going down.

He shakes his head in disagreement. "You left Max at home tonight, buddy."

My heart is starting that insane tempo again. I think I'm really gay now, because this has gotten totally surreal. "Guess so," I grumble.

"It's the game, Hunter. You got to play it right. It's what they like."

"They?"

"When they cross-dress, they want to play it all the way, really do the role, you know?" Okay, so now I'm getting a crash course in how to be a successful queer from the king of the gaytraders.

"Oh, well, thanks for clarifying that," I snap. Of course, my reaction has nothing to do with the way Brian's been staring at Max all night long. He's not staring at his own damned boyfriend that way.

"Look, I know you're new to all this," he says, and I hate the jealousy that's knotting its way all through my stomach. "Just thought I'd explain a little."

"Yeah, well you know, keep your explanations to yourself," I bark, feeling incredibly sulky as I watch Max laughing with Peter, looking so amazing I can hardly stand it. I'm captivated by the way his legs are kind of dainty with those pumps, the way they emphasize his strong calf muscles, yet make him look all girlish and curvy at the same time.

Brian turns to me, a little shocked. "What's the problem,

Hunter?" he asks with honest confusion. "Have I done something to offend you?"

"You're way too interested in Max." Go me! I finally put it out there.

"What are you talking about?" he laughs, shaking his head. "Max is my good friend."

"Like hell," I say, staring out at the dance floor. "You're into him."

"Hunter, you're talking crazy. Max and I were over long ago, before we even got started."

"Oh, that's not what Max said."

"No?" He seems genuinely curious now.

"He was smitten with you, that's what he told me. Smitten." I draw the word out for massive emphasis.

Now Brian's just smiling, shaking his head in amusement. "He broke up with me, you know," he says and that's when I realize he's staring at Peter while he talks. Not Max. "After telling me all about his straight best friend, the one he just couldn't shake. The one he thought about constantly, but had no idea how to ask out, or feel out, or whatever."

"He told you about me?"

"Yes, Hunter. In fact, you owe me a little thank you, I believe."

"What for?" But I think I already know what's coming next.

"Because I'm the one who told him to ask you out."

Now why the hell didn't Max ever supply this handy bit of information? But then I remember how pleased he was with me being all jealous, how much it seemed to light him up. The little bastard, he's let this possessive streak in me simmer for a long damned time.

"Never knew that," I say, nodding like a dope, and feeling

completely mortified.

"I told him that if he didn't, he'd wake up one day and his straight best friend would have a wife, two kids and a mortgage, and he'd have lost his chance forever."

Okay, it's true. Not only are John Ramirez and Max's clingy T-shirt my two new best friends, but Brian Edwards's name has just been added to that growing list.

"Thanks, man," I mumble, staring down into my beer glass. "I owe you big time."

He laughs, shaking his head. "Not at all. I just didn't want you thinking I was after Maxine or anything. Although she is a pretty little piece of tail."

"Well if you lay a hand on her, I'm kicking your ass."

"There you go," he grins. "You got it now. Defending your girl's honor and all that."

"Maxine's mine, man."

Who knew? Not only is Brian a total standup guy, he's funny as hell, too. Good thing I'm already in love.

And, man, am I in love, I think when Maxine cozies up next to me. "Hey, sweet thang," I purr in her ear, slipping my hand around her waist. "Can I take you home tonight?"

The golden eyes narrow and she leans right against me, looping her hands around my neck. Pure kitten, and I want to lap her all up. "Counting on it, sweetheart."

"Good. Soon though, okay?" And I sound every bit as desperate as I feel, fingering that sequined waist beneath my calloused fingertips.

Soft, girlish voice in my ear, she says, "I'm betting that forty-five minutes from now, we'll be making love."

Now how's a guy supposed to resist a come on from a girl like that?

Chapter Ten

When I wake the next morning, it's to find Max snuggled up close against me. His eyes are still lined with dark green and one of the sequined combs is tangled in his hair. Guess it's pretty evident that we didn't bother with a damn thing once we finished making love, just kind of collapsed into bed, a heap of loving exhaustion.

As I lie there watching him, I can't resist stroking the soft curls that still frame his face. I swear it absolutely staggers me what a gorgeous woman he made last night.

A year ago, it would have terrified me, him looking that way. Hell, probably even a few months ago. Maybe it should shake me up now, but it just doesn't. Because the thing about my Maxine, that lovely little kitten who pounced on me last night?

Well, she's still my Maxwell, just a slightly different angle on my baby, that's all.

So I lie beside him now and run my fingertips down his backbone, drawing the sheet back so I can really see his sinewy shoulders and rippled arms. God, he's one hell of a handsome man too. No wonder he drove me fucking mad in that cocktail dress.

Ah, the dress. Sequins and shimmering blackness, clinging to the curvy figure of the one I love. Well, I know one thing about that damned dress, and the person who wore it last night.

I will never forget the first time Maxine and I made love. Never. Not if I live another hundred years, not if I die tomorrow. Last night is just burned into my memory with all the power of forever.

The way we danced for so long in the darkened living room after we got home, with only the moonlight whispering between us. How I lost myself in those feline eyes as we swayed together to the music. Not too close, a little apart, enough so that certain mysteries stayed clear between us. We both made sure of that.

Lovers' music she chose, a little androgynous. Dakota Staton. The kind of music you put on when you want to seduce someone against a very slow groove. I never realized Max knew about Dakota, but guess I was wrong on that count.

And then how forbidden it all was, especially once I slipped my hand beneath the hem of her dress, lifting it gently upward, easing it higher until I caressed her smooth, nylon-clad thighs. Then discovered those lacy little garters, so damned unexpected—it was enough to bring this farm boy to his knees.

I snapped those clasps open with loving care, one at a time, just holding my breath. And only then did I find Maxine's sweetest secret of all, the silken panties right beneath.

I spun her around then, so I held her in front of me, and she became a little faceless to me, even more like the woman I felt her to be, as I dipped my fingers low along the edge of that lace. For endless minutes I just stroked the curly patch of hair there, nothing more. I refused to explore too much, because nothing could break the spell she'd cast over me.

Honestly? For a few moments I don't think I ever wanted that illusion to end.

We worked our way to the sofa, and she kept whispering

girlish secrets in my ear, until she curled right up on my lap like some gorgeous Geisha girl. She was so delicate as I stroked her hips, the length of those smooth arms and legs; I thought I'd never breathe again.

Then, almost like the sun inevitably fills the nighttime sky, things shifted back between us, became recognizable.

But it definitely took a while. Not until all the layers kind of peeled away—the cocktail dress, the garters and panties—until finally I held Maxwell in my arms again. His whisper smooth legs and arms muscled tight around me as we made love, his voice still kind of breathy and soft in my ear.

He was Max again, but...not quite.

So now I lie here, blown away as I watch him sleep, a little amused by the pink painted fingernails poking out from beneath the pillow. And a lot aroused just remembering the night before. For a moment, I stroke his soft curls again, taking care to untangle the fragile sequined comb that's still twisted there. God, when did I manage to fall even deeper in love with him?

That's when the phone rings on the nightstand, jarring me from my dreamy reverie. A quick glance at the clock tells me that it's well past ten a.m. Undoubtedly Louisa is calling to see how Maxine's big debut went. So I fumble for the receiver with a sleepy hello, only to be met with silence.

Crackling, electric silence.

Then Phillip Daniels's hard voice finally says, "Hunter, may I speak to Max, please." No greeting or pleasantry, just down to business. Hell, I guess I'm lucky he even remembers my name at all.

"Yes, sir," I answer with forced brightness. "Just one moment." I begin nudging Maxwell, but he just kind of rolls away, so I cover the receiver with my palm.

"Baby, wake up." I poke him in the ribs, hard. Finally his drowsy eyes open, still lined in that lovely green and he just blinks at me in sleepy confusion.

"Your father," I whisper hoarsely, indicating the phone. For a moment he stares, then sits right up in bed, rubbing at his shadowed eyes as he takes the receiver.

Shit, if Phillip could see his son right now, all curls and makeup and discarded silky underwear, he'd probably come after me with that shotgun after all.

"Dad," he says, and the voice has dropped right back down in timbre. "How are you?" No more Marilyn Monroe, which is a bummer for me, but probably good for his dad.

I settle back between the sheets and roll onto my side to listen to their conversation. Max's whole body tenses as he listens to whatever his father is saying on the other end.

Seems Phillip is asking about our Christmas travel plans, because Max says, "Well, we're coming in on the twenty-third. I told Mom when I ordered the tickets."

Long pause, dark eyebrows rising as he listens. Then, "But Hunter is coming with me. I told Mom that when we talked about the holidays." Max's mother had been quite welcoming, actually, encouraging him to bring me along.

Another long silence follows on Max's end. I watch as his eyes dart wildly, and then his hand begins to shake where it's cradling the receiver against his ear. "I won't come without him. You have to know that."

What the hell? I can't believe what I'm hearing, what it seems my future father-in-law is trying to do, but then Max's voice becomes eerily quiet as he says, "If Hunter's not welcome in your house, then neither am I, Dad. That's what you're really saying. That you're not going to let me set foot in there again."

And then his eyes suddenly well with tears. "No, whether

you know it or not, that is what you're saying..."

Seems his father tries to cut in, but Max shuts him down, barely saying goodbye. He hangs up the phone, kind of staring at it for a long moment, as I touch him lightly on the back.

"So what did he say?" I finally ask after a long silent moment.

He shocks the hell out of me when he takes the phone and hurls it hard against the far wall of the bedroom with a pained little cry, something terrible like a wounded animal might make. I shake at the sound of it.

I reach toward him, trying to hold him, but he's out of the bed before I can even make physical contact. "Max, stop," I urge, but he falls to the floor, just kind of collapsing in quiet tears there, grabbing at the broken pieces of the phone.

"Fucking asshole," he hisses through the tears.

I've never seen him like this, not once in the four years that I've known him. He just kneels there on the floor, completely naked, trying to put the smashed receiver back together, his shoulders quaking with quiet sobs.

I drop to the ground beside him, gingerly touching his arm. "Baby, what happened?"

He looks at me, his face twisted into a horrible expression of agonized pain. And that image just rips at my heart—Max naked there on the floor, crying, the makeup running down his face.

Especially when he says, "My father won't have me in his house if you're with me, that's what he said. He's disowning me, for being gay."

I try and shush him, touching him with incredible gentleness on the shoulder. "No, baby. You misunderstood. No, no."

"He said that if I bring you, I'm not welcome there." Then he buries his face in his hands. "My father just disowned me...God, I can't even believe it."

"He didn't, Max. He didn't...he just, just..."

Just what? Won't have his own son home if he brings his lover along for the trip? Yeah, well, that probably is pretty much being disowned, seeing as how I'm a permanent part of Maxwell's life now.

I'm all intent on reprisals, and for a moment I even think of flying out alone to Winchester for a big showdown with his father. But then there's the shrill sound of the phone ringing again, and Max's eyebrows lift with a hopefulness that nearly kills me, as he wipes at the dark streaks that line his cheeks. "Maybe it's him," he says, trying to make the smashed phone work so he can answer it. "Maybe it's my dad calling back because he's sorry."

But the receiver is beyond repair, so I sprint to the kitchen, and I see right away who it is on caller ID, as I snap up the receiver.

"Is he okay?" Leah asks, breathless and upset, before I even say a word.

"No, he's not."

"I can't believe my dad really did it. Mom just called me in tears. Please let me talk to him," she begs, sounding as desperate as she should. "Please put him on."

"Not now, Leah," I say, feeling incredibly protective.

"Hunter, I'm on your side, you know that."

I lower my voice and whisper into the phone, "He's too upset, Leah. Okay? Just give him a while."

"Please tell him that we're here for him. Tell him it's going to be okay."

I hang up the phone and move back to our bedroom. Max is just kind of kneeling there still, hugging himself, and when he stares up at me, his face is a total mess. The makeup has run terribly, and his eyes are swollen with tears.

"I never thought he'd really turn his back on me," he says, sounding remote. "Just didn't."

I kneel beside him, as naked as he is, but not nearly so vulnerable. "Yeah, well, guess families are full of surprises."

"Not yours."

"No, because I don't have one, baby." I shrug. "If I did, they'd be fucked up too."

"Your aunt's not fucked up," he says, wiping at his eyes. "She loves me."

"Well, she's just one. You have an army there, Maxwell," I say, trying to get him to laugh, but he only stares into the space over my shoulder.

"When I was seventeen, my dad found a Playgirl in my room. Under the bed. Did you know that?"

"No, I didn't." Of course I didn't, because he's never told me, but he's talking a little out of his mind, and I get that.

"Know what he said when he found it?" he asks, and I just shake my head, feeling something strange choke at my throat. "He told me that it would kill him if I turned out to be one of those people. That's what he said. Those people."

Now what can I even say to this? I have no clue, and good thing he just keeps talking. "I'm one of those people he prayed I'd never be, Hunter. Don't you see what a disappointment I must be? I'm still the guy with the Playgirl...only it's you. The living, breathing truth."

I try to pull him close within my arms, but he shoves at me, wrestling free. Apparently, he needs to move, to pace, and he's on his feet again, roving the length of our bedroom in agitation.

Until he reaches the pile of Maxine's clothes in the chair, and he lifts one of the garters, clenching it within the palm of his hand.

For a long moment, he stands like that, not saying anything, and it kind of scares me. I'm not even sure why, but the look on his face, the raw anger is unsettling.

"What's wrong?" I ask, trying to look into his eyes, as I rise to my feet.

He shakes his head, but a dark expression shadows his face. "Hunter, I love you," he says quietly. "You have no idea how much. Honestly, you don't."

"Yeah, I do. Because I love you like that."

"Your acceptance means the world to me," he whispers, gazing at me with tears shining in his eyes. "It makes me feel so loved."

I nod, wondering what's really going on in that complex mind of his. Sometimes he just leaves me a few paces behind, and this is one of those times.

"You know, Hunter, this problem with my father, him finding that Playgirl," he says, dropping the garter onto the chair. "That wasn't the only thing that happened when I was seventeen."

Oh, no. I think I know exactly what's coming next, and my heart just clenches hard within my chest. "No?" I ask, encouraging him. "What else?"

"My dad came home early from work one afternoon. When I thought I was alone in the house," he explains, gazing up at me meaningfully. "He found me in one of Leah's dresses, decked all the way out."

"Holy shit, baby."

His lip begins trembling, and I get that he's not even with me. He's back ten years earlier, staring down the barrel of his father's steely scrutiny. "He told me that if he ever caught me cross dressing again, he'd kick me out of the house. And I don't know," he says, wiping at his eyes. "I guess I said something stupid because I was so angry, so hurt, but then he shoved me. Hard. And I remember just kind of sprawling on the bed, and him looking at me with such...disgust. He was revolted by me."

"Oh, Maxwell," I whisper, stepping close to him. "I'm sorry. Sorry he reacted that way."

"I ripped Leah's dress when I fell, and I didn't know what to do, so I threw it away," he continues, gazing backward into his past. "For months, she kept mentioning it, looking for it, and every time she did it was like it opened up everything between my dad and me all over again."

"Sure, of course it did." I don't know exactly what he needs from me, maybe just to listen, so I keep encouraging him.

"I graduated that May and started UCLA the very next month. I couldn't get out of his house fast enough."

"What about your mom?" I'm not sure why, but something makes me ask about her.

"After the big blow up with my dad, I went to Louisa's. I slept on her parents' sofa for almost a week, until finally my mom came to get me."

"So she knew?" I'm thinking of Louisa, but he assumes I mean his mother.

"Yeah, she knew. Didn't say a word when she showed up at the Carters', just that my dad's heart was breaking because I wouldn't come home," he explains quietly, glancing up at me. "Then in the car, she said she loved me, no matter what choices I made. That it was harder for my dad, but that he loved me, too."

"She was right."

"Maybe so, but it never felt like it. Felt like I lost him that day, because of being different."

It's literally like a light goes off for me then, almost like I can see it flashing right over Maxwell's head. And I get what this has all been about between us, ever since Winchester when he admitted he'd wanted men for such a long time—even the cross dressing last night and the clingy white T-shirt the week before. I get the whole damned thing.

"Baby," I breathe, stepping behind him. I place my palms on his bare shoulders and kiss the top of his head. "It was a test, last night. Wasn't it?" I whisper fiercely, catching his reflection in the mirror across from us.

At that precise moment, his gaze locks with mine, and I know I'm dead on right. "You had to know that I wouldn't run. Wouldn't turn away from you like your dad did."

He bows his head and his strong shoulders slump forward, but I won't let him hide from me on this. I tug at his elbow, forcing him to turn within my arms, until he stands facing me. Then with incredible gentleness, I cup his face within my hands and tilt it upward, until he's looking me right in the eye.

"I will never leave you, Maxwell," I vow, my voice intent and thick. "I accept all the parts of you, even the crazy little pieces, okay?"

"Maxine turned you on," he admits, and he doesn't sound too happy about that fact. "I saw what she did for you. Maybe you're not even into me, maybe deep down, you're still straight. Maybe you wish I were a woman," he blurts, the words tumbling out in a painful rush of emotion. "Hunter, you went wild for Maxine." He sounds jealous as hell, and I ignore the fact that he's worked up about another version of himself. I know the feeling that's haunting him; I remember how it felt from just last night.

I stare at him, hard, because he's got to get this, and say, "Because of how goddamned much I love you. Not because I need a woman, or need you to...to change. She made me hot because she's a part of you!"

I'm starting to feel vaguely angry, and I'm not sure why. But then I realize it's because Phillip's betrayal all those years ago nearly drove a wedge between the two of us right now.

"But...but my father loved me, Hunter," he stammers quietly. "He loved me, and he-he couldn't, couldn't stand that I'm this way. Seeing me in that dress." His voice breaks, a piercing little sound, as he buries his head against my shoulder.

"Yeah, and I thought you were beautiful last night, okay?" I murmur against the top of his head. "You turned me fucking on, all the way."

For a long time, we hold one another, with me petting his hair, stroking his back. And over and over, I say one thing. "Baby, I love you. All of you, and I'm never leaving."

That's what I say, because right then, it seems like the only damn thing that matters.

Hours later, he's showered and carefully removed all the remnants of the makeup. He's wearing jeans and a T-shirt and he's transformed back to his totally masculine self. His father's timing just kills me, because I can't help but think if he'd chosen any other morning, then his dad wouldn't have gotten this over on him.

But that's not what happened. His father called him when he was still halfway in drag, still feeling a little delicate and vulnerable.

Fuck his father. Fuck him for hurting the person I love

most in this world.

But Max is strong again now, and although he's withdrawn and pretty quiet, he's actually talking about going down to Williams Sonoma just to make Leah happy.

"You need to call her," I suggest carefully, and he gives a shrug of forced indifference.

"Why bother?"

"Because she's worried about you, man."

"I'll call later," he says dully, looking back at the newspaper where he's spread it on the kitchen table.

"How 'bout I call her then? Tell her you're okay," I offer, reaching for the phone.

"Since when did you and Leah get so tight?" he asks tartly, and I feel like a stranger is staring up at me.

"Maxwell, what's going on?"

Again, he just kind of makes a face of indifference. "I mean, she wasn't so keen on you back in Winchester."

"I don't know what the hell you're talking about. She's planning our whole wedding," I remind him. "I mean, you're the one talking about the registry thing, all to get her to lay off of us about it."

"I don't want anything to do with my family. Not at all," he says. "Okay? Not any of them."

He's being incredibly unfair to his sister, and to John and his mother for that matter, lumping them in with his father. But I know it's not the right time to say that, so I just nod, folding my arms over my chest. "Okay, sure. But you do owe your sister a call."

"Later," he grumbles in a sullen voice, leaving me there at the table by myself.

Later finds us at Williams Sonoma, just as planned, and he's prowling the aisles like a wily hunter. Sometimes I swear that Maxwell's more turned on by the sight of a good bread machine than he is by me. Watching him finger all that chrome and steel, I practically see the hard-on he's getting from across the store. My Maxwell loves his cooking gear, of that there's just no doubt.

I wander around a little aimlessly, wondering why in hell a set of measuring scoops should cost more than thirty dollars, when my cell phone rings. I've got it shoved in my back pocket because of a problem down at the studio, something I'm trying to sort out between the stunt coordinator and my construction foreman.

But when I answer, it's Leah again. "Why hasn't he called?" she asks before I have a chance to really answer the phone. "He thinks I'm part of it, doesn't he?"

"Part of what?" I ask, scratching my eyebrow in confusion. Max is on the other side of the store, scanning mixing bowls into the registry. I swear, he's found his way straight to heaven in this place.

"My dad's rejection. He thinks it's a conspiracy, doesn't he?"

"No, actually, he doesn't."

"Because, I could see this playing into his feelings about me," she says in a rush, and I hear the pain in her voice. "Problems we've had in the past, that kind of thing."

"Leah, he's just really upset with your father, okay?" I explain, and wish Max had called her earlier. "He's really hurt."

"I know he is."

"What was your father thinking, anyway?"

She sighs, and it's a broken, weary kind of sound. "I really don't know, Hunter."

"Well, he's about to lose his son if he doesn't get his shit together."

There's silence for a long moment, and then she says, "You'll still come, won't you? To Winchester?"

"Like hell."

"No, Hunter, seriously. Use the tickets and come stay with John and me."

"I don't think that's such a great idea right now, Leah."

"Why not?"

"Because I don't think I need to see your dad, for one thing. And Max doesn't either, for another."

"We wouldn't see him. We'd celebrate at my house."

Is she saying what I think she really is? I have to be sure, so I ask, "You'd blow off your parents? Take a stand with us?"

"Yes, I would, Hunter."

"Why?"

"Because my father's wrong on this. And because Max needs me."

"Okay," I manage, but my throat is tight as a wire as I watch Max from across the store. His expression is so melancholy, a little hopeless, and as Leah starts chattering about how we'll spend the holiday, I add another best friend to my ever-growing list.

Chapter Eleven

'Tis the season, and what do you know? I'm in love for the very first time in my life; and I mean really in love, that soul-shattering, breath-stealing kind of love that Max Daniels has worked on me. No doubt about it, I'm definitely doing my part to make the yuletide gay. Complete with secret Christmas packages for my fiancé, tucked in the corner of the rental SUV.

He's asleep beside me, cranked back in the seat with his hand dangling over the armrest between us. Soft little snoring sounds keep coming from his direction, and I'm glad he can rest. Between those long hours at the office and planning our wedding, he's been working his ass off. Well, and shopping his ass off, too. Aunt Edna was right about that—my boy does love to shop.

We're almost to Winchester, and as I click off the miles, a strange nervousness builds inside me. My palms are sweaty, my throat's gone dry; I can only wonder what the hell is wrong with me. I mean, we've found true allies in Leah and John, and on top of that, we're spending the holidays with all our closest friends. And that's just it. Max and I are truly a couple now, everyone knows, so I should feel secure about going back to Winchester.

Instead I'm white-knuckling the steering wheel like it's some kind of adversary. The only conclusion I can reach is that maybe I'm worried about my baby, afraid his father will somehow manage to fuck with him again. No way in hell I'm going to let that happen. Phillip's days of hurting Maxwell are over, end of story, and if that means some kind of showdown between the two of us, so be it.

Yeah, so I'm in hyper protective mode, and it's no wonder. Max finally seems to be enjoying our engagement, not fretting so much about family and all that shit. Thanks to the Wedding Nazi's coaching, he's become fully consumed with our nuptials, just having fun with everything.

Hell, he spends every night with his nose poked in those bridal magazines or surfing gay wedding sites on the Internet. Around our place it's all wedding, all the time. Like last week, when he popped into the bathroom where I was shaving and out of the blue announced that he'd written his ceremonial vows. When I asked if he was going to read them to me he blushed wildly, protesting that there was no way he'd let me hear them until the rehearsal. I smirked and reminded him that everybody would hear them then, so maybe he'd want to practice on me beforehand.

All that got me was the suggestion that he could think of lots of things he'd like to practice on me, but none of them included those vows. Five minutes later we were laughing and rolling in the sack, practically ready to make love. See? I'm crazy about those vows already and I haven't even heard them yet.

So, yeah, he's doing the wedding thing full tilt, and I have to say it clearly suits him; he's downright radiant about it all. But it's more than that. Something in his whole demeanor has changed in the past month—he's become bolder, more confident. Like maybe in the wake of Maxine's big debut, Max came out of himself a little bit more, too.

He's even sporting a new, super-short haircut that's driving me fucking mad. Every time he catches me staring at him, he just grins, running his palm over that spiky hair with a little shy gesture. Shy my ass. Every time he does that, it's an invitation that makes me want to sprint to his side and do the exact same thing with my own hands. And while I restrain myself most of the time, occasionally I move in for a quick kiss and run my fingertips over the bristly hairs along the back of his neck.

He's hot as hell, and he knows it, which is just fine by me. He deserves to know how beautiful he is, that the new haircut works its magic over me like a damned voodoo charm.

Of course, Maxwell always glows this time of year, anyway. He's like a little boy when it comes to Christmas; I saw that from the very beginning of our friendship. I'd only known him a few months when he and Louisa threw a big holiday bash at her house. Between their two guest lists there were probably seventy-five or more people crammed into that place, and Max was in the thick of everything, right in his element. He moved easily through the noisy partygoers, serving up elegant hors d'oeuvres on trays, and making fancy sausage balls in the kitchen.

He never even broke a sweat, just kept smiling and chattering with all their friends. In fact, Louisa was the one who looked vaguely panicked by it all, but not Max, not even close. He loved every minute of it, right down to placating the cops when they showed up around midnight because the neighbors had complained.

But more than anything, it's those fantastic little sausage balls I remember. I can practically taste how spicy they were, even now. I have a funny memory of plucking a handful of them off of his platter while he was arranging them, just to be irritating. Even then, I had to pop his proverbial bra strap—that's nothing new at all. I probably managed to swipe half a

129

dozen of them before he could stop me, and he kind of swatted at my arm as I darted out of his reach. He had this confounded expression on his face as I glanced at him, so I turned back for a moment.

"What?" I wondered if I'd truly pissed him off. Figured I probably had since I was constantly pissing off Veronica, but honestly? I really hoped I hadn't because I wanted him to be happy with me.

He gestured me closer, smiling at me innocently. I loped over to him, and when I was just a couple of feet away, damn if that debonair, polished guy didn't suddenly hurl two more sausage balls right at my head. "Thought you might want those," he teased, pushing past me without another glance.

So the little devil flirted right back. Funny that I never realized it for what it was at the time.

Especially since I remember thinking how killer that suit looked on him, with that pinkish-colored tie. That he was sophisticated and smooth in ways I'd never be, and probably had girls all over him wherever he went. I wondered if Louisa ever got jealous about that fact, 'cause I knew I would...if he were mine.

That's what I was thinking as I watched her take the silver platter out of his hands, leaning up on her toes to kiss his cheek, a tender gesture, and an oddly innocent one between two people who I assumed were lovers. He sure as hell struck me as a beautiful man that night, and even way back then, some small voice inside me was willing to admit that fact.

And glancing at him beside me now, sleeping so sweetly, he strikes me as even more gorgeous than four years ago. Probably because I don't have to figure anything out now, don't have to translate the confusing, rogue voices inside my head.

It's very simple: I know I'm in love.

It feels a little weird, not being alone at Christmas. For the past seven years, I've spent every holiday back in L.A., all by my lonesome on the big day. Bowl games, frozen pizza and loads of beer. Not a bad way to pass the time, but it had gotten old. Edna never stopped trying to get me home, but with the short hiatus from the studio and the frigid temperatures back in Iowa, I just couldn't muster much enthusiasm for the trip. Besides, Ed always had plenty of company between her church friends and neighbors.

The past couple of years, the Winchester Contingent—Max, in particular—kept trying to convince me to head home with them. I was pretty tempted, especially last year when Max and I were already damned close, but still I stuck it out alone.

Yet the solo gig didn't fit anymore, either. I think maybe that's why I called him at his folks' house on Christmas Day to wish him a happy holiday. Strange to think we were still just best friends then, because I definitely remember that he sounded a little breathless to hear my voice. He told me he'd missed me, I blushed when he said it, and then mumbled something lame back to him.

Then there was the gift he kind of thrust at me, right at the LAX curbside when I dropped him off last Christmas. One moment he was plunking his bags on the sidewalk, the next leaning back through the passenger door with a foil-covered box.

I pointed at the big, flouncy bow on top. "Louisa wrap that?" I teased, and he smiled a little sheepishly.

"Nope, just me."

"Cool," I said, stalling for a moment, not sure what to say, because I didn't have anything for him. "Thanks, man. I didn't, you know..." I gestured awkwardly at the gift, and he nodded, stepping back onto the curb.

"I know. I just found something you needed."

"Well, uh, thanks."

"Have a great holiday, Hunter. Wish you were coming to Winchester. We all do."

With that, I was left in his car alone, fingering that glittery package and wondering why I felt so squirmy and strange all over. Why my face had flushed hot at the sight of that big, girlish bow.

And wondering why I suddenly wanted to go to Winchester, Virginia with all my heart.

During the haul back to my place that day, I kept wondering what Maxwell might have bought me, what I might need, at least in his estimation. Max's "needs" are much more on the par with most people's desires, I knew that even then, so I figured it was something highbrow and fairly useless in my ultra-utilitarian, blue collar world.

Even though we'd never done the gift thing before and it wasn't part of our friendship, his gesture made me wish I'd taken the time to find him something too. At my apartment, I set the package on the kitchen counter—there wasn't a tree to put it under—and kept staring at it, stalking it, really. The tag on top said, "Don't Open Until Christmas!"

How could I possibly wait? That was two days away and I was so freaking curious. I only had two other gifts, both from Aunt Edna, and I hadn't saved them for Christmas. They were clothes, flannel shirts, just like I figured they'd be. Well, and Veronica had baked me a huge batch of cookies, more than half of which I'd already consumed. She knew that the sprinkled kind were my weakness, God love her.

But with Max's present, somehow I did manage to wait,

thanks to that little admonishment on the tag. Probably, too, because I knew how seriously Max takes Christmas, how much he loves it, and I didn't want to do anything to spoil his surprise.

Christmas morning I woke to just another smoggy L.A. day—sunny and far too quiet outside my apartment. Rolling over in bed, I thought about my friends back in Winchester, wondered what they were doing, if they were together.

And of course, I thought about Max. Why I hadn't just tagged along? Because I missed him, a lot more than I could comfortably admit.

Truth, baby! Sometimes it's a cunning thing, especially when you're not quite ready for it. Those little moments of clarity, the kind when you realize that you're aching inside because your male best friend is several time zones away, well they can be pretty damned unsettling.

What I did with my own burst of realization was pad into the kitchen, bare feet swishing on the carpet, and tear into that wrapped box like a little boy on Christmas morning. Like it might be a train engine or a fire truck, something thrilling and unimaginable.

A card was on top of the tissue paper, just peeking out at me, and I set it aside. Folded carefully within the box, wrapped with incredible loving care was a china tree-topper, a handmade, delicate star that shimmered gold and purple and red. Maxwell knew I never had a tree at my place—we'd talked about it when I helped him wrangle his own home on the top of his Explorer. He knew I just didn't *do* Christmas, had never been into it growing up, despite Edna's endless coaxing.

Tears blurred my vision, as I opened the card and read his words.

Start making some memories, Hunter. Life's too short

without them. Maybe you'll spend next Christmas in Winchester? Love, Max.

I don't know what struck me more, the gesture or what he'd written, though I definitely noticed one word in particular. Couldn't look away from it for the very life of me. *Love.*

And I think I opened my heart to the possibility of it with him just a tiny bit more that day.

As we make our way up the steps of John and Leah's house, I can't resist pointing at her holiday flag, flapping in the chilly breeze. Three green elves are wearing red and white fur, but manage to look more like aliens. Kind of like Santa's helpers meet *The X-Files*. They look really silly, as if someone unexpectedly sprang those suits on them, someone from a bad wardrobe department for a B-grade movie.

"Look, they're cross-dressing," I murmur in his ear, as I drop two shopping bags filled with packages on their front step. I expect him to laugh it up with me, but instead, he answers by slugging me. Hard.

"Hey!" I protest, rubbing my arm.

"You deserved it." But he's smiling, and I know he's just playing right back with me. He loves that I can't quite get Maxine out of my head; that I keep bringing her up in offhand ways.

"Maybe it's just a Winchester thing. You know, drag queens," I say, right as the door flings open. And there's Leah, wearing a similar Santa's hat, all red and white faux fur.

"Max!" she squeals, flinging her arms around his neck, and he leans in close for a heartfelt hug. What a difference from last time, I think, as Leah holds on to him, eyes pressed shut like she's savoring the moment.

Finally, they step apart, and she turns to me. A little cooler, but still my friend, she smiles and draws me into her arms for an embrace. It's different than last time. It's real and warm and makes me feel oddly uncomfortable. I've never had a sister, so I'm not sure how to do this. "Hunter, I'm so glad you're here."

I break the hug, feeling awkward. "Yeah, uh, good to be back." She doesn't seem to notice my discomfort, because all her attention zooms back on to her brother as she tugs him inside the house with a stream of questions.

I follow dutifully behind, carrying our suitcases and thinking that she's still my new best friend, for reaching out to Max like this, for saving his Christmas. Even though I never thought I'd say it, I definitely love her.

I just have to get comfortable with being part of her family.

John appears from the kitchen, where I hear a chorus of familiar voices. I make out Louisa's laughter and Veronica's giggles, right as the warm smell of home-baked cookies hits my senses.

"There you are!" Veronica pokes her head out of the kitchen with a generous wave in our direction. "The boys are back in town!"

"We thought you'd never get here," Louisa chimes, and blows us both a kiss.

"Long flight, you know," I kind of mumble, glancing all around me. Max sails right to the kitchen, hugging Veronica and Louisa, and I suddenly feel stranded. Like a stranger in the middle of what should be familiar territory.

That feeling of panic from the car intensifies. It's rapid and suffocating, only now there's nothing to white-knuckle except the suitcase that I'm left gripping in my hand.

"Can I take that for you, Hunter?" John asks, patting me on the back. "Show you the guest room?" For a moment, I feel a little dazed, and wonder if he means that I'll be staying in a room by myself again, without Max.

But I can't possibly voice that question, and instead I find myself following him toward the back of the house, kind of agreeing to a long series of his friendly questions. What a great guy, it's still true; he just chatters along about how glad he is we've come, that we didn't let "things" keep us away. That Leah's thrilled we're staying with them.

Then we're in the guest room, and I see that there's a king-sized bed, piled high with downy comforters and feather pillows. Totally inviting, with no doubt about the message it all conveys. He confirms my thoughts. "This is where you and Max are staying."

Together. No arguments, no confusion, and certainly no shame.

"Thanks, man," I mumble, feeling slightly embarrassed. Not sure why, I mean, hell, he toasted to our wedding just a couple of months back. Maybe it's just that he's so freaking open about us being together.

He leaves me alone to settle in, and I sink to the edge of the bed. My heart is racing and I've broken out into a cold sweat. For a long moment, I stare at the rug and wonder what the fuck is wrong with me. I'm with my soul mate, home for Christmas, part of his family.

I should be happy, because for the first time in years, I'm not alone. But the problem is, I've spent my whole life alone, so maybe I can't do this. Maybe I'm just no good at being part of a tribe.

"Hunter?" Max pokes his head into the bedroom, and his eyes are shadowed with worry. "You okay?"

I'm lying on the guest bed, staring up at the ceiling, feeling cranky as hell.

"Just tired." It's more of a grunt than an actual statement.

Max shuts the door behind him and steps close. He runs his hand over the top of his head, and I know that look on his face; he's not sure how to read me or what I need.

"That all?" he finally asks, sounding uncertain.

"'Course that's all. Think I'm gonna take a nap." Never mind that I've just blown off everyone back in the kitchen and living room.

Max settles on the mattress edge and reaches to brush my hair away from my face. "Hunter, talk to me." I recoil from his touch, jerking my head sideways, and he withdraws his hand like he's just been burned.

"Everything's fine." My voice is tight, like the rest of me feels.

"Doesn't seem like it."

"Leave it alone, Maxwell. I'm okay."

He licks his lips and still just stares at me.

"What?" I finally cry, meeting his intense gaze. "What's the problem? I'm tired, all right?"

"And you're being a dick."

"Oh, thanks a lot, man."

"Hunter, I realize this is new for you, that it feels different being with everybody for Christmas." His voice is soft and patient. "I know that, but you're going to have to try."

"Stop it."

"Stop what?"

"Trying to read me, to analyze me like some goddamned shrink."

He laughs, which seems odd, seeing as how we're

launching into a full-scale argument. "*What?*" I cry again, my eyes growing wide, because he doesn't seem angry at all, just a little sad, as he reaches to cup my face within his palm. This time I don't pull away.

"Hunter, you're an open book," he says with a faint smile. "You always think you're such a mystery when the whole world can read everything about you. Especially me."

"Oh, that's just fucking great. I'm transparent." I grumble the words, but I find my anger fading. God, why does he have to be so gentle with me? So loving and clued into all my emotions, especially when I'm being such an asshole.

"You're perfect," he whispers, leaning low to kiss me. His lips are soft, and a little salty, as they brush against mine. "And beautiful and I love you. You know how much I love you."

"You taste like...nuts," I observe.

"Roasted chestnuts. John did them out on the grill."

I shake my head in disbelief. "This really is going to be like some kind of Dickens Christmas, isn't it?"

He smiles a long moment, leaning in to kiss me again. "You can do it."

"But what if I can't?"

"Then you still have me."

I know he understands, that he gets how hard this is for me. How my whole life I've felt like an orphan—hell, I've been one, despite Aunt Edna raising me. But there are things at play here that he doesn't know, that I've never told him, and I think he understands that too.

I rake a hand through my long hair, blowing out a heavy breath. The crazy nervousness is fading now, because he's with me. "I'm trying, Max, I really am. I mean coming here, and, and..."

He cuts me off. "I know that."

"It's weird, that's all. I'm not used to all this traditional stuff."

"You're used to me. Well, at least, a little bit by now," he says, gazing at me through his thick lashes, and I pull him hard against my chest.

"Very used to you. And to loving you," I whisper, pressing a tender kiss against the top of his head. I trace my fingertips over the luscious, short hair. "'Cause I do. So much, and I want to get this right."

He leans up and smiles gently, nuzzling his mouth against my cheek, whispering, "The only thing you have to get right is just being you."

"Then let's go find a beer," I say, and he laughs, rising to his feet again, as I sit up on the bed.

"Sure," he agrees, narrowing his eyes at me. "Just don't expect any frozen pizza, okay?"

"Damn, baby, that's what I came for."

"Bowl games, yes. Frozen pizza, no."

"Then I'll survive," I laugh, as I follow him out of the bedroom, gathering my nerve to face the others. "Give me my football and I can definitely survive."

Unexpectedly, he turns back toward me, and says, "Hunter, you were surviving for a long time. This is being with the people who love you."

And he doesn't even wait for me to respond, just leaves me there, his pointed words ringing in that hallway like bells from some Christmas lost long ago.

Chapter Twelve

"Okay, so we're going to divide into groups," Leah announces, giving her red Santa hat an adjustment as she speaks. She's gathered us into the kitchen like efficient holiday troops, pairing us up into teams. Maxwell and I will work together. Veronica will go with Louisa, and Ben will head off with John, while Leah goes to oversee a pageant rehearsal downtown.

Work. That's what this seems like to me, but for some reason everybody else is laughing and making jokes. Apparently, they really love this drill.

Leah thrusts a huge plate of cookies into my hands. "Hunter, you and Max are going to the retirement home, then meeting Veronica and Louisa at the orphanage afterward."

"Why?" It's not what I mean to ask, but still the word pops right out of my mouth. What I really wonder is whether or not Maxwell put her up to this, me going to the orphanage.

"Because it's what we do every year," Max explains evenly. His eyes lock with mine, and I glimpse a flare of understanding in his gaze. I can see that it's not a setup by the kind reassurance in his expression.

Veronica slips her arm around my waist, hugging me tight. "It's what we always do, Willis, only you're a part of everything now."

"Lucky for us, because otherwise Max would be sulking again like last year," Louisa says, tossing a pointed glance in Max's direction. He smiles guiltily, tugging at the zipper on his leather jacket. It's a nervous habit of his, one I know from experience.

"I wish Hunter had come with us," Veronica mimics melodramatically.

Louisa places an exaggerated hand over her heart, adding, "He's all *alone* back in *Los Angeles*."

"Maybe we should call him!" Ben laughs.

Poor Max just shakes his head at all of them, glancing at me a little shyly as he shoves his hands in his pockets.

"You missed me?" I blurt before I can stop myself. I'm thinking of how damned much I missed him all last Christmas.

The look on Maxwell's face says it all, as he kind of gives a strangled cough. "Well, I told you that when you called here, remember?"

Yeah, baby, I definitely remember. How clammy that receiver felt in my hand as I kicked back on the sofa with a beer. How I never wanted our conversation to end, that I kept replaying it in my mind for days afterward.

"Oh, God, was *that* why my brother was so testy last year?" Leah groans, staring at Louisa and Veronica in sudden understanding. "Because he missed Hunter?"

"Bingo!" Ben says.

"We're talking major crush." Veronica spreads her hands wide in explanation. "Huge. Bigger than big."

Max looks really sheepish and stares at his shoes for a minute, rocking heel to toe. "Guys, I wasn't that bad."

Leah stares at her brother, aghast. "No, Max, I distinctly remember pulling you off of the sofa to help me in the kitchen.

More than once. I just didn't know why you were so morose."

"Are you sure that wasn't me the first Christmas we were married?" John asks, grinning at me. I swear he nearly gives a wink.

"No, that would be me most every year," Ben says. "Forget good deeds. I'm all about pure, unadulterated holiday laziness."

The jabs continue until Leah reaches for her coat, shaking her head. "Hunter, they're just impossible, every last one of them. Thank God you're here to shake things up for a change."

"Why, Leah? To increase the body count?" Max teases, following after her, laughing like a little kid. "So we can hit ten charity events instead of eight this time? Or would that be twelve with Hunter's help?"

Leah tugs on a pair of expensive leather gloves with the precision of a Marine Corps commander. "I'm not listening to you, Max Daniels. Not listening at all." But I hear amusement in her voice as she swings open the door with a flourish and announces to us all, "Report back at seventeen-hundred hours."

"As you wish, Captain." I flip a sharp salute her way.

"Willis, don't even start."

Gauging by the collective groans from our friends, I'm pretty sure I'll have to take my place in line if I do.

At the orphanage, Veronica plays guitar and sings Christmas carols for the kids. Max sits on the floor, holding a golden-haired toddler on his lap, softly stroking her hair. They're cuddled up like lifelong friends, just listening to the music together. She kind of reminds me of that kid at the beach last summer, the one he befriended. Man, Max has got a way with children. Watching him work that room, I feel alternately awed and clueless. I decide to stake out a place by the window and stand there on the edge, where it's safe.

Problem is, I know the expressions I see here far too well, the shadowed loneliness in the eyes of these children. I can't look too closely at any of them, because if I do, I won't be able to stick around. Instead I focus on Maxwell, on how amazing he is with all these children, so gentle and kind. He makes them laugh by pulling faces and crawling around on the floor after them.

He'd make a fantastic dad. Realizing that kind of causes my heart to ache—yet leaves me feeling oddly hopeful, too. Like maybe one day we could adopt or something. Who knows, but I love seeing this side to him. He's so carefree with these kids. After all, nobody here gives a crap if he's queer, a cross-dresser or a millionaire. Nobody cares if he cooks like Emeril or makes money like Donald Trump.

He's just a guy who can give killer pony rides and make a Santa puppet sound convincing and funny.

God, I love him. He's all I ever wanted in a wife.

He's all I ever wanted in a father, too. That's what I realize, watching him be so loving with all these kids. Hell, I'm not sure what I'm thinking—certainly not that he's my dad or anything creepy like that. It's more like I have some weird memory flash, as I watch him cradle that little girl close on his lap, whispering in her ear.

The memories fold around me and I remember my own daddy, how he always made Christmas such a big deal. It's one of the four or five things I even recall about my parents apart from the day they died.

That last Christmas, my father took me out into the woods. I followed him in the snow, stepping into his huge footprints until we found just the right tree. I can hear the sound of that buzz saw powering up, filling the wintry silence with a loud roar. Then there's the soft thud of the fir branches hitting the damp earth, and my father dropping low to the ground, touching the prickly pine with me. There's my small hand beneath his large gloved one, stroking the branches.

Son, it's a living thing. You gotta respect the nobility of that.

He was just an autoworker, an assembly line guy, yet he had a total grasp on the universe. Maybe it's why I love working with a block of wood so much, that same simplicity. Sometimes I wonder if I'm nothing more than the sum of who they both were. Even worse, I worry that I don't add up nearly so well, that I'm just a shadowed reflection of them. Now that question hounds me a lot more often than I like to admit.

But what scares me the most is how close Maxwell's come to figuring it all out, pounding me with those direct questions of his I can't quite evade.

With a snap of Louisa's camera lens, I'm slammed back into the moment. Good thing, too, because Maxwell's watching me. Carefully. I plaster on a smile for his benefit and shake off that memory—before it can penetrate me. Or open me up too much.

Somehow, though, as Max studies me from across the room, I'm sure he isn't finished with me yet. Even worse, I suspect my memories aren't either.

Our group has converged on a big downtown park where there's a Santa village, complete with elves and helpers. Naturally, it comes as no surprise when I spot Leah in the crowd, handing out candy canes.

"Those are the kids from the Y program. The one for underprivileged kids," Max explains, leaning close to my ear. "Leah arranges for them to get free pictures with Santa every year."

"That's great." I nod, watching a knot of little people squealing in laughter about some shared joke.

As for me, I'm working hard at being sociable for Max's sake, but damned if I'm not becoming more reclusive by the moment. I feel like an outsider, an observer as my lover and friends convene across timeworn territory. Then again, maybe I'm still haunted by those children at the orphanage.

I was one of the lucky ones; I never spent time in a place like that. After the accident, I was kept at the home of a neighbor, someone who picked me up from kindergarten that day and simply said, "Your mommy and daddy had to go someplace. They sent me instead."

Cowards. God love 'em for what they did to help, but what kind of asshole tells a kid who's just been orphaned that his parents sent them?

Edna hopped the next flight out from Iowa City and by nightfall had arrived in our Detroit suburb. The minute I saw her gentle brown eyes peering at me from the doorway to the neighbor's den, I knew something was wrong. I think I realized just how bad it was when she swept me into her generous arms and rocked me against her chest. "Hunter, I love you," she whispered. "I'm going to take good care of you. I promise."

After that, she explained about the solid, Detroit-built automobile that had failed my father's unwavering confidence. She left out words I learned much later; words like "drunk driver" and "death on impact". No, that day, she spoke to me like the five-year-old I was, using simple words to convey the truth. "Mommy and Daddy won't be coming back, sweetheart," she said.

Kind of hard to forget something like that, even after all these years.

Thing is, I have far more memories of their death than I do

of their lives. And that's always seemed more than slightly fucked up to me.

"Horrendous, isn't it?" Max asks, giving me a tentative smile.

I didn't realize that I'd begun staring off into space. Correction, my unfocused gaze has apparently centered itself on an alien Santa helper. It's something of a lawn gnome, there in the middle of the park. Ugly as sin, like about a million other items in this freaky desert town.

"Been an annual fixture in this park for my whole life."

I nod, feeling numbed by the memories that have cloaked themselves around me like a gauzy web. Maxwell's not daunted, though, and presses happily along with his story. "When Louisa and I were fifteen, I dared her to steal it one night. To keep it until the next day," he admits. "What do you think she did?" he finally asks when I say nothing.

"No clue," I half-grumble, aware that he's too bright. Working too hard to be sure I'm really okay.

"She planted it on my parents' lawn."

"Huh."

"I was grounded for the rest of the holidays."

I just nod along with him, barely listening, because for some reason I'm remembering the tacky manger scene at Richman Brothers Funeral Home.

"Hunter, are you all right?" he asks after a long silence falls between us. We're walking around the park together, strolling aimlessly. It's the kind of thing that would've made me feel really close to him normally. Made me feel like his lover, the way his elbow keeps brushing mine, the way he's touching my arm in concern. We're a hell of a lot closer than two macho guys out for a walk. We're together, and anybody who looks our way can see it.

But I'm not in that moment. I'm light years away, back in my past.

"Fine, baby. Promise." I turn to watch the children scampering around Santa's village. A mother holds her small son's hand. She's pregnant, probably due in a month at the latest, and my heartbeat quickens painfully as I watch the boy touch her large belly.

Max steps even closer into my space, clasping my forearm. "I'm worried about you." He's serious as a heart attack, and I can tell he's not gonna mess around about my bad mood anymore.

I scowl, feeling irritable with him that he won't let it go. "Look, I don't want to do some autopsy on my mental state, Maxwell," I say. "Don't push me like this. Told you that earlier."

"I'm not pushing." His voice kind of breaks and I literally see hurt shadow his handsome features. "I love you and I'm worried, that's all." We fall silent for a long moment—me gazing anywhere but into his melancholy eyes, him trying hard to stare into my own.

Finally he gives a weary sigh. "I just wish you'd talk to me, Hunter. It's not like you to shut me out like this. You've never done that before."

"Shit, Max, don't be such a goddamned girl," I bark before I can stop myself. He looks like I've just slapped him hard across the face, as he takes two steps back from me.

God, he was right earlier. I am such a first-class dick. I don't deserve him, or my friends. No wonder I've spent most of my life alone.

"I'm going for a walk," I finally mutter into our shared silence, staggering past him.

I move across the park, toward a covered picnic area. It's far enough away that maybe I can breathe a little. Maybe I can regain my equilibrium instead of feeling like my life's just been smashed all to hell.

"How about Havana's finest?" John asks. He's standing on the edge of the picnic gazebo, extending two gorgeous looking Cuban cigars toward me. Yeah, it's bribery, plain and simple. I wonder how Maxwell sent him home that fast.

"Maxwell's?" I ask, lifting an eyebrow as I lean back against the picnic bench. I've only had about ten minutes to sift through my wildly careening emotions, and so far I haven't made much progress.

"I brought them along in case we needed them. I hear you have a wicked appreciation for a good smoke." He hands me a nicely trimmed cigar. "You want this? Or should I save it for Leah?"

That actually manages to get a snort out of me. "She smoke these things very often?"

"Oh, man, all the time. She's worse than me," he says. "But then again, she's a Daniels. They're all pretty intense, don't you think?"

Intense. Not a bad way to describe my sweetheart, even though Max seems to possess a more lighthearted side than his twin does.

Then we kind of start gabbing about the loves of our lives, comparing notes like a pair of girlfriends. It would be comical if I weren't so depressed.

"Did Max send you over?" I finally ask, going on a strong hunch.

White teeth flash against that very dark skin. "He's concerned, that's all."

"Did he send the cigars, too?"

"No, those are all me."

"Cool," I say, taking a long drag. God, nothing tastes better than a smoke on a cold, gray day like this one.

I'm about to voice that thought, when Max says, "You love smoking when it's cold." He steps into the cabana, and I can tell he's wondering if I even want him around me at the moment. My heart clenches tight, and I urge him closer. "Baby, you can share."

"Oh, I've got one for Max, too," John volunteers. "I brought them along figuring we would need a decent Leah escape."

"God, I feel like I owe you both some huge cosmic apology for Leah's Christmas mania," Max says, dropping onto the picnic bench, close beside me. His jean-clad thigh brushes very close against mine, way closer than a mere friend. It's so freaking cool that we can be real around John.

"It makes her happy and that's all that matters to me," John says.

Max glances at me, a heavy-lidded look into my very soul. "Yeah, when you're in love, that's all you want." Bingo, the boy just nailed me good. "For them to be happy."

Max brushes his fingers against the back of my hand. He won't actually reach to hold it with John here, no matter how open his brother-in-law is. But the subtle gesture tells me everything about how much Max wishes that he could.

I take another long drag on the cigar, staring into the distance at the Santa village. The pregnant mother and little boy have finished with the pictures; now they're walking across the park. She holds his tiny hand within her much larger one.

Something about that sight just burns hard into my mind, like an afterimage from staring at the sun.

Thing is, Maxwell needs to know the deeper places inside me. Otherwise our union won't mean as much, because he won't have come all the way in. After all, he's made himself vulnerable as hell with me, trusting me with all his little broken pieces. Kind of makes me wonder why I've held out on him for so damned long with my own crazy shit.

And I want him to know everything now, even the secrets I've fought so hard not to tell anyone. I want him to walk into those hidden chambers and smash them wide open with me.

After all, who better to make that journey with than the love of my life?

Chapter Thirteen

Thing is, once I decide to tell Maxwell the truth, my mood improves instantly. Secrets are like that. They weigh you down, burden you, shut you off from those you love the most. Just knowing I'll tell my lover everything, that someone in my life other than Edna is gonna know exactly how it is, well it catapults me right into the holiday spirit. Even though I haven't told Maxwell a damned thing just yet.

That's probably why I give him serious hell once he takes hold of Leah's kitchen, because I'm feeling a little frisky now. Flour flies in every direction, the blender whirs. Kind of like our place most any night of the week, except to quote Max's buddy Emeril, he's "taking it up a notch". I'm not sure I've ever seen him labor quite so long over any one meal.

I keep circling his way, poking my head into the kitchen. "What're you making now?" I ask, brushing a dab of flour off his cheek.

"Gravy." He smiles at my questions, 'cause he loves it when I get interested in his cooking. "Trying something a little different this time," he adds, and then I get a detailed explanation as to the benefit of a thinner sauce on the Yorkshire pudding he's been slaving over. I nod dutifully, then wander back to the living room, sinking onto the sofa beside John. He and I are watching bowl games with Ben, while Leah helps her brother in the kitchen. It's just us for now, because Louisa and Veronica have gone home to do the family drill until later, when the meal's on deck.

Frankly, it suits me to have some down time because I'm all worn out from Leah's charity stuff. I'm telling you, it was more work than a typical day down at the lot. Thank God for John's generous beer supply, which I dove into soon as we returned from our rounds. I've been drinking and watching football ever since, which has definitely helped my season to be jolly. That, and seeing how relieved Max is that I've shaken off the darkness.

And he's definitely relieved, so much so that he's kissed me about a dozen times since we got back from the park. In the powder room. In the hallway. Beside the refrigerator. That's one thing you discover about being gay—so long as you're clandestine about it, you can still get some serious ass.

Max whistles as he moves around the kitchen, and although I've sunk way down into the sofa, my boots propped out in front of me, I'm still studying him. I've got a perfect view from the great room into the kitchen. What a beautiful man, I think, watching him scowl at the open cookbook propped on the bar ledge. He catches me and gives a shy smile that makes me blush unexpectedly. That only makes his smile grow much wider. Good, 'cause the last thing I wanted was to give him hell today, not when he was already dealing with his family shit. At least he hasn't mentioned Phillip so far, and I can only take that as positive sign.

For a while, I settle back into watching the game and chatting it up with John. I'm telling you, my future brother-in-law is a great conversationalist. We can talk about nothing much at all, and I'm still left feeling like I've made a true connection. That's what I'm thinking when I glance up from the television again, only to find Max manhandling a blowtorch.

Obviously it's time for me to find out what the hell my boy's doing, so I lope in there right as he powers the thing up, blue flame darting wildly. Leah's watching from where she stands at the center island working on a casserole.

"Whoa! Maxwell, what's this?" I ask, and Leah makes a face over his shoulder, the kind that indicates she's glad I'm butting in.

"Making crème brulee. It's our dessert later."

I nod at what he's doing. "Yeah, well you don't have a freaking clue how to use that thing."

"Thank you, Hunter," Leah agrees, planting a hand on her hip. "Maybe he'll listen to you."

Max lifts up a small soufflé dish toward the flame. "I know exactly what I'm doing," he announces slowly. "Don't be so overprotective."

"Hold up, Maxwell," I blurt because he's got the torch way too close to his face. "Let me do this."

"No."

"Baby."

"No." This time he sounds really pissed about it, and I'm certain that familiar temper's about to kick in.

"Have you even operated one of these puppies before?" I ask, trying not to worry about how close he's got the torch to his beautiful eyes.

"I saw this on the Food Network."

"Well, Maxwell, I wouldn't trade stocks based on reading the *Wall Street Journal*, either." I reach for the torch again. "This is my thing. Come on, let me do this."

The golden eyes narrow and for a minute I think he's going to give me hell. Then, the strangest thing happens. He starts laughing, as he shuts the torch off. "You realize how ridiculous this is? We're fighting over power tools."

"In the kitchen, no less," Leah agrees. "Talk about two worlds colliding. I mean, Max, you do realize they sell special gourmet torches, right?"

"But they're not as effective," he explains in a patient voice. "The flame doesn't distribute evenly or properly."

"Uh, huh," I say, sounding as skeptical as I can manage when he looks so adorably befuddled, caught between us both this way.

"It's true!" he argues, smiling faintly. Yeah, he knows he's whipped.

"You gonna let me help with this thing or not?" I nudge him with my shoulder. "Or is the kitchen your sacred domain?"

He stares down at the torch, and then back up into my eyes without saying a word. God, he's gorgeous. The black cashmere turtleneck he's wearing only makes him look even hotter than usual. I blink, aware that I'm blushing slightly because of how hungry I suddenly feel for him. Just like earlier, when he gave me that faint smile from the kitchen. I'm a goner for him when he wears black, no joke.

"You do it," he finally says with an offhanded shrug. "You're good with a tool."

"Oh, God, I so did not hear that." Leah steps past us, toward the oven.

"Don't mind our innuendo." Max's gaze never leaves my face. "We're just two guys in love."

Okay, so now I'm blushing like a maniac, feeling embarrassed in front of his formerly homophobic twin sister.

Except, she seems genuinely amused, and plays right along. "Wow, Max, I had no idea. Here I was thinking you and Hunter were just having a power tool moment."

"Have to hit Home Depot for that action," Ben shouts from the living room, obviously having followed our exchange. "It's gaydar central over there, guys!"

Inspired, I take the blowtorch, kind of sticking it between my legs with an exaggerated flourish. Assuming my most effeminate voice I say, "Well, if you want to talk power tools, sweet pea, you can check mine out anytime over on aisle sixty-nine." At that exact moment, I wriggle my wrist, allowing the torch to give a little thrust of flame for dramatic emphasis.

Max bursts out laughing, raking a hand over his short hair in a sexy, jittery way. Hard to believe, but I think I've finally managed to unnerve him.

Leah gives a little sniff, tossing her ponytail primly over her shoulder, and says, "Hunter, if you care to operate your tool, then proceed at your own risk."

From the living room, I hear Ben call, "Here, here! Watch and learn!"

More laughter, and my face burns, as Leah hands me the first dish of crème Brulee with a smug smile of satisfaction. She's managed to get me good, it's true.

"What's a nice tool doing in a place like this?" I ask, staring right at the blowtorch.

And for a moment, I half expect the freaking thing to answer me.

Much later, there's only Maxwell and me still awake. I find myself sitting in the dark living room, staring at the Christmas tree. Max collapses on the sofa beside me with a weary sigh, and I reach for his hand, threading my fingers together with his. Feels good to finally make that physical connection with him, especially after such a long day without it.

For a while neither of us even speak, we just sit together, holding hands by the shimmering lights of the tree.

Leah and John have already turned in for the night, so I'm certain we're all alone when I get inspired, and say, "I wanna give you something, Max." I kneel down beside the tree and dig around for one special gift that I've tucked away for him. Takes me a minute to find what I'm after, then when I glance back at him, he's vanished.

Turns out he's got a surprise of his own, because he reappears in the doorway with an open bottle of Dom Perignon and two champagne flutes balanced elegantly between his fingers. Apparently he'd already iced down the bubbly a while ago.

"What's that?" I ask, grinning up at him. The slow, seductive smile I get in return tells me all I need to know about his intentions for later tonight.

"A little holiday cheer."

"Looks like," I say, sliding the foil-wrapped gift across the rug toward the sofa where he settles. "And this is for you." His dark eyes widen at the sight of the package.

"Hunter, I thought we were going to exchange tomorrow night," he argues, but he's smiling like a little boy.

I shrug, scratching my eyebrow. "Well, it's Christmas Eve," I say. "And I wanted to give you something special tonight." I've done his holiday right, and I know it. It's only a matter of time until he does, too. "Maybe this could, well, become a new tradition," I add. "For us, I mean. You know, a holiday thing." Something about that thought makes me realize it's my first Christmas as his lover—and our first Christmas as a couple.

His eyes glitter in the near darkness. "I'd like that."

I nod, trying to regain a little of the composure I feel slipping from my grasp. "Cool."

He drops down onto his knees beside me, and whispers. "You should open something, too." He bends past me, practically leaning right into my lap, as he searches for the gift he apparently has in mind.

I can't resist stroking his hip, not with him pressing so close against me, so I reach for him, my calloused fingertips meeting the soft wool of his cashmere sweater, the thick denim of his jeans. For a moment, he stills beside me, and I slip my hand beneath the sweater, lifting it. Until my fingers stroke the warm skin of his abdomen.

A little audible sound escapes my lips before I can stop it. He drops back beside me, studying my face seriously as he places my present on the floor. I take my cue and lean in for a slow, simmering kiss. His lips barely touch mine at first, even though my mouth opens hungrily. Then, I feel his tongue dart with my own, as my hand closes around his waist.

"Oh," is all I can say. "Oh, oh." The kiss deepens as he laces his arms around my neck. I'm not even worried about his family, I'm only thinking about how goddamned much I suddenly want him.

My hand finds its way into his bristling hair, stroking it, as our kiss grows intense and a little desperate. In the space of a heartbeat, my cock's aching for release, but then a soft gasp punctuates our silence, as he pushes apart from me. "Hunter," he pants, brushing at his disheveled hair. His gaze tracks toward the kitchen, then the hallway.

"Stupid, I know," I admit, wiping my damp mouth. I know what he's thinking—Leah or John could easily have discovered us.

"No, that's not it," he says, his chest still rising with uneven breaths. "Just, well, we're opening presents now." That's what he's so worked up about? "I mean, aren't we?" he asks, looking uncertain.

I can't help laughing a moment. "Baby, is that why you're putting on the breaks?" I still hold him close by the waist, practically drawing him right onto my lap where I sit on the floor.

He laughs softly, too. "I guess it's silly, but I'm really excited about you opening my present." My heart beats a little bit faster; I can't believe I'm with someone who wants to please me so damned much. Who wants to give me so damned much of himself.

"Sure, Max," I say, my voice coming out strange and thick. I can't think of anything else to add, nothing that will sound meaningful like I want.

"Don't get me wrong," he rushes to explain. "I-I want, well, you and all..."

"I know that."

"Because I wouldn't want you to think..."

"Maxwell, get over yourself and open this damned thing," I say, shoving my own foil wrapped gift his way.

He nods, settling beside me on the floor, and begins opening it. The wrapping unfolds delicately, until he's clutching a small leather-bound book within his hands. His dark eyebrows draw together, as he thumbs through the volume, fanning the blank pages.

"Is it a diary?" he asks, clearly confused. I reach for it and turn to the front page.

"Here, look." I show him my inscription. *Maxwell's Kitchen: A Book of Treasures*. "It's for your recipes. The ones you come up with yourself." Then I flip to the first few pages, where Louisa has recorded some of his originals in her very neat handwriting.

For what seems like forever, he doesn't say a word, just stares down at the pages, tracing his fingertip over my writing, then Louisa's. When he looks up again, he gives me a fabulous smile, leaning close to kiss me. "Thank you, baby," he says, his voice hoarse in my ear. I rarely get any endearments out of him; maybe he's afraid I'll laugh them off or something. So when I do, I know his emotions are at a fever pitch.

I close my arm around his waist, holding him against me for a long moment. "Lots of blank pages, so you can fill them up when you go to cooking school."

"I love you, Hunter," he whispers in my ear, resting his cheek against my shoulder. "You are so kind to me."

For some reason, his words remind me of what a bastard I was earlier, of how impossible and mean I was in the face of his unconditional love.

"Maybe every now and then," I mumble, stroking his hair. He doesn't budge, just folds his arms around me, snuggling close.

"Oh, you are very good to me."

"Not today."

He doesn't miss a beat, just rubs my lower back. "You were hurting. I knew that." How does he understand me so goddamned well? I shift a bit, trying to slip out of his grasp, but he won't let me. Just stares hard into my eyes.

"You were hurting because of the orphanage," he presses. "I never should have let you go with us."

I shake my head, dismissing his concerns. "Maxwell, I never spent time anywhere like that. No big deal, really."

"But it reminded you of losing your parents."

I don't answer him for a long time. Try to decide if I'm really ready to be this honest yet.

I choose a different tact, and while it's not what he wants to hear, it's still something I need to say. "I shouldn't have made that comment. About you being such a girl."

"You're changing the subject."

"I didn't want to hurt you. About Maxine and...all that."

"How could you possibly?" he asks in a sharp voice. "The only thing that hurt me was knowing that today made you remember losing your parents."

"Maybe." I shrug noncommittally.

"Okay, well when are you going to talk to me about it? I've known you almost five years," he says, slightly breathless. "I've been your lover all these months, and you've never once opened up to me about losing them."

"Never talk about them period. It's not you."

"But I'm your lover," he says again, eyes growing wide with emotion. "If you can't open up with me about it, then I'm not sure we'll ever really be a family."

God, he's shot me right in the heart with those words, felled me like a giant to the freaking earth. I can only stare back at him, blinking, fighting tears.

"I want children, Hunter," he says finally. "I want to make a family with you. But how can we possibly do that if you can't face Christmas?"

"Don't you fucking get it, man?" I shout, not even worried about how loud I am. I'd planned to tell him everything, but now that the moment's here, the feelings come storming out of me, boiling over like hot poison. "That's when it happened." The words are out before I can stop them. Just out there, hanging, shooting him right back in the heart. "They died on December eighteenth. How's that for a goddamned holiday memory?"

He lifts a hand and slowly strokes my hair. "That must

have been so hard," he whispers, nodding, as hot tears spill down my cheeks uncontrollably.

"My mom was pregnant," I admit in a hoarse voice. "I was gonna have a little brother."

"Oh, Hunter," he murmurs. "I'm so sorry. So sorry that you lost your family."

"Thing I remember most are all those presents under the tree. After the funeral."

I stare into the distance because I need him to know what I'm not able to verbalize. That once they were gone and buried and my life had ended, the toys were still wrapped up, waiting for a Christmas that would never come. The things they bought for a little boy they loved, the things they knew I'd hoped for since summer. Memories I'd never share with them.

"No wonder the holidays are so difficult," he acknowledges, still stroking and petting me. Soothing me. In one burst of movement, I bury my face against his strong shoulder.

"I hate this time of year, Maxwell. You have no idea. I can't ever seem to shake this shit."

The funeral home with its giant artificial trees and tacky manger scene. The scent of flowers mingled with fresh pine; a sickly sweet smell that has haunted me all my life.

"We can make it new together," he promises softly, kissing me on the cheek. "That's what we can do, Hunter. Make it our very own. Like you said earlier, about starting traditions."

I nod, blinded by the tears, as he just kind of rocks me in his arms. "I never told any of you," I say. "I couldn't."

"You could always tell me. You just weren't ready."

For what seems an eternity, he comforts me beneath the twinkling lights of that tree, etching a new Christmas memory into my heart. One where a strong man holds me until I sleep, beating back all the demons that would have my very soul.

One where I'm loved like perfection until the ghosts fade away, that's the Christmas memory Max Daniels makes for me beneath that tree.

Chapter Fourteen

Staring at myself in the bathroom mirror, I understand why Max wanted me to open this particular present tonight. Ralph Lauren satin pajamas. Royal blue. Damn, baby, you know how to dress your fag up right. I feel kind of faggy in them too, so I adjust the pants, pulling them lower down my hips. Anything not to seem like such a bad imitation of Thurston Howell the Third. I mean, Maxwell can pull this look off without batting an eyelash. But me? I'm an Iowa kid who grew up sleeping in long johns on cold nights and buck naked in the summertime.

Another glance in the full-length mirror, and I unbutton the top, opening it across my chest. A soft tuft of dark hair appears, and funny enough, I get a little more comfortable with the get-up. I do actually look kind of sexy. Maybe even fuckable, though I'd never have bought something this flashy for myself. Max looked pleased as hell when I opened the package up too. Apparently, when he imagined the pajamas on me, he had to disguise his hard-on right in the middle of Neiman's.

So he wants me as a boy toy for Christmas? No problem, I can deliver.

My hair's wet from the shower and I rake my fingers through it, trying to comb it into a neater mess. Maxwell's waiting for me in the bedroom. The room they gave us is something of a suite, with bathroom and fireplace included.

When we came to bed, we discovered that Leah had turned on the gas logs for us. Damn, I couldn't help wondering if she didn't want me to do her brother right in her very own home.

With one final, appraising glance in the mirror, I open the bathroom door. I find Maxwell sprawled in front of the fire, with nothing but a bath towel hiding his natural gifts. His hair is soaking wet, spiky and delicious, but his body is what I can't tear my gaze away from. He's lying on his stomach, kind of just warming himself, the towel contoured to his muscled physique, outlining every last glorious detail.

I step toward him, giving my pajama pants a tug because my groin tightens at the sight of him. He gives me a coy glance over his shoulder, closing the men's magazine he's been reading. *Details* or something like that. "Wow, Hunter. You look really...lovely."

I cough, feeling my face burn as I walk toward him. "Why not brand me queer right off the bat, baby love."

"You *are* queer, sweet cakes."

He rolls onto his side, propping his head on his elbow. I drop to my knees beside him. "I feel a little ridiculous," I admit, fingering the hem of the silken top between my rough fingertips. "Like a girl or something."

"You look like one gorgeous man to me." He slips a hand beneath the shirt and gives my stomach a gentle rub, just a loving touch to reassure me.

"So, I'm macho enough to pull this look off, huh?" I ask honestly.

"Hunter, macho has never been your problem."

"No, that would be you. My problem, I mean. Wanting you for all these years."

"You complaining?" he asks, his expression growing a little uncertain.

164

I close my eyes, shaking my head. "No, baby. No complaints out of me. Never." Truth is, I'm feeling such a glow of love that I swear I must be shining from the inside out. I'm fairly certain he must be able to see that.

Slowly, I open my eyes again. Maxwell doesn't say a word, just watches me for a moment. His gaze flickers with a strange mix of erotic need and compassion. I know what he's thinking; he's worried I'm still upset, too upset to make love like he obviously wants. So I take his hand and draw it between my legs, letting him feel how aroused I am. Having opened up with him about my past, all the pain, has only stoked my need to epic proportions, even with how weird I feel in this Ralph Lauren get up of his.

His golden eyes narrow hungrily, as he slowly strokes the length of my erection. Without my boxers on, the silken material just glides across it, causing me to quake with desire. "Oh, baby," I murmur, aware that I'm kneeling eye level to him. That he's staring right at the swelling bulge in front of my pants. He rolls onto his back, beckoning me to follow, so I straddle him, as he continues the caresses.

Everything grows hushed between us; he's more silent than usual, maybe because we're in his sister's house, or maybe because of how tender and intimate we've been tonight. I'm not sure, but I follow the lead he's establishing, planting my knees on both sides of his chest, so that I'm facing him. Without a word, he tugs on my waistband, drawing it low until my cock springs free. There it is, exposed perfectly to him and he doesn't waste a moment. His fingertips close around my shaft, and he draws it right between his lips.

My whole body stiffens at the contact, my back arches as his warm mouth closes around my tip. God, it's almost more than I can take, his tongue teasing me, coaxing me like this. He lifts his head, sucking me all the way into his mouth, which

165

causes a sharp hiss of pleasure to form on my lips. I lift onto my knees, thrusting forward, anything so that he can take me deeper.

My heart pounds its way right out of my chest, my hands claw at his muscular shoulders. Despite myself, I begin thrusting my hips, even though what I really want is just to feel more of me within his mouth. He clasps my thighs, stilling my motion, and for a moment my eyes open, locking with his hooded ones. I cover his hands with my own, and our fingers thread together.

I'm dangerously close, about to lose it all; I make a little groaning sound, one I hope will cue him in to my state, but it's too late. Suddenly my whole body quivers and I feel my warmth shoot into his mouth as I find my release. He takes all of me, until I'm left panting, my hands splayed across his chest.

I grow limp within his mouth. "Sorry, I-I meant to..." I murmur, pulling out.

He shakes his head firmly. "I wanted to do that."

"I wanted to make love."

"We're not done," he whispers, giving me a threatening glance. "Not by a long shot."

I gulp, feeling a little wicked as he pushes me off of him. "Stay there," he commands, leaving me by the fire. He rises gracefully to his feet, wiping at his mouth; I wonder if I taste as good to him as he always does to me. Salty perfection.

I tug my pants upward, as he tosses pillows onto the floor. What does my little seducer have in mind?

All the mounds of soft throw pillows now spread before the fire, creating a bed of sorts, a bed of tassels and soft velvets and plush crinolines. Once he's done with his handiwork, Max turns to me, the towel falling loose from around his hips. Then there's only him, my beautiful Adonis brought right to Earth.

"Lie down, Hunter," he instructs me, and my mouth goes dry. "On your stomach." He doesn't mince words, not one bit. Baby knows what he wants, and he's about to go right for the gusto.

I nod like the dutiful lover I am, slipping to my knees, and he's right behind me, urging me downward onto my stomach. "I'm going to make love to you, Hunter. Long and slow," he promises, slipping one confident hand low around my waist. "That's why I wanted you...relaxed. To begin with."

"Oh, okay," I mumble, swallowing hard. I feel my cock stiffening already, as he drapes his body low across my own. I'm spread across those soft pillows, sliding against them, with the fire warming my body as he forces his erection between my legs. There's the sensation of him, pushing hard against the satin there, the sensation of only that thin slip of material separating us at all.

Our hips cradle together and he begins a rocking motion, all the while kissing the nape of my neck. This is love making as I've never quite known it with anyone before, not even him. I mean, between the fire and the satin that's covering my body and the pillows, I feel a little like I'm in some Arabian sex fantasy. Like he's my prince, and I'm being made part of his harem. Initiated by firelight and seduction.

"Hunter, relax," he urges me. I didn't even realize how I'd stiffened beneath him. He slides the satin pajama top all across my torso, using it to pleasure me. Reaches between my legs and caresses the hardening length of me.

My eyes press closed, as he slips one palm beneath the top, stroking my chest. Teasing my nipples until they're taut against the cool material. Then, as I rest my cheek against the pillow, he's unbuttoning that shirt, until there's just my bare chest resting against all the sensual fabrics.

His gentle fingers thread through my hair, stroking it back from my cheek until our eyes meet in the near darkness. "Are you comfortable?" he whispers. "Tell me how you feel."

"Amazed," I sigh, closing my eyes. "Amazed by you, Maxwell."

"I love you."

"God, don't I know it."

"Feel it, Hunter. That's what I want." Then he's pulling my pants completely off of me, and I'm just bare beneath his lithe body. I have a passing thought that we'll mess with Leah's pillows, me coming and all that, him coming inside of me. But he's already anticipated that problem, because he coaxes me upward with one hand, sliding a soft sheet beneath us both. "Boy Scouts' motto," he murmurs in my ear. "You know, be prepared."

I'm about to make a snappy comeback when I feel his preparation right where it counts. Cool fingertips stroke me, massaging lubricant into my opening, and I can't help but squirm at his touch. My hips kind of writhe as I feel one finger push inside me, followed by another. Then, he urges me upward and slips another pillow beneath the sheet, underneath my hips, so that I'm raised just like he needs me to be. So that I'm poised and ready to take everything he's got for me.

Staggered breaths pass between us as he lowers atop me again. A loving hand rubs my shoulders, caresses my arms as he pushes all the way inside me. I don't realize I'm holding my breath until I'm full of him, then I kind of sigh and moan all at once. My cock throbs against the pillows as his weight settles atop me. He's so thin and gentle that he's easy to take this way. I buck a bit, eager for all of him, and he's pleased at that. "Yes," he breathes in my ear, licking it with his tongue. "Yes, love."

I'd never let him call me that outside this room, but it

sounds beautiful right now. Especially when he presses up against that place inside me, the one that feels like sheer ecstasy when he goes deep into me. When he does it a second time, I can't help but groan damned loudly. "Oh, Hunter, yes, yes," he murmurs. "Ah, yes." His hands wind through my hair, and he begins talking. Just talking and talking; cooing in my ear and loving all over me. I can't say a goddamned thing. I'm utterly speechless because of what he's doing to me.

Speechless, but about to come all over this sheet. Our hips grind together, desperately rocking, and I feel how hard his sinewy thighs are, how very masculine. My eyes close and I think of what an odd mix he is, completely male, yet soft and beautiful at the exact same time. Makes me needy as hell for him.

That's my last thought before my whole body shudders beneath his. Before I lose myself in Max Daniels's arms one more time tonight.

Satin. Head to toe, slippery, draped across my body. That's what I feel as I turn over in bed, feeling for Maxwell. I blink back the morning light. The bed's empty, there's just me and these luscious pajamas he gave me last night. He made me put them back on for sleeping, said I deserved a night of indulgent rest. Apparently that's what I got, because he's already up and out of our bed.

I nuzzle against his pillow, shifting my hips because of the erection that's pushing against my sleek pants. Sure, I wake with a hearty salute every morning, but I swear it's a little more intense today, probably because of how he took me by that damned fire last night. Or maybe it's just this silken, sinful state I'm in, like some harem-girl-in-waiting.

For a moment, I just cozy up to where he's slept, thinking

169

about how much deeper I've fallen for him, just since yesterday. I'm also thinking about how loved I feel, all because of how he handled the heavy shit about my past. He amazes me, period. That he can give this much of himself, and do it so freely, leaves me feeling vulnerable this morning. Leaves me feeling shattered and a little shaky. But I'm not going to step back again, not on your life. I don't care if I'm scared shitless by all this intimacy with him, I'm right where I want to be.

His running shoes are discarded on the floor beside the bed, a familiar, comforting sight. Funny how something so practical makes me ache for him a little, reminds me of how much I love that he's all mine. He's obviously gone for a run this morning and didn't want to wake me. We run together sometimes back in L.A., but he's damned hard to keep up with, especially with all those hills. He just laughs at me too, calls me a couch jock, as I huff and puff along beside him.

When he does that, I usually quip right back at him, something about how I'll be the jock of his couch any night of the week. I love teasing him about sex, because he's so easy to unnerve, and always blushes like some kind of virgin. Something about that turns me flat on too.

From the living room, I hear his muted laughter and I smile, thinking of all the presents I've brought along for him. One or two are hidden here in this bedroom, for later when it's just us. But it's going to be fun seeing him discover all my surprises underneath the tree.

So I roll out of bed, and decide to just waltz right out there in my new pajamas. After all, Leah loves giving me shit about things, so why not give her the perfect fodder?

I was right about Leah, too, because no sooner do I appear in the living room doorway than she gives me one of her cool, appraising stares. She finally coughs and sputters after what feels like forever. "Wow, Hunter, you're looking very..." Queer? Gay? Rich and studly? "Satiny." She offers me an innocent smile and I roll my eyes at her.

"I'm in my kept man persona." I invoke my best construction worker posture and point down at the pajamas. "Don't they rock?"

"I'm sure my brother thinks they're fabulous," Leah teases, lifting a suggestive eyebrow.

"They look great on you," Max agrees, not even missing a beat. God, the expression on his face as he tosses a knowing glance my way. That glance is nothing short of a reminder of what he did to me last night by the firelight—that and a promise of what he'll do back in L.A. My satin and his bare skin once again.

I drop to the floor beside him, a lot closer than I ever would have dared last trip. "Morning."

"Merry Christmas," he says with a boyish grin, and I fight the urge to give him a sloppy holiday kiss. It's in my heart, and so I move my lips almost imperceptibly, blowing him one instead. He glances toward Leah and John, both of whom are busy with their own presents, then touches my hand, giving it a warm squeeze.

"I've got something for you to open." His eyes assume a mischievous gleam.

"Oh, really?"

He reaches for a small present and hands it to me. "Something you'll love," he assures me.

I fiddle with the wrapping, tugging at it, and get a memory flash of last Christmas and the tree topper. Maxwell has this incredible way with his gift buying and it always leaves me feeling adored. The paper unfolds and I see a little ornament box, the kind with commemorative lettering.

"I'll be damned!" It's a freaking Harley Davidson ornament, a 1971 model. "Super Glide?" I cough and he just smiles at me, the picture of pure innocence.

"Well, you've always loved the old classics."

"Uh, huh." I tear into the box, feeling like he just gave me the toy I'd been waiting for all year. "Baby, this is amazing." It's an actual replica, complete with kickstand and a moving front wheel.

Leah looks up from across the room, where she's holding a book that she's just opened. "What is it with you guys and the Harleys? Is it like a gay thing or what?"

"It's a *guy* thing, Leah," I say, feeling defensive about my lifelong obsession with bikes. Then I get an idea, and reach under the tree for one of Maxwell's prizes. "Open this one next," I advise him. Yeah, I'm gonna get her good.

Max struggles with my bad wrapping job for a moment, then the package finally opens to reveal his special Harley T-shirt. "Cool!" he says, unfurling it. Then he gives me a conspiratorial look and I nod in agreement.

"Isn't that a little bit small?" Leah frowns at the shirt her brother is examining. I'm sure he's already down at the club in his mind, showing off his beautiful biceps in his brand new Harley shirt, clinging like pure perfection.

"Just his size," I say. "No doubt about that."

"But it's so...tiny," she says, scrunching up her nose.

"Trust me, Leah, your brother loves a tight T-shirt," I explain and then I think she gets it, because she stares down into her lap, looking a little embarrassed.

But then she regains her composure, smiling faintly as she says, "So it is a gay thing, then. Harleys, tight T-shirts..."

"Leather, you name it," Max adds, laughing. He's just giving me shit now, getting even for my T-shirt remarks.

I'm gonna set the record straight. "Look, the T-shirt's for my stud muffin, but the Harleys are an all guy thing, okay?"

"Sure, Hunter," Leah teases me, grinning at her twin. "Stud muffins won't have anything to do with motorcycles, now will they?"

Max sniffs indignantly. "I got engaged on the back of a Harley, thank you very much."

Then Leah turns to him, genuinely curious and they begin talking like a pair of girlfriends, exchanging notes on their respective big moments. My heart kind of gives a leap when I see her reach for his hand, examining his ring for the first time as he tells about the Mulholland Drive proposal.

For a moment, she glances my way, smiling as Max explains how I popped the question and all. It's funny, but I'm certain that Leah has come to love me a little; I see it in the way she glances at me. And I understand exactly why—she loves me because of how well I treat her brother, because I love him like he really deserves to be. Which is no tribute at all to me, and every acknowledgement of how special Maxwell really is. He deserves the fairy tale, to quote "Pretty Woman". He deserves to have the whole shebang of a happily ever after.

I'm nobody special, just an ordinary guy from farm country who's gonna give him that fairy tale.

We spend all afternoon laughing it up, watching bowl games, then late in the day, Max throws together a fantastic meal of leftovers that leaves us all ridiculously full. Louisa drops by afterward and cozies up with Max by the fire, sharing a glass of brandy.

So when the phone rings well after our fabulous meal has

settled, it jars us all. John nearly staggers toward the receiver, thick with brandy and wine like the rest of us. He picks it up in the kitchen, mumbling a hello that's then punctuated by a strained silence.

"Leah?" he calls, and when he pokes his head back into the living room where we're carousing by the fire, I know right away that something's wrong.

She smoothes out her hair, then her skirt, and I'm sure she senses it too. John's gaze tracks right to me. There's a good reason why he's my new best friend, and when he gives me a slight nod, I'm certain that it's Phillip Daniels on the line. Hell, it's almost eight o'clock on Christmas night, for crying out loud. At this point, couldn't he have let another day go by?

From the kitchen I hear Leah's murmured conversation, a few muted remarks. Max is oblivious, laughing by the fire with Louisa. They're sipping their brandy and strolling down memory lane.

"Max," Leah says. Her voice is thin and Max's head snaps up in immediate familial recognition. "Will you come here, please?"

He's dutiful and doesn't even question her, just brushes himself off as he rises from beside the fire.

He's calm, so why the hell is my heart pounding like a motherfucker? After what feels like forever, Max reappears with the quiet announcement, "Mom and Dad are on their way over. They were in the car."

"What?" I bark. "What the hell?"

Louisa places a calming hand on my forearm, just watching Max. "They want to bring something over. For us, Hunter." His voice wavers a bit, but he remains composed. "A Christmas gift."

No fucking way. What does this mean? Are they serious? I

look from Max to Leah and get the feeling they're sharing one of their Super Twins communication moments, as they kind of nod without saying a word. "Baby, are you sure?" I blurt, feeling my pulse skitter like crazy.

"I'm okay with it," Max says with a nod, settling back beside me on the sofa. "Weird, but yeah, I am."

No sooner has he said that, then a pair of bright headlights pierce Leah's front window. "They're here," Louisa announces. Tugging at the hem of her hand-knit sweater, she seems every bit as nervous as I feel, every bit as questioning of Phillip's motives in suddenly insisting upon seeing Maxwell tonight.

I want to ask her why the Daniels would do this, why they would have rejected Max so completely, seeing as how she's known them for a lifetime and all that. I want to press Louisa for some kind of reasoning here.

More than any of that, I want to pull Maxwell right into my arms and hold him fast so his father can't hurt him one fucking bit.

Instead, Max stands like the grown man he is and takes that room with confident strides.

Talk about seizing the situation by the balls. I'll be damned, but he's gonna meet his old man right at the front door.

Chapter Fifteen

It's a tense scene with Phillip and Diane poised on the sofa opposite us. The Christmas music on the radio seems much louder with their arrival, intrusive, as we all kind of stare at one another in awkward expectation.

Battle lines have definitely been drawn here. Louisa sits just beside Max, holding his hand. I'm on his other side, wanting to hold his hand, and poor Leah just kind of flits around the room trying to make everyone comfortable. John has vanished into the kitchen, evidently pouring glasses of brandy for the folks.

"So, did you have a nice day?" Diane asks in a voice that's far too bright. I feel for her, I really do, because she loves her children. Of that there's no doubt. She never asked to be thrust into the middle of this dispute, forced to choose sides between Phillip and their son. Then again, maybe if she had stood up to Phillip years ago, we might not even be gathered here like this, so she's not entirely blameless, either.

"Yeah, Mom, it was great," Max says, his voice softer than usual. "Very nice day." Then he and Leah begin to recount the presents and good times we've shared this holiday, while I just sit back and listen.

I notice that while Max talks, he stares only at his mother, avoiding his father completely. Not me, though. I'm eyeballing

Phillip Daniels for all I'm worth, because I want him to know he won't get away with hurting Max again. Not on my watch, no fucking way.

Phillip meets my bold gaze, assessing me, and I'm reminded of that time in his study two months ago. The night he tried to send me out on a rail. Hell, I'm still surprised he didn't pull out a checkbook that day and try to bribe me right out of Maxwell's life. Just like then, I feel a surge of protectiveness for my lover, only it's more intense now that I know how deep the hurt really goes between these two.

Phillip and I are two strong guys, and neither of us is used to backing down, so maybe that's why I refuse to look away from him. He watches me in turn, silent, maybe even curious about this farm kid who's managed to steal his son's heart. I glimpsed that same curiosity last time and it's in his expression now, but something's changed. Phillip Daniels is tired, worn out. There's an undeniable glimmer of melancholy in his weathered eyes that wasn't there before. Strange, but it makes me want to help him out a little, maybe even broker some kind of peace between him and his son.

"Mom, look at what Max and Hunter gave me," Leah says, reaching for an open box under the tree. "It's cashmere!"

Diane begins to laugh, lifting the hot water bottle out of the box, examining it. "What on Earth?"

Max chuckles, rubbing at his eyes. "A hot water bottle wrapped inside a cashmere sweater for cold nights."

"It's even semi-moth proof!" Louisa laughs. "Semi being the operative word in that sentence."

"I thought it was pretty ridiculous," I say, glad for something cheery to distract us. "But Max is the gift czar in this family."

"Kind of like Leah and her Christmas list," John agrees as

he enters the room, and presses glasses of brandy into his in-laws' hands. "You don't dispute the Mistress of Mistletoe."

"Leah and Max always did love the holidays," Phillip reflects and I'll be damned if he doesn't look regretful.

"I loved being with my family," Max says, his voice sharp. "That's what the holidays are about, Dad."

"Yes," his father agrees, nodding as he stares at the floor. "You're right, son."

"Phillip, don't you want to give them their gift?" Diane prompts him, sliding the large package at their feet toward us. "To Max and Hunter? Now's a good time." Leah and John's present had already been nestled under the tree, brought over some time in the past weeks to be opened on Christmas morning. There'd been nothing for us, not a scrap of a mention and I knew it had broken one more bit of Max's heart. So now I wonder what they've got planned, showing up like this at the eleventh hour.

The gift is a large one—so big, in fact, that it's kind of begged my attention ever since they plopped it down on the floor beside the sofa. When they entered, Phillip had clutched it close within his arms; almost protective in the way he clasped it in that bear hug. Good thing, because it spared Max the awkwardness of an embrace as he ushered his father into the house.

"Sure, you're right. Now is a good time," Phillip agrees, looking up at Max. "Son, you want to come over here?"

Max glances at me, then back at his father, uncertain. "You and Hunter?" his father amends and my heart gives a hopeful leap.

I rise from the sofa first, clueing Max in that it's okay, that I'm right with him. We cross the floor together, staring down at the box for an awkward moment. I drop to the ground, squatting there as I examine the present.

"Say, Maxwell," I remind him, "you can use your new knife."

"You're right." He reaches into his back pocket. I gave him the knife this morning, wrapped up in one of those little blue boxes that he adores so much, a sterling silver Swiss Army knife from Tiffany and Co. He glowed when he opened it, too, as if I'd given him secret treasure. Like we'd cart it off together to our backyard tree house and use it for slashing vines or something.

His father leans forward, elbows propped on his knees, interested in our reaction as Max uses his new blade to slice open the paper. When the Williams Sonoma logo comes into view, Phillip explains, "It's from your gift registry."

Max's head snaps upward. "Really?" I know what he's thinking because it's the same damned thing I'm thinking. For his old man to pick something from the registry is a blessing of sorts. There's nothing else it can possibly be.

"Well, I wanted," his father pauses, turning to Diane before he continues. "*We* wanted to get you something for the apartment. Something you could really use. Something you both wanted." Both. That word's not lost on me, not for a minute.

"We know how much you love to cook, sweetheart," Diane says.

"Maxwell's a genius in the kitchen," I agree, pride in my voice.

"Better watch out, Hunter," John says with a laugh, dropping onto the sofa beside Leah, patting his stomach. "You know what happens in the first year of marriage."

"Yeah, man, you get fat. I'm already kicking in overtime at the gym."

Max studies the gift box, then cuts the sealing tape with a deft turn of his blade. "Wow!" he cries, staring down into the open package, and I try to peer over his shoulder. "I can't believe it! I've wanted one of these for forever. Look, Hunter, it's a bread machine!"

The joy in his voice is undeniable, as is the glimmering look in his eyes. "Mom, Dad, this is amazing. Thank you," he says, reaching down into the box.

Maxwell is the one who's amazing. He has all the money in the world, yet when someone takes the time to buy him something special, even if he could afford it in a heartbeat, it pleases him so damned much. It makes him feel like they've put some kind of value on him, because they thought of something he really wants. But as he drags the giant processor onto the floor, and Louisa kneels there, examining it with him, I know this moment represents far more than that.

His parents have just given us a tentative first blessing. Merry, Merry Christmas to us.

When it's time for them to go, there's an uncomfortable moment at the doorway when I'm not sure if his father is going to shake my hand or if his mother will hug me. We've made serious headway tonight, yet things are still far from easy. Max's mother has already embraced him three separate times and right now I don't think she plans to ever let go. "I love you so much, sweetheart," she says, drawing him close.

I watch them, feeling thankful for our breakthrough, and that's when it happens. Phillip clasps my shoulder, giving it a surprising squeeze and says, "Hunter, when do you leave tomorrow? Early?"

"Yeah, we're rolling out of here right after breakfast."

"Well, maybe you could have that breakfast at our house,"

he offers quietly. "I mean, if there's time."

Max steps apart from his mother, his mouth falling open. For a moment he says nothing, the golden eyes just kind of darting between his dad and me. I know my Maxwell and what he's thinking, because I see a spark of anger flash in his eyes. Maybe it doesn't make sense, not with the obvious overture his dad's just made, but it's there nonetheless. *Don't say it, baby. Just don't,* I think, willing him not to react out of anger. Not to say what I know is coming next.

"Oh, so we're invited to your house now?"

Damned telepathy. Guess it doesn't work no matter how much you love your soul mate. "Hunter and me both?" Anger tinges every word.

Phillip kind of coughs, frowning at his son because there seems nothing else he can say. So I say it for them both.

"Yeah, that would be great, Phillip. We'd love to come by for breakfast tomorrow. What time you have in mind?"

The look of relief in his father's eyes stirs something strange inside of me. Relief and gratitude, that's what I see in his weary expression because as bizarre as it is, I've become a connection of sorts for him. A tenuous link to the son he obviously loves very much, even though he's made scores of mistakes with him.

"How's eight?" Diane chimes, slipping her arm around Max's waist.

I glance at Max, and he gives a tentative nod, gratitude flickering in his own eyes, maybe even despite himself. "Good, we'll be there," I say.

Phillip extends his hand then, taking my own firmly. "Merry Christmas, son," he says to me and for some really weird reason, I fight the urge to cry right on the spot.

Max is a nervous wreck. He circles the bedroom, checking things, zipping and unzipping the suitcase. I haven't seen him so worked up since we came home to Winchester last time. Hell, I'm getting nervous just being near him. "Will you stop it, Maxwell?" I finally sigh in exasperation.

He turns to me, all innocent and unaware. "Stop what?"

"This. This nervous fidgeting shit. It's making me crazy."

He becomes still, right there in the center of the bedroom, raking his hands over his dark hair. "Max," I say, soothing him with my voice. "It's okay. Really."

"What if he's asked us there to gang up on us or something? What if he's going to try and talk us out of the wedding? What if it's all a set-up?" He's talking madness, so I just draw him into my arms, holding him close.

"You know that's not what it's about, man."

"No, Hunter," he says, wrestling out of my grasp. "I don't know that at all."

"Why'd you get so angry at him last night?"

"What?"

"He's making a peace overture, Maxwell. Don't you get that? The bread machine, the invitation to the house."

"It's too late for opening his home to you." The steely voice makes me glad he's on my side.

I get quiet as he moves back to the suitcase, heaving it onto the floor. "No, it's not," I say. "Not at all too late."

"Oh, Hunter, I don't want you as my voice of reason on this," he nearly thunders, throwing his hands into the air. "Since when did you and my father get so cozy?"

I roll my eyes, starting to get a little pissed. "I'm on your team, don't forget that."

"Huh, funny. I don't see it that way."

"He gave you a goddamned bread machine, for crying out loud!" I shout, not caring what Leah or John think. "He's trying to make things right, but you're as stubborn as he is."

All that observation earns me is stony silence and a withering glare from the love of my life. Great. Fucking great. "I'm gonna go pack the car," I say, huffing past him toward the hallway.

"Hunter, wait."

I turn back and see that tears have filled his beautiful eyes. "I'm scared," he admits, staring down at his loafers. "Scared that I'm getting my hopes up again for nothing."

I drop the bag in the hallway, then step back into the room, closing the door behind us. "You know, for somebody who's got so damned much, how can you expect so little?"

"I don't get it."

"You're amazing, Maxwell. The best person I know, and you deserve their love."

"I-I never thought I didn't." He shoves his hands into his pockets with an offhand shrug.

"No?"

Our gazes lock for a moment and I know he's working at something, an important thought when he says, "I'm not sure my dad thinks I deserve his love." Okay, now we're getting somewhere.

"Why not?" I ask, using the most derogatory word I can think of to drive my point home, hard. "'Cause you're a faggot?"

He nods, the tears obviously threatening again as he just stares down at the floor. "Yeah, well you're definitely queer as they come, sweetheart," I say, using that endearment on purpose. "So fucking what? Your old man's gonna have to deal if he wants you in his life, and he obviously does."

"How can you be so sure?" he asks, anguish in his quiet voice.

I step close, stroking my fingertips over the short, bristling hair that I love so much. "He ever give you a cooking utensil for Christmas before?"

"No."

"Okay, well you think a homophobic dad typically does that? Chooses something off his queer son's wedding registry, for chrissakes?"

He blinks at me, processing what should be so easy for him to see, then after a long moment, he begins to giggle. Kind of girlish, definitely relieved. "God, I'm an idiot," he says. "Aren't I?"

"He hurt you. Really damned bad, and that's tough to get past."

"The thing is, I want them to love you like I do," he says, stepping near and wrapping his muscled arms around my neck.

"Baby, that's never gonna happen. I'm your lover, not theirs."

"Well, I want them to get you. To understand why I love you."

"Yeah, well that's fair enough, but it starts by opening up to them, despite the bad history."

"I have a present for them, too," he admits, turning toward the bed and I see a small gift tucked beside his briefcase. "I lost my nerve in giving it last night. I was going to leave it with Leah for them."

I'm burning to know what it is, but I don't ask. I give him space to share in his own time. "You gonna bring it then?"

He picks it up, handing it to me. "You give it to them, Hunter. I think that would be great. Perfect, as a matter of fact."

Interesting that he doesn't tell me what it is, just sends me off to the car, wondering what in the world we're giving his folks.

"Come on in!" Diane says, giving me an affectionate hug. "I'm so glad you came, Hunter." She pats me on the cheek again, like last fall, and any barriers I had against this sweet woman definitely crumble a little bit more. She's just way too Aunt Edna for me to keep resenting her.

"Smells great," I say, sniffing the air. Eggs and bacon hold a special place in this farm boy's memory bank and this morning's no exception. Their siren call draws me right toward the Daniels' family kitchen. My feet assume a life of their own, zigzagging me right to where the good stuff's cooking up.

"Good morning, Hunter." Phillip looks up at me from where he's preparing the eggs on the stovetop. Surprise number one— I had no idea that Maxwell's dad liked to cook at all. Max follows on my heels and gets another bright greeting out of his father. "Son, good morning. You sleep well?"

It's almost as if we'd stayed right here, the way his father's talking to us. Somehow I get the feeling he wishes we had.

"Yeah, Dad, it was good. Leah's got a great guest bedroom."

"Rolled out the red carpet for us." In a shared bedroom. That's what we're both implying and it doesn't even earn us a blink from his father. Instead, he proceeds to show us the fresh juices on the counter, the coffee in carafes. It's a great spread he's laid out for us, so I don't waste a minute availing myself of it and reach right for a buttery pastry.

"Cool, is that skillet a Le Creuset?" Max asks, stepping close to his dad.

"Leah gave it to me for Father's Day last year. I haven't used it much."

"Well, Dad, you really should. They're great for all kinds of things."

Then they start chitchatting about all the cookware's potential uses, the joys of a skillet made by artisans in northern Italy, while I lean against the counter, listening in surprise. Surprise that they have this to share between them. That is, until Diane joins me, holding her mug of coffee close between both hands. "Almost like when Max was a little boy," she says, just for me to hear.

"How's that?" I ask.

"Well, Phillip used to make breakfast on weekends and he always got Max to help him. Would put him up on top of the chair and let him stir the eggs. Let him pop the bread into the toaster. That's how Max first learned to cook. With his father."

I can't fucking believe it. No way. I could have guessed a million different possibilities and never once realized that Maxwell's most beloved hobby comes right from his own father.

"Maybe they'll find they have more in common than they think," she says on a sigh, sipping her coffee. Listening to them talk endlessly about the damned skillet, I can't help but hope she's right.

So after all these months, I'm back at the family table again, sitting right beside Maxwell. Only this time, he talks and gestures with his hands and nobody's paying a damned bit of attention to his ring. His parents are being great, asking loads of questions about his job, our apartment, even the plans for the spring. Max gets withdrawn when they ask about the inn where we're holding the service, kind of clamming up a little. It's not that he's punishing them; I understand that. He just feels protective of what he holds most dear.

"Well, are you having music?" his mother asks after several

of his shorthand answers, obviously trying to get him to open up some more.

Max kind of coughs, sipping his coffee, and so I answer for him. "A band, yeah. For the reception. The whole thing's going to be a blast from the get go. Lots of food, booze, dancing. Not to be missed, I can tell you that."

Uh, oh. Shit, shit, shit.

Nobody says anything for a moment, and I'm just grateful that the whole room hasn't imploded because of my tactless comment. Without meaning to, I just created some kind of expectation for them to respond. To explain why they aren't coming, precisely, if we're throwing such a damned good shindig.

"I'm sure that's true." That's his father's reply, as he stares down at his plate of food, anywhere but at either of us.

"You could still come." Max's voice is quiet, gentle. Not accusing or desperate like it could be and I close my eyes, bracing. Bracing for the hurt to come, the rejection that I really don't want him to experience yet again.

"Son, I don't think that's what you want. Not really."

"Of course it is," he blurts, leaning forward, hands flat on the table. "You know I'd kill for you to be there."

There's a long silence, but then his father blows my mind with what he says next. "Max, I should never have told you Hunter wasn't welcome here for Christmas. I owe you both an apology for that. I'm, well, just very sorry." Phillip glances eagerly between us both, then folds his hands into a neat little pyramid, as he continues. "Hunter, you are welcome here in our home any time. Any time, son. You and Max, please know that."

I swallow hard, nodding. My voice is nowhere to be found, so I don't bother with speaking. It's Max that does so instead. "Thanks, Dad. I appreciate that. We both do."

"I've been a little crazy about all this," he admits, looking at his wife.

"Does this mean you'll consider coming? To Vermont?" Max presses again, but I don't have time to become hopeful before his father shakes his head.

"I can't, son. I wish that I could."

Max stares over his father's shoulder, at some unseen point across the room. Maybe he's staring into his past, at a teenage boy in drag, confused. I'm not sure, but he tilts his chin upward, proud, and says. "Yeah, Dad, I wish you could, too."

We're halfway back to Los Angeles, when I remember the present Maxwell had for his folks. "Damn, baby." I glance beneath the airline seat in front of me. "We forgot your parents' gift."

"I didn't forget," he says with a vague smile. "Just wasn't ready to give it after all."

"So what'd you get them?" I squint into the winter sunlight, bright outside the plane window.

"It's a picture. Of you and me out at Long Beach."

"That one Brian took?" I ask, pretty certain I know the shot.

"Yeah." He grins sweetly. "That's the one."

In the picture, I've got my arm right around him, holding him close, the ocean wind whipping my long hair until it clings to my face. His own short-cropped hair is sexy and tousled, his hand around my waist. That one picture says a lot about our relationship. We look married in it, in love. Like two people who've found the rest of their lives. It's a couple snap shot, the kind proud parents might put on their mantle if they were supportive enough.

"Maybe some other time," I suggest with a knowing nod.

"When they're ready for it." I'm thinking about our wedding and that it's still not too late for them to come.

"Maybe. If they're ever ready, yeah, it'll make the perfect gift."

No, I think with a wistful smile. That wouldn't be the perfect gift, at least not to me. My perfect gift would be Diane and Phillip Daniels there in the front aisle on wedding day, sitting with Aunt Edna when we're joined in civil union.

But maybe gifts are like that—best when you're only dreaming about them, not opening them up to discover what's inside. At least that's always been Max's philosophy; it's all about the unknown and the possibility of what still remains to be discovered inside the box.

So that's how I think I'm gonna take this situation with his parents and my secret hopes for our wedding day. Kind of think that the best just might be yet to come.

Chapter Sixteen

I'm dreaming about water. Warm, salty ocean water, and it's lapping around my bare waist. And Max is with me. He's with me, just standing in the middle of the waves, naked and beautiful.

I lift my hand to his chest and slowly trace my fingertips down the length of him. From his nipples to his navel, I have to touch it all. Especially the rippled muscles of his abdomen, sculpted tight in a way that I'll never be disciplined enough to achieve.

Then his hips, narrow and perfect, they fit right within the palms of my rough hands. He's just my size, just what I need in a man.

I draw him much closer, until our chests press together, until my mouth tastes brine on his lips.

Waves push and draw against our bodies, urging us closer together, then easing us apart. Warm, like summer rain, like the way it feels to be inside of him.

I need this, I murmur into his mouth, as he opens to my kiss. All of this.

The sun is low on the horizon, and I know that the day is nearly done. A quick glance at the beach shows that we're all alone, thrust close within the rolling waves.

Take me, he cries, warm hands closing tight around my thighs, until we're so near that his cock brushes against mine. Until I'm moaning into his mouth, kissing him as deeply as I can.

Not here, baby. Not just here, I protest.

Then the dream skips ahead by a few absent moments until we're on the beach, adrift on the wet sand. Bare, completely bare in one another's hard arms. Muscles and sinew and tendons wrap together, until I work him beneath me.

Until his slender body quivers below mine, frantic for fulfillment that I can't seem to give him. Gritty sand burns my knees as we writhe and beg and ache to join our bodies.

But we can't have one another, not completely.

At least not here on the beach, not in the open, where anyone might see.

Wait, I suddenly realize. Anyone can see.

That's when I spy Leah and Phillip, off to the side, just watching us in what seems an offhand manner. Not disapproving precisely, despite the fact that they've discovered me buck naked atop Maxwell. I stare down into his eyes, panicked, but he only smiles at me, a little conspiratorial.

Baby, would you look? I advise, nodding toward his family. Now his mother's there, and Veronica. Shit, Ben and Louisa, too. It's getting worse by the moment, but despite the way I've begun shaking, Max seems so freaking relaxed.

It's okay, he assures me, not even glancing toward our gathering spectators. *Hunter, you're okay.*

But, but...I'm sputtering because now Julie Bernard is there. She's the first girl I ever kissed, at a dance in eighth grade and she's whispering with Aunt Edna and Marianne Langley. I lost my virginity to Marianne in a barn behind her father's house when I was barely more than fifteen.

Max lifts his hand to my cheek, cupping it within his palm and says, *They all know.*

I don't want to be this out!

Max points at the crowd studying us there on the beachhead. They stare like we're a pair of odd starfish washed up on shore, not gay lovers tussling together in the foamy waves. *But, Hunter,* he explains. *Nobody cares.*

I keep shaking my head, writhing against him, needing him so goddamned much, even with all the people watching. That's when I feel his hands pinning me hard. *Hunter! Hunter!*

"Hunter," Max says loudly and my eyes flutter open. "Wake up!"

"Fuck."

He's leaning over me, gazing down into my eyes, as naked and smooth as in the dream. As perfectly gorgeous, too, only nobody's watching us. For a long moment, I can only blink.

"Some dream, huh?"

"Was I making noise?" Panic courses through my system as I remember just how erotic the dream was. No telling what kind of sounds I made, especially wrapped right in his arms like that.

"You kept moaning like you were in pain, and kind of shaking. Frightened me, actually."

"Anxiety dream." That's all I grunt, because I know there's no way I can explain it all without seeming like I'm getting cold feet about our nuptials, just two weeks away.

"Are you anxious?" he asks, serious as he props his head on his elbow, studying me.

"Let's just say that thirty people were watching us make love."

"Was the sex good?"

"Not nearly so satisfying as last night," I purr, leaning in to kiss him. Guess I can forget the dream with the reality so close in my arms.

"No?" he teases, stroking my chest slowly. "Maybe I'm starting to spoil you, then."

"Not a chance in hell," I say, rolling him right onto his back. "What time is it?"

"Nine-thirty."

Great. That means our final premarital counseling session isn't for another two hours, so we have plenty of time for a long, slow seduction scene. We can even reenact our own version of "From Here to Eternity" right between the sheets.

Maxwell suckered me into the premarital counseling over martinis and cigars at a swanky little place near his office one night back in January. He had me meet him, decked out in my suit and tie, so of course I had that first date on my mind. I would've done anything for him, smoking those stogies and remembering the night we began to fall in love.

"So what's up?" I asked him that night, leaning back against the banquette seat. My legs fell open, my thigh resting against his. I'd come to love doing shit like that, being flirty in public with him.

Before he answered, he reached for the smoke, smiling at me through his long lashes. That damned charcoal-colored suit looked hot as hell on him that January night. Someone from his office passed by, and he lifted the cigar in greeting. I moved my leg back to dead center.

"Nothing's up." He took a long drag.

I studied him. "Expensive cigars, martinis and a big date

out. What's up?"

"Does something have to be up? I wanted to take you out, Hunter."

"I love it when you do, but I know you, Daniels."

Under the table, he reached a discreet hand and stroked my leg. "Well, this is just a date, but I did have something to ask you." He leaned close, his shoulder pressing into mine. Public, obvious. Another office worker passed by and he offered a nod and a smile. I reached for his hand, touching it.

"Tell me."

"Well, the Unitarian minister who's performing our ceremony requires something of all the couples he joins."

"First born?" I laughed at my own joke, even though Max remained serious and directed.

"Counseling. Premarital counseling with a local psychologist or minister."

"I'm not a Unitarian. Not gonna do it."

"I figured that." He reached inside his jacket, retrieving a piece of paper from the pocket. "So I planned ahead."

He handed me the paper with an optimistic smile, as I took the cigar out of his hand. "What's this?" I asked, staring at his neat handwriting on the page.

"The name of our premarital counselor."

"Oh, fuck."

"Gladly."

"Shut up, Maxwell. I'm serious. I don't want to do this," I groaned. "We don't need this. We're fine together, crazy about each other."

"Of course we are. But Reverend Donnelly says it really solidifies things, forces a couple to examine their motivations for joining."

"I'm motivated to be with you." Max smiled at that one, and this time, he was the one who let his thigh press hard against mine. Being public can be so damned sexy, especially when your boyfriend is attracting the attention of every gay male in the place. Hell, every girl for that matter, but he's always oblivious to that kind of notice.

"Then will you do it for me? Because I'm asking, Hunter?" He looked into my eyes hard with that question, penetrating me on the molecular level with his gaze. "You know I can't refuse you a goddamned thing."

And just like that, I found myself on tap for ten premarital counseling sessions. Who knew?

Dr. Erickson loves me. I managed to wrap him right around my finger at our first counseling session when I told him that I was straight, just happened to be in love with a man. I think he got a big, fat kick out of that one, because he smiled knowingly, then proceeded to dismantle a whole bunch of my illusions about sexual orientation. Only after I'd let him go on for a while about "gender identification" did I admit that I'd been yanking his chain; that I knew for a fact I was queer with some fairly latent hetero tendencies.

During the past weeks, Dr. Erickson has assessed me as being blunt and honest, but gentle in my relationship with Maxwell. I kind of dig that, because it seems about right. I think he's more concerned about Max than me—he's pursued the cross-dressing stuff a lot, especially as it relates to his dad. One time he even asked if Max wished he were a woman. That got a pretty rattled answer out of Maxwell, as he tried to explain that what he'd always wished was that he were more comfortable with being feminine. That he's often felt like a girl, not so much that he ever wanted to be one. I was a little surprised by that revelation because, yeah, Max can get a little girlish sometimes, but mostly he's a total dude in my book. Guess it's all about how you feel on the inside.

Dr. Erickson made some notes about that, nodding his head. But he also says that my acceptance of Maxine has been critical to Max's "gender integration". Not sure exactly what that means, except that apparently I'm good for Max. And our relationship is, too.

None of this is very romantic, but it's the hardcore stuff we're supposed to focus on in this gay union of ours. There's also been a lot of talk about how hard it is for a couple like us because we don't have any true role models, which means we have to figure shit out on our own. Kind of make our own rules up about making this marriage work. Those are the things we've been discussing over nearly two months of counseling sessions, so I kind of figure our last one is going to be the graduation moment—you know, easy and all that.

"This is our final session before the union ceremony in two weeks," Dr. Erickson begins, studying Max and me carefully. "You are about to embark on the next phase of this relationship."

I nod and get the strangest feeling that something big is coming yet.

"I believe you are more equipped for union than before these sessions began, gentlemen," he says with a faint smile. He rubs a hand over his graying beard, glancing between us. Our good doctor's queer as they come, by the way, self-proclaimed "life partner" of a Studio City attorney. They opted out of the union thing, but he loves coaching committed couples like us "into that joining of selfhood".

"Hopefully you're stronger in your partnership as you embark on your marriage."

Max and I nod, and he reaches for my hand. I give it a gentle squeeze, holding it fast as Dr. Erickson asks mildly, "So tell me, any last issues? Any pressing concerns?"

"Nah, don't think so," I say with an offhand shrug, and Max gives my hand another little squeeze. Almost like he's encouraging me. I glance sideways at him, about to ask what he has in mind, when he says quietly, "Your anxiety dream. You should mention that."

I wave him off. "Maxwell, that was nothing." But the doctor's all over it in the space of a heartbeat.

"Anxiety dream, Hunter? What sort of anxieties are you struggling with?" He lives for this kind of shit, no doubt about it.

"It was nothing, honest." But our counselor's not fooled for a minute.

"Anxiety is normal just before making a formal commitment like this, Hunter."

"Yeah, well it was no big deal." I shift around in my chair, unable to settle or get comfortable. "We were naked on the beach and a whole bunch of people were watching us get it on. Or not, actually. We kind of stopped when I realized Marianna Langley was watching us."

Max turns to me in surprise, releasing my hand. "Marianne was there?" I swear I detect a hint of jealousy in his quiet voice.

"Along with Leah, your father and a whole other crowd. Julie Bernard, too."

"Julie?" Max asks, more than slightly breathless. I scowl at him.

"Baby, it was a dream, for crying out loud!"

"Marianne and Julie are obviously important," Dr. Erickson observes, studying Max more closely than me over the rims of his glasses.

"I don't see why you'd dream about them now," Max says, rubbing at his eyes. "Veronica there, too?"

"These are past girlfriends?" the doctor asks and I nod, not answering for a moment.

"He lost his virginity to Marianne," Max informs him, staring down into his lap. This hurts him for some reason; I don't get it, but it obviously does.

"Max, look, it was just a dream."

"Were you ashamed to be seen with Max?"

"No!" I cry defensively, and tap the toe of my hiking boot on his polished wooden floor. Nobody speaks for a mini-eternity, until finally I admit, "I felt really out. More out than I wanted to be, being seen by all those girls. Family and all."

"Family," the doctor repeats, nodding. "That's interesting."

"Why?" I ask.

"Because you want a family with Max," he observes. "It's why you proposed, isn't it?"

"Yeah." I shrug, folding my arms over my chest. "Your point?"

"Hunter, we've focused on Max's issues a lot during these sessions. But we haven't talked much about your own family situation."

I give a little groan, rolling my eyes. "I don't want to do this drill, okay?"

"You were orphaned, Hunter."

I give him my best macho posturing. "Don't I know that?"

"Max and you are forming a family together, so it's important that you recognize your abandonment and embrace
198

it. That you accept the part of you that needs family now."

I stare up at him, and for some reason flash on Aunt Edna's kitchen. On sitting at her table, fooling around with my little motorcycle models that I loved to build as a kid. In my memory, Ed looks at me, giving me one of her rosy-faced smiles, the kind that always made me feel protected and safe.

"So why're you making that point to me now?"

"You're no longer alone in the world. Marrying Max means that you are embracing family, even if it's not in the most conventional of ways." I feel the doctor staring at me, but I won't look at him, or at Max for that matter. My boot becomes my obsession; I use it to make a scuff pattern on the varnished wood flooring.

"Hunter, you described yourself as gay at the outset of our sessions, yet you've repeatedly referenced your heterosexual relationships. Even your dream references them," he says. "You, in fact, are the one who perceived this relationship in traditional heterosexual terms. Marriage. Family."

"So?"

"That has an impact on what you want with Max, on what you want from the relationship."

"I'm not expecting him to be a girl or anything, if that's what you're getting at." I think of Maxine, and how much she turned me on that night months ago.

"But you are expecting a traditional relationship. To make being gay work within those confines."

"Anything wrong with that? Why shouldn't we have what everybody else has, huh? Yeah, so I want to settle down, what the fuck is wrong with that?" I shout, feeling my hackles rise unstoppably. But the doctor just smiles in what appears to be satisfaction.

"Pissed you off, didn't I?" he asks, using my own kind of

language. I'm smart enough to know he's trying to talk on my level.

"Damn straight."

"What angers you, Hunter, is that you've finally found the family you've yearned for your whole life. The love you've craved. That's why you're defensive. Because I seemed to challenge that."

"Oh. You didn't?"

"I wanted you to see what you're looking for in marriage. That it's okay to be gay or bi and still want what the rest of the hetero world has. That's fine. More than fine."

"I never thought that it wasn't."

"But you're not entirely comfortable with your sexuality."

"Sure I am," I say and glance at Max. He looks oddly nervous, shaky as he fiddles with the label on his bottled water. I still can't believe how jealous he got over the girls in the dream.

"You dreamed that your first girlfriend, and subsequent ones, were watching you with Max."

"I-I felt...confused. Really out," I stammer. "More out than I ever want to be."

Dr. Erickson taps his pencil on the desk, leaning toward me. "Hunter, think about the setting. The beach. What happened at the beach for you and Max?"

I give a knowing laugh. "Commitment."

"Precisely. Your first steps of commitment, of coming out. They happened at the beach."

"Why the girls?" Max asks, not looking at either of us. "Watching us?"

"Because Hunter's subconscious is trying to sort out his bisexuality, Max. That's all," the doctor explains patiently, and

Max looks upward in relief. "It's nothing personal against you. He's giving you everything."

"Baby, you know how I feel," I say on a whisper. "This was just some crazy ass dream."

"Max, how this relates to you, though, is that just because Hunter's marrying you, his heterosexual side won't simply shut off, any more than a straight man stops noticing other women just because he's married. It's your job to validate his heterosexual aspects."

"How?" Max asks, his golden eyes widening as he stares at the doctor. "I-I'm not sure, well how to do that."

"Maxine," Dr. Erickson says with a faint smile. "Hunter, you responded quite well to her, didn't you?"

I hold up both hands in protest. "Wait, now that has nothing at all to do with this."

"Everything, actually."

"Yeah, I was into her, but that was because of Maxwell, and..."

"Maxine accepted you, Hunter," the doctor disagrees. "As equally as you accepted her. She played to both sides of your sexual pendulum."

Maxwell and I fall deathly silent; we've never brought Maxine out again, not after our one night of going wild together. My face burns beneath the doctor's eager gaze, at what he's suggesting. Finally, he continues, "Role playing is a vital part of every couple's sexual experience. You do realize that, right?"

I grunt, squirming inside. Max gives something of an answer, and I have the feeling he's about as mortified as I am by this discussion.

"Hunter, answer me honestly. Have you felt attraction to a woman in the past month?" he asks. "Be truthful."

I think for a moment, then start laughing. "Yeah, on *Will and Grace.*"

Max gasps audibly. "Grace?" he says, turning to me with wide eyes. "Tell me it's not true."

"She's hot, man."

"But Eric McCormack!" Max snorts, the picture of easy betrayal. You have to understand, Max is a hardcore, totally devoted Will fan. Will all the way. I think he secretly visits Eric McCormack fan sites, which I give him major shit for whenever I get suspicious.

"Baby, I'm a Grace kind of guy," I explain, touching his arm, but he jerks away from me testily. "I mean, Will is sexy and all, but Grace..." I make a guytown gesture with both my hands, the kind that illustrates her shapely figure. "Yowsa! Grace has the goods!"

Max sniffs indignantly, tossing his dark hair away from his eyes. "I'm shocked."

The doctor starts laughing, shaking his head in appreciation of our sudden marital dilemma. "Max is about Will, you're about Grace," he says. "What better explanation of my point could there be?"

"I'm all about Maxwell!" I cry, nearly rising out of my seat in sudden frustration. "Let's get that much clear."

"Of course you are, Hunter," he agrees. "Extremely loyal, too, I might add. All I'm suggesting is that you must embrace both sides of your sexuality. Max isn't like you, he's been queer for as long as he can remember."

"Whereas I'm a homo convert, thanks to Gorgeous George over there," I grumble, gesturing toward Max. That does get a lovely smile out of my baby.

"All I'm saying is that while you may call yourself gay, it's a lot more complex than that. So long as you both realize this is a major difference in your sexual identities, all should go fine," he explains methodically. "And maybe, just maybe, Maxine might come out and play every once and a while. I don't think there's anything wrong with that. Not for either of you."

Huh, come to think of it, I've been entertaining some serious Maxine fantasies for a while now, just hadn't been sure how to explain them to Maxwell. So maybe this last session of counseling accomplished something significant after all. Either that, or at the very least, all those "Will and Grace" reruns just assumed a whole new meaning.

After our session is over, we spend the day biking it down to Long Beach. This is the last Saturday we'll do this as single guys; next week we have final tuxedo fittings and a dozen other details to cover. So our ocean drive is a special time for just us. No work, no wedding plans, just Max and Hunter together on that Harley.

By the time we get back to the apartment, I'm feeling a little windblown and tired as Maxwell hits the shower. I open drawers, looking for a change of T-shirt, and spying a hidden package, get inspired. It's a Christmas present, one I kind of lost my nerve about giving him once his dad showed up on the scene. I've been holding on to it ever since.

I remove it from the bottom of the drawer, fluffing the smashed bow and wrapping. It's a small, flat box, and I'm thinking that now might be the right time to give it to him, when Maxwell steps into the room.

"What's that?" he asks, toweling off his dark, wet hair. Damn, he's luscious when he's wet like that. Another towel is draped around his waist as he settles down on the edge of the bed. "This is Christmas wrapping," he says, surprised. He picks up the box, grinning, but clearly confused.

"Christmas in April," I say with an awkward laugh, reclining on our bed. I prop my head on my arms, just studying him. "No time like now."

"Okay," he says, sounding uncertain.

He picks up the flat package, running his fingers over the paper. He's so easy to please, I know it wouldn't matter to him if there was only paper inside; he just loves the mystery of it all. I begin to wonder if he's ever going to open the freaking thing up, though, because he just keeps tracing his fingertips over the ribbon, kind of shaking the box.

"Baby, you gonna open it or what?" I tease him, and he looks up at me through those long lashes. It's a flirty glance, and it causes a tightening in my groin just like he means there to be.

"Just checking it out," he says with a soft smile, and then begins untying the ribbon.

When the wrapping opens like a flower, a thin black box with glittery lettering appears, with only the words *For Him* in cursive on the front. Just the sight of that box nearly gives me a raging hard-on. Sexy, demure, it says a whole damn lot.

Again, Max glances up at me, his eyebrows forming a curious question mark, as he opens the box. He peels back the thin layer of tissue paper, smoothing it with his fingertips, and then his eyes widen in disbelief. Apparently that's the first time he notices the inside of the box lid, where the silver writing teases coyly, *Or...For Her?*

"Wow," he says, as with incredible care he removes the lace lingerie. It's white and unbelievably feminine, in fact, I ordered it because it was called "Bridal Suite".

"That all you gonna say there, Max?" I gloat, feeling damned proud of myself because I see how pleased he is. Hell, he's grinning from ear to ear.

The tips of those ears, by the way? They've turned bright red, and he's sexy as hell when he gets that flustered.

"I-I can't believe you, well, thought of it," he admits a little breathlessly, just teasing his fingers over the extremely generous material on the front of the panties. "Or found this at all."

"Internet, baby. The key to all of life's mysteries." I don't share the details of my surreal venture into crossdress.com, or talk about those tantalizing pictures of guys with bodies a lot like his, kind of slightly built and waxed to girlish perfection.

A little like Maxine did during our one night together.

No, I don't share those details at all. I just lean back against the pillows, studying his reaction.

"I guess so." He lifts the bra out of the box with a wildly curious expression, drawing in a sharp breath as the cascade of silk and lace unfolds across his lap.

"For you," I assure him. "And I mean really for you. Designed that way."

"I can see that," he agrees with a nod. But then he's back to the panties, because they're what fascinate him most, something about how roomy they are, built just like he needs them to be.

"I had to remember my girl, you know," I admit softly, and for the longest moment he won't even look at me. Just keeps staring into his lap where he holds the lacy lingerie. Until he finally meets my gaze there in the semi-darkness, and I see how furiously he blushes. "Maxine. Had to think of her," I explain and wonder when my voice became rough as malt whiskey.

"She's thrilled." His voice has literally changed, pitched upward, as he stares at me with sultry, feminine eyes, kind of fanning his lashes slightly.

"You know, I was kinda thinking I'd like to see her again," I admit, avoiding his gaze as I toy nervously with the box lid. "Soon, you know?" I feel like I'm asking a girl out for a very first date, that's how bashful I suddenly am about the whole damned thing.

"She'd like that." Full on Marilyn Monroe, right there in the near dark with me.

"You think?" I ask, finally looking into those feline eyes. "Would she have anything to do with a big lug like me?"

"Any time, sweetheart." Lashes flutter and fan, lips part almost imperceptibly. I can't fight what I'm feeling for another minute, I swear it.

I lean in close, brushing my lips against his, and my heart is hammering an insane rhythm, as I whisper, "I'd really love to see my girl." I release a nervous breath, feeling like I've scored big time with the gift, as he wraps his hands around my neck, nuzzling close.

But my chest thumping is cut short when he reflects, "You're really into Maxine." Unlike months ago, there's no jealousy in his voice, just unabashed curiosity. "I know that Dr. Erickson encouraged this, but I'm still surprised by how taken you are with her."

Taken with her? Is that like being smitten? Fuck, I'm smitten with Maxine. That's what he's saying, and suddenly I find that I'm blushing like an imbecile as heat creeps downward into my neck. I'm on fire with shame, because he's pulled back the curtain on our clandestine illusion; he's thrown on the stage lights, and I'm the one left exposed for everyone to see.

"I mean, you've definitely responded to her more than I ever imagined," he adds, and I know he's studying me, even though I refuse to meet his pointed gaze.

"Guess so," I manage, cursing myself a fool for making over the whole damned thing so much. I should have left the goddamned gift hidden in the bottom drawer.

Maxwell reaches for my hand, cocking his head sideways. "Hunter, I like that you're so into that side of me," he admits, his voice thick with obvious emotion. Soft, yet ragged all at once.

I nod, but the warmth just keeps spreading across my face. My shame is stupid, with all that we've shared, with how much I love everything about him. "Hunter?" he asks uncertainly, stroking my hair. "I wasn't laughing at you or anything. Just observing, okay?"

Finally, I allow my eyes to track upward, until they lock with his. "Yeah, well, I do dig Maxine. A whole fucking lot, okay?" I'm testy now, feeling really pissed at him for making some big deal out of it all.

"Hunter," he presses, his voice still incredibly gentle. "I get it. I really do."

"Okay." I have no idea what he means, but I feel so vulnerable, so raw. Like that night last summer when I first understood that our coupling wasn't just some short-term fling. The night when I realized I'd fallen in love with him.

I feel the same spiraling, choking panic right now. Like I want to hide from him for eternity. Please just anything but this burning, insistent shame.

I rake my hands through my hair in frantic desperation, looking at the ceiling, the floor, everywhere but into the eyes of my lifetime lover.

Funny, but Maxwell isn't backing down an inch; in fact, he moves even closer to where I'm huddling on the bed. "Hunter, I get why you respond to Maxine so much, okay?" he says, his voice quiet and soothing. "I totally get it. So why don't you?"

"Why don't I what?" I snap, rubbing my palm over my chest. My heart is beating like a fucked-up clock, and all I can think is that I want to bolt. I mean, what kind of freak responds so strongly to a drag queen?

The simple answer traipses across my heart—a freak that loves someone as deeply as I love Maxwell. Simple, simple answer, yet it feels complex as hell.

"Why don't you realize the truth of what you told me that day? That you accept Maxine because of how much you love me."

"I said it 'cause it was true."

"But, Hunter," he says, reaching a tender palm to my cheek, and caressing it, soft skin against bristling stubble. "It's more than that, don't you see? It's like Dr. Erickson said. You love Maxine because she accepts all of you."

Oh, shit. He's right. Of course he is, and I wonder how the truth never hit me before this moment, not even earlier in our session. But he's Maxwell, and he's not stopping now. Before he opens his mouth, I know what he's going to say next; I hear the words flash through my mind like lightning before he even utters them.

"You said yourself you were straight as an arrow until you got with me."

"I wanted you from the moment I saw you."

"And Maxine, well, she embraces that in you."

I nod, unable to speak as he just keeps touching me, loving me. So unbelievably gentle, so kind even when I'm a straight up bastard.

"I told you before, I don't wish you were different," I whisper, closing my eyes as he strokes my hair, pressing a sweet kiss against my jaw. "I've never wished you were a woman, or anything like that. No matter how bisexual I am."

"Hunter, I know that. I was just freaking out a little that

day. But I know how you feel about me," he says. "And I do mean *me*."

"God, you can turn me on just by walking in a room," I blurt, my voice kind of cracking over the words. "Everything just gets all electric whenever you're near, baby."

"You've never loved anyone the way that you love me. I know that." So confident, so absolutely sure—hell, I must be pretty freaking obvious in how much I love him. Easily, he draws me right into his arms; I don't fight him at all.

"'Course not, baby," I mumble against his shoulder. "Never wanted anyone this much, either. I'm just lost to you. Totally lost."

"You're not lost, Hunter," he disagrees gently. "You found love. So what if it was with someone surprising?"

"I don't want women anymore. Only you."

"And Grace, right?"

Before I can even answer, he blesses me with that soul-rending smile that always spells my doom, and whispers, "Until a year ago you'd never even kissed a man. Now, you're marrying one. I'd say you're entitled to feeling weird at times. Especially when it comes to sweet Maxine."

"Sweet," I laugh, a little begrudgingly, and his eyes widen in reaction.

"Isn't she?" he teases in a husky, seductive voice, becoming a coquette right there beside me. "Isn't she sweet, your girl?"

"Oh, you bet, baby," I growl and then I'm just all over him. Nothing could stop me as I take him, tumbling in his arms across the length of our bed.

My hands stroke his silky hair, loving the feel of it beneath my fingertips. Loving that I've got a man in my arms as we roll and tug and nip at one another in a flurry of intense desire.

Scratchy beard brushes against my cheek, Ralph Lauren cologne mingles with the smell of salty brine and fresh air. He's a man, all right, and even though I couldn't have anticipated being with him until a year ago, there's one thing I know for sure now.

Sometimes you find love where you least expect it; and hopefully when you do, you're smart enough to grab it.

Chapter Seventeen

When I hear the words "bachelor party" I immediately think of Tom Hanks and a bad eighties movie. So when Maxwell tells me he's planned a secret shindig for me, I instantly balk at the idea.

"Nah, baby. Let's not." We're heading to Vermont in ten days, and the thought of some wild night doesn't do much for me. I think I'd rather cozy up under the sheets with him and have wild sex. Screw everybody else. Well, so to speak, which is kind of my point.

"Hunter, are you kidding me?" he asks, reaching for the toasted bagel I made for his breakfast. "You really are joking, right?"

"What do you mean?" I hand him a napkin and small thermos cup of coffee, which he sets on the counter with a smile of gratitude. Papers are shuffled together, arranged neatly as he tucks them into the side of his Coach briefcase.

As always, Maxwell looks like a million bucks as he gets ready to head downtown in his designer suit, but you'd never guess it by the critical way he turns to examine himself in the mirrored refrigerator.

"Well, you strike me as the bachelor party type guy," he says, adjusting his tie with an assessing gaze.

I shrug, sipping my own coffee. "Never married anybody

before. Especially not a guy." It's a little early for gazing this closely at my swinging pendulum of sexual orientation.

"Ah, so that's it."

"What?" I ask, padding after him barefoot, clad only in my boxers and T-shirt as he heads toward the apartment door.

"You're scared."

"Like hell," I protest as he turns to kiss me. He's crisp and clean, and I feel less than adequate as his lips linger against mine.

"You look gorgeous all rumpled like this," he laughs, running his fingers through my unkempt hair. Funny, it's almost as if he intercepted my telegraphs of insecurity.

"Humph."

"And you are scared about the party." He gives me a sly look, and I know he's just trying to push all my macho buttons, working to get his way. "Worried that it might be more bachelorette than bachelor, Hunter?"

I choose to ignore his little dig at my bisexuality, especially because he gives me another slow kiss.

"You don't kiss like you're scared," he teases.

"I like to know what to expect, that's all," I whisper against his smoothly shaven cheek. "I don't care what you've got planned, baby, really. Just don't like being surprised by it."

He pulls back and his eyes narrow. "You're going to love this party. I promise you, Hunter." He's still running his fingers through my hair, combing it back from my eyes with a gentle gesture.

"I'm not getting out of this, am I?" See, I'm just a sucker when he strokes my hair, little more than a puddle of mush, I tell you.

"Sorry."

"No, you're not, you asshole. You're not one bit sorry."

He grins at me mischievously, waving the bagel as he turns to open the door. "Thanks for the breakfast. I love you!"

"Yeah, yeah," I grumble. "You're just in it for the bagels."

"No, that's not true," he disagrees over his shoulder, stepping into the hall. "I'm in it for the sex."

"No, I'm in it for the sex. You're in it for the Harley!" I say, snapping the door shut before he can answer.

Truth is, we both know the score. We're in it for our lives.

"So, isn't this something we're supposed to be doing separately?" I ask, staring at my reflection in the mirrored closet doors. We're getting ready for the dreaded bachelor party, switch hitting on clothes and preening like a pair of girlfriends. I've tried on a couple of his polo shirts, but nothing works, so I'm back to my ever-reliable flannel shirt.

Max, on the other hand, is still practically naked. He traipses past me in nothing but his boxers, and I give his ass a playful fondling. "Hey, hey, sweet thing," I laugh, squeezing his generous behind.

He tosses me a lazy-eyed look that makes me want to fuck him on the spot. "Separate?" he asks, his voice all husky as he watches me. He even has the nerve to run his tongue across his upper lip. "You would rather be separate tonight?"

It takes all my willpower not to bed him then and there, especially when he kind of thrusts his chest out at me.

"Don't play innocent with me, Maxwell."

"I'd never claim innocence in this relationship," he admits, stepping past me into the closet. "Not with the way you make love."

"Answer my question, Daniels. Traditionally speaking, shouldn't we be having separate bachelor parties?" I stare at his back, at the defined cordons of muscle that appear and bulge as he pulls a pair of pants off the hanger.

"Well, we're not exactly traditional groomsmen, are we?"

"Nah, not really." I fold my arms over my chest, just watching him move in those boxers.

"So why not enjoy partying together?"

Good question, and he's right. Nothing about our wedding runs the gamut of typical, so why should I start worrying about it now?

"It's something I'd like to give you, Hunter. This party."

A little light blinks on for me then, and I finally get it. This night is one of Maxwell's sweet little gifts. If he could've done it, he'd have wrapped the whole thing up and plopped one of his flouncy bows atop it all. What did I ever do that he loves me so damned much?

"Cool. It'll be really...special."

"That's what I want it to be," he admits. "A real wedding memory."

With that pronouncement, he steps into a crisp pair of black jeans that are undoubtedly the single sexiest piece of clothing I've ever seen on my boy. My heart gives a desperate leap as he pulls them onto his slender body.

"Whoa!" I kind of karate-chop my hands, my gaze roving down the sinewy length of him.

"What?" he asks, running his palms over the pants self-consciously.

"Danger, Will Robinson. Those are fucking tight, man."

"Yeah," he grins boyishly. "I know." He's pleased as hell with himself that they look so amazing on him. His gaze wanders to the mirror and he gives a little turn, studying his appearance.

I clasp his hips, tugging him close by the waistband. "Baby, can you breathe? 'Cause I don't want you passing out on me or anything. Blood supply is critical for some of my favorite parts down there."

He plants one hand on his hip indignantly. "Excuse me?"

I burst into a roll of laughter. "Oh, shit, Max. You look ridiculous when you flame like that!"

He swats at me with his white T-shirt, popping my arm hard, so I yank the damned thing right out of his hand. He lunges at me, but I bounce away from him on the balls of my feet, playing keep away.

"So what's this?" I dangle the shirt over my head like a stolen basketball. "The tightest shirt this side of San Francisco?"

Max strains to grab it out of my hand, reaching for it, but my height advantage makes it impossible for him to succeed.

"Give it back." He scowls at me, all testy, and that flat turns me on.

"No way in hell." I hide the thing behind my back as he grabs at it unsuccessfully. "So you're dressing all the way out tonight?" I am definitely getting the picture of the kind of party he has planned for me.

He reaches over my head again, slightly winded. "Maybe," he admits, as I pull him close into my arms, and suddenly find myself pressed chest to chest with him. Well, with him and those damned tight jeans.

"You're looking very sweet," I murmur in his ear, as I run my hands all over his bare back. "You've been working hard in the weight room too."

He only laughs like a coquette, holding me close, so I say, "Yeah, you're laughing, but it's no joke how hot you're looking there, Maxwell."

"I'm getting married. I'm supposed to look beautiful." Beautiful. That seems an appropriate description for my blushing groom-to-be.

"Well you damn sure do."

"Good," he says, and then he's laid hold of that shirt. Ripped it right out of my hands, and he kind of pirouettes away from me in victory.

"Hey, no fair!" I chase him across the bedroom, and he stops long enough to give me a frisky gaze, as he slips it over his head, sliding right into the clingy thing.

"Tough break, Willis."

No fucking joke. I'm supposed to stare at that all night long without jumping his ass? Yeah, right. Somebody give me a time machine—fast forward about ten days, would you please?

Wedding night sounds great right about now, thank you very much.

Turns out I was right: We've hit clubland full stride, with the gaytraders and even Bruno the pickup basketball player in tow. I ignore the momentary pang of jealousy I feel, thinking about Bruno having stolen Max's first gay kiss. Kind of wish it'd been me, but hell, I got the rest and that's all that matters. Besides, without Bruno neither of us might be here tonight, so I owe him a bow of gratitude for Max's initiation into the queer nation.

First thing I do when we enter the club is grab myself a beer; that and wonder what Max has planned. After all, he brought me here blindfolded, with the promise that it was going to be "one hell of a night to remember". God, I love him. That's what I'm thinking with a dopey smile while I wait for the bartender to notice my existence. I never feel quite so straight anymore as I do standing at this club, surrounded by other gays. Not sure why exactly, but something about this place makes me feel really macho.

I am curious why our straight friends are absent from the event, but don't question Max since he's in charge tonight. Maybe he figured they'd be weirded out or something, even though that makes no sense. Louisa and Veronica have always loved clubbing, straight or no, so long as the dancing is good. Besides, they've made their acceptance of our lifestyle undeniably clear, so has Ben.

The bartender hands me my beer with a wink and a thank you for the generous tip. That's when I spot Maxwell and can hardly believe my eyes. He's snaking his way out of that shirt, tugging the damned thing right over his head, so that he stands in front of this whole crowd of strangers practically naked. I can't even say a thing, just point at him, working my mouth.

He laughs, giving a modest glance downward. Beautiful, perfect, no question about it, and definitely no need for modesty on his part, either. He's got the body, no wonder he'd want to flaunt it.

But I can't believe he's actually going for the shirtless thing. I mean, I've seen it countless times in the clubs. Gorgeous guys strip out of their shirts to show off their bodies, but those guys are usually looking for it, aren't they? Or maybe they've just been flirting all along and somehow I missed that point.

Maxwell tosses me an alluring gaze, reaching for my hand, and I know he's leading me straight into pure temptation, right out on that dance floor.

Max knows from experience that I'm not too keen on

dancing at this place. It's one thing to hold him in my arms when it's just us, when it inevitably leads to so much more than an embrace. It's another thing altogether to pump and grind with him out in the open. Something about that always makes me feel like an oaf, a little self-conscious, too. Like I'm really pushing the envelope of my sexual orientation or something.

So usually I lurk by the bar or stick around upstairs watching the show. The show that has always included hundreds upon hundreds of half-naked gay men, pummeling their bodies to house music, and it never once occurred to me that my exhibitionist lover might want to join their ranks.

Until now, when he's ditched that T-shirt of his, so he's part of the tribe. My heart is in my throat as he leads me onto the crowded floor, shouldering his way into the writhing masses.

At last he turns to me and slips one thigh between my legs, stepping inward. For a moment, he stares up at me, a question forming on his face. I'm not entirely sure what he's asking, maybe if I'll go as far as he's obviously willing to lead. Not sure at all, but I nod slightly. He knows I've acquiesced, because his smile broadens; he presses inward, sliding together with me.

Then, just like that, it's happening. Some kind of vortex opens, swallowing us whole and I'm spinning right into my lover. Into our moment, together.

Our hips lock fast, and there's nothing separating us except noise and heat and sweat, as we start to grind to the droning beat. It hardly matters that we're in a crowd; there's only Max pushing against me, his thighs, his groin. I'm hard as they get, baby. He slips his palms onto my hips and draws me even tighter against him, right as he launches into an amazing gyration of rhythm.

That lovely bare chest shimmers beneath the flashing lights

like something primal. He's my very own tribal dancer, pushed close against me amidst hundreds of strangers. His eyes drift shut for a moment, as he raises his hands high like an offering. Shimmying, he separates a bit, our hips drift apart. This time it's me who reaches, drawing him back.

"Oh, no you don't," I growl in his ear, and he laughs sexily, pushing in close again. Thrusting a bit, we disguise it as dance while our bodies slide and gyrate. We're pressed hip to hip, abdomen to abdomen. My hands rove all over his velvet chest, touching, claiming. God help me, if one of these other shirtless boys try to make a move on him, I'll kick their ass.

More grinding of our hips, more flailing of arms and bodies as we pulse with the music. His hands wander all over my thighs, upward onto my waist, urging me into a pounding rhythm. Right here on the dance floor, and nobody gives a shit. Still, I glance around self-consciously, and Max leans in close against my cheek. His breath is warm, familiar.

"There's only us," he assures me.

"And a thousand other people," I shout back into his ear.

"Like I said," he laughs, lifting his arms again with a beguiling look. "Just us."

For a moment, my own eyes drift closed, as I feel the rhythm. Our rhythm, pounding out between us. I'm startled when a draft of cool air hits my chest, and even more so to realize that Max is carefully unbuttoning my flannel shirt.

"No," I insist, shaking my head as I cover his hands with my own. He thrusts his hips faster, moving his hardened cock against mine. Making me aware of how blatantly he's aroused.

I can't breathe. I swear to God, I simply can't. Maybe that's why I don't fight my lover, as he slowly unbuttons my shirt, until it falls open. A frigid waft of air conditioning causes my nipples to grow taut; he keeps rocking and grinding, drawing the shirt off of my shoulders.

He's undressing me, that's what my lover's doing. Anyone can see. As if anyone really cares.

With a slow, wicked grin, he hands the shirt to me, leaning to shout in my ear, "Tie it around your waist." He points at his own T-shirt, looped over his belt and dangling down his back.

With an awkward, frantic gesture, I secure the shirt around my hips. Glancing downward, I'm dismayed by how strongly I resemble some Seattle grunge refugee. Again, Max leans close, his breath fanning my cheek as he teases, "I always had a hard-on for Kurt Cobain."

I just roll my eyes, and say, "Shit, man. Courtney was the hot one."

We rock and thrust; we step apart and slide that floor. Then we spin right back together again, and I hold him fast against my body. Cradling our hips together as we make our need clear to one another.

"Baby," I gasp, fighting for air as he runs his fingertips over my chest silkily. His eyes have narrowed and I know that bedroom gaze. For a fleeting moment, I actually think of dragging him off to some dark corner, and glance around.

I think he knows my thoughts, because he throws his head back with a wild peel of laughter. Those muscular arms fly overhead, as he spins a wicked little turn.

His motions catapult him backward from me, and I'm left grasping for his slender, alluring body. But with one quick glance that explains everything, he's gone. Swept away in that whirlwind of movement, then suddenly paired with someone else. Okay, I feel jealousy choking me like thick bile. I'm fighting it, beating it back as that stranger presses in close with my baby and they begin a quick dance movement of their own.

He's mine, goddamn it. What the hell is going on?

But then someone's in my own space, shoving inward, making a move. Oh my God. I'm being hit on by a strapping, great-looking guy! Someone other than Max. I hardly get a look at him because I just keep staring toward the floor, watching the way our hips kind of push and move. I'm entranced by our motion; most especially that I'm dancing so boldly with a stranger. That I'm this gay. Except—I'm getting married in less than a week. Doesn't get any fucking weirder than this.

With that thought, finally I look up, and in the flashing neon meet the stranger's gaze. Only he's not a stranger. My dance partner laughs at the obvious recognition on my face, and leans in close to say, "What do you know, huh? It's never the ones you expect."

I'm speechless, because it's Robert from swing gang down at Universal. Holy shit.

"I had no idea," I manage back in his ear, over the sound, looking around desperately for Maxwell. I see his dark head bobbing in a sea of bodies, and it looks like he's moved on to dance with someone else, the little fucker.

"Me neither." He's laughing while moving in closer until we're barely separate at all.

"I'm with somebody," I shout, kind of gesturing in Max's direction. Robert doesn't even bother to follow my gaze.

"Kurt or Courtney?" he jabs, tugging on my flannel shirt with a lopsided grin.

"I'm with my boyfriend."

He just cocks a curious eyebrow, his gaze roving across my bare-chested state, and I blush a thousand shades of red. "Well, isn't he the lucky fellow?"

I clarify, "This is my bachelor party." It only gets me more wide-eyed curiosity, and I curse myself for the four or more beers I've already tossed back. "Commitment ceremony next week," I grunt in his ear, by way of explanation.

"Well, are you boys into the free thing? You know, open relationship? 'Cause if you are, then maybe we could…"

I cut him off with a bitter scowl. "Just dance, for crying out loud."

He laughs at my grumbling, shaking his head. "I'll remember this Monday morning, Willis! Down at the studio."

"Well guess what, Roberto?" I lean in close, exaggerating my hip motion for effect. "So will I, man."

But somehow, on a really weird level, this is insanely gratifying. To just know that I'm attractive to other guys—hell to guys I work with, apparently. Even as Robert and I are kind of thrusting and swimming along with a thousand other sex-crazed dancers, I realize this is important. It's like a Grade A stamp of approval on my queerness.

Maxwell is the shit for knowing to do this. I am marrying a guy who is literally, completely and totally the shit. Go, Me! I have excellent taste in husbands.

A thousand tribal beats later, Max finds me again. He's damp from his exertions out on the dance floor, and grinning like a besotted fool. "You're amazing," he pants in my ear, wiping at his brow.

"How's that?" I ask with an aloof shrug. I'm trying to look pissy and sullen because he left me on my own, when really I can't believe how sexy he looks. His face is flushed, his dark curls clinging to the nape of his neck. Kind of like he's been doing something else entirely.

"The way you opened up to all that. Just dove in and totally went for it."

"Yeah, yeah," I complain with a reluctant grin, as he kisses me on the lips. His warm hand grazes my cheek, drawing me much closer.

"I love how open you are. To things with me."

My eyes narrow on instinct. "You're buttering me up."

"We're not done for the night."

"How come I knew you'd say that?"

Brian suddenly appears, slinging an arm over my bare shoulder. "Hunter, ole boy, the best is yet to come. At least as far as you'll be concerned."

Then Max, Brian, Peter and Bruno have formed a knot around me and it seems they're all just howling with laughter. At my expense. I don't know what's so damned funny, but there's an adorable twinkle in Maxwell's eyes that makes me feel safe. Especially when Brian claps my shoulder, saying, "Come on, buddy. Time for the blindfold again!"

Then Max shoves a clean white T-shirt into my hand. "But first you need to put this on."

I unfurl it, and read the silver, glittery words embossed across the front: I'm not gay, but my boyfriend is!

"Oh, fucking great," I manage, as I tug the shirt over my head. The damned thing must be at least two sizes too small, pulling at my biceps and chest. Max gives me a knowing glance, cocking one eyebrow as he strokes my upper arm in appreciation.

"Perfect. Just the right size."

With that pronouncement, the silken black scarf goes back over my eyes again. God only knows what Maxwell has planned next.

Somehow, I can't help but wonder if the night won't be swinging more toward the bachelor side of things, considering how he's just branded me with that T-shirt.

Turns out, I had no idea just how right I was.

That is, not until they shuffle me out of Brian's SUV and my boots hit pavement with a scuffling thud. Then the blindfold is peeled away, and I see a curving neon figure displayed on a marquis. Girls, girls, girls! We're talking Bada Bing all the way, not Louisa or Marilyn wannabes at all.

"What the hell?" I ask, turning to Max, who just grins like a Cheshire cat.

"Bachelor party, Hunter." He shares a quick glance with Brian, then his gaze cuts back to me.

I start shaking my head in instant protest. "Maxwell, I don't know about this," I say, brushing anxiously at my hair. Never thought I'd see the day when a strip club would make me unsettled, but somehow this feels weird. You know, coming to a girly club with my gay lover.

Max doesn't miss a beat, though, as he slips his arm around me, and draws me close. "Hunter, this is for you. A last night out thing before our wedding."

"I'm queer now," I blurt defensively. "This isn't my deal anymore."

Before Max can answer, I see several familiar faces emerging from the parking lot. Veronica lets loose a high-pitched whistle as she sails to my side. "Hellooo, boys!" she bellows in her best Mae West imitation. "Ready to have some fun?"

"Ah, shit!" I announce. "This is like a total setup."

"You bet it is!" Veronica laughs, flinging her arms around my neck. "Love the shirt, Willis." She tugs on the hem, and it barely springs back at all it's so skin tight. This wins me a dramatic wink, as she teases, "Just in case they didn't believe what it says, huh?"

224

"I hate you," I grunt at Maxwell, but he's too busy sweeping Louisa into his arms for a tender hug. "And you two? You're both straight, okay!" I shout, gesturing at them. "You just need to go have wild sex, make babies, and get it over with already." They turn to me, a little surprised, still clinched in one another's arms, as I add, "Maxwell Daniels is straight as folk, people! He's straight! And I'm outing him right now!"

Every last one of our friends howls with laughter, and for a long moment I stare indignantly. I mean, I meant it to be funny, but I really was a little worked up and jealous, too.

Then Louisa skips to my side, and sweeps me into her small arms for a hug, pressing her face close against my shoulder. She smells like the earth, natural and sweet, and I sense how much she loves me. It's not just Maxwell anymore; I'm really important to Louisa Carter, too. Unbelievable.

"You do realize that I've seen him in a Ninja Turtle bathing suit, right?" Louisa laughs, still holding me. "In the long run, that does make sex slightly problematic."

I have this bizarre flash of our honeymoon, and Maxwell appearing poolside dressed just that way.

"Got a point there, Carter. Kind of a strong visual."

"Stronger than you can probably imagine." She giggles, stepping apart and grinning at Max.

"Turn about is fair play, Mr. Daniels," she says.

Then I start snorting with laughter, because the whole setup is hysterical. You know, the idea of tagging along with my gay lover to a decidedly macho strip club. Bringing our closest friends along—most of whom are either girls or gay guys. Pretty oddball, but also a riot, too.

So, I decide to get into the spirit of things and sling an arm around Max's shoulder. I waltz right up to the entrance, feeling vaguely hetero and queer all at once. The bouncer gives our crew a strange glance and I stare him down, flipping my I.D. as we walk right in the club. Hell, maybe not this particular place, but I've been this way before. Makes a strange kind of poetic sense, then, that I'd come here one last time.

Yeah, Maxwell's scored a hit big time, because this is one fucking night to remember.

My millionaire fiancé must have bribed someone big time because I find myself with the best seat in the house. I'm talking, right up front, hands in easy "dollar distance". So I take advantage of that fact, teasing the dancers and stuffing fives and tens into their slinky lingerie every time Max shoves them into my hands. Which is frequently, by the way. He's like some dad at the Midway keeping me hooked on pinball or something.

Of course, his encouragement has nothing to do with the way Louisa and Veronica squeal loudly every time I poke more money into the dancers' panties. One of the girls actually leans low, tracing her fingertip over the glitter lettering on my shirt. God, I feel like a first class fag, too, as she kind of smirks, shimmying her hips at me, making her point.

I'm feeling slightly aroused by her, by the dark showering hair that falls down her back. My jeans are kind of starting to tighten down there because of hot she is, when she looks right at me and mouths, "Gay." She smirks about it, too.

Well, something about that feels like a challenge, so I turn to Max, "Give me a twenty, baby." He doesn't hesitate, just slips one between my fingertips.

I wave my girl back over, grinning for all I'm worth as I tuck the bill right beneath her garter. Max even stands with me, and I mouth back at her, "Bi!"

The girl smiles at us, enjoying the gag as she works it for me. Guess she's used to all kinds of people yanking her chain;

in fact, we're probably tame by a lot of comparisons.

Then I settle back down at the table, and drape my arm right over Max's shoulder for good measure. I don't give a shit if anybody thinks we don't belong here. Thing is, even with all the testosterone running wild in this place, I want the world to know one damned thing.

I'm with my guy.

Must be two a.m. when we stagger back through the door of our apartment. I'm flat exhausted, but still horny as hell. Max drops his wallet and keys on the kitchen counter, and I seize my moment, wrapping my arms around him from behind.

"You're a very bad boy," I murmur in his ear, raking my palms over his chest. The tight T-shirt allows me to feel every ridge and ripple of his body, and he arches backward into my arms.

"How's...that?" he asks, breathless already.

"Planning so much temptation for one night. When you knew how long it'd be until right now."

I work my hips behind him, kind of half-pinning him against the counter where he can't move. My erection bulges through my jeans and I make sure he feels my hard-on.

"Pocket protector?" he laughs, as I slip my fingers down beneath his waistband. "Or is that a cell phone?"

"Daniels, you're a cock tease."

"I resent that," he purrs, reaching back to grab my thighs. "I'm just a gay man with a strong sex drive."

"A beautiful, perfect..." I spin him in my arms, so we're facing one another, "...extremely gay man."

"With a healthy drive for his lover."

The kiss that begins between us conveys the need we've felt

227

all night long. On the dance floor, at the strip club. Hell, just watching him dress at the beginning of the night.

I drag him toward the sofa, tugging at the button on his jeans. "Drive this, then, sweet thing," I suggest, popping open my own fly as we collapse onto the sofa in a tangle of desire.

He's on top of me, kneeling between my legs, and makes quick work of my jeans. Before I can blink, they're halfway down my hips, and he's got his greedy hands inside my boxers. Warm fingers close around the tip of my erection, stroking, loving. Oh, no, this feels so fucking good that I know I won't last long.

"Baby," I groan, lifting my hips to meet his strokes.

He doesn't answer, and as my eyes open, I see a satisfied gleam in his eyes. "I have plans, Hunter Willis."

"Oh, Max," I cry, unable to stop the crescendo of need pummeling through my body. He drops his dark head low, and the familiar wetness suddenly circles my cock as his tongue snakes around my tip. "Maxwell!" I can't possibly be quiet, not with the way he's shattering me.

My fingers grope at his muscular shoulders, comb wildly through his hair as my groin tightens and aches for him. The sucking sensation is unbelievable. How can this sophisticated, smooth guy give such unbelievable head? Unrestrained is the word for my sweet baby once we're together this way.

When I know I'm near the end, he suddenly stops, shimmying right out of his jeans. "Ba...by?" I gasp, reaching toward him as those tight black jeans drop to the floor.

I don't even get an answer, just a smug, gorgeous smile as he straddles me, positioning himself.

"Lube?" I mumble, holding him with trembling hands, but he shakes his head.

"I'm very relaxed," he explains with a sly smile. "And very

drunk." Then he gives a giddy laugh, pushing down onto my shaft before I can argue against it. My cock is a straight, obedient little arrow, even if I'm not anymore. And I'll be damned if it doesn't nearly glide right into him without one bit of help.

I'll be damned, too, if I'm not gonna come in ten seconds flat, not with the way he lifts against me, that gorgeous erection of his glistening and jutting straight out. I clasp it within my hand, closing my eyes as I begin to stroke him straight into his own sweet oblivion.

Maxwell talks and moans and I just lose myself in the ecstasy of his perfect, tight little body. Then everything gets delirious, a little maddening in its intensity, as for a moment I swear our honeymoon has already begun.

Chapter Eighteen

So here we are. The big day and it's like somebody's turned me inside-fucking-out. I'm just a mess and a half, standing here in this dressing room. I keep pacing the floor, mopping my brow with Maxwell's handkerchief. It's an embroidered one he loaned me for the day; tucked it right into the box with my tuxedo. It even has his initials on it, so I clutch it like a lifeline, as if I'm holding on to him for real.

This is all Veronica's fault. She's my "best person" and she's late. I glance at my watch and realize that, actually, she's not late yet. It's only noon just now. But she is supposed to be here any minute to make sure I've got this tuxedo on right, and God love her, if she doesn't get here soon, I might fall apart. It's not about how the suit fits anymore; it's about keeping me together at the seams.

I stare out into the garden, at the flower-draped gazebo, the folding chairs lined in neat rows, the dream-like cascade of cherry blossoms. I lean my forehead against the wooden frame of the window, bracing myself for my future. This is it. An hour from now and I'm gonna be down there, taking Maxwell's hand in my own. I'll be taking him as my very own, in front of God and our chosen witnesses. I'm ready, I really am; I've never been more ready than I am right now.

Then how come I can't stop this crazy shaking inside? It's

not like I haven't wanted this day for the past nine months. I reach beneath my unbuttoned dress shirt and place a calming hand over my heart. Damn, it's racing like a mad fucker. *Still, boy,* I coach the overactive muscle, but it does no good at all. The thing still pounds like it's going to leap right out of my chest.

A knock comes on the door, and I rush to open it, relieved that Veronica's finally here. I know she'll be able to make sense of this nervousness, explain away how crazy and stupid I suddenly feel. For all our bickering, Veronica really does understand me, and I know she'll have just the right words for me today.

I jerk open the door, already grumbling at her, "It's about time you got..." My sentence fades on my tongue. It's not Veronica, not even close. I'll be damned if it isn't Phillip Daniels, all dressed up in a nice suit and standing here in Vermont. At our inn, on our wedding day, just like I've secretly dreamed he would be for months. Only now that he is, I'm not sure whether I should whoop for joy or search him for a shotgun. Wait, that's if he wanted me to marry his son, and with all his past objections, he might be toting one just to stop this blessed event.

"Hunter?" he asks, smiling uncertainly at me from across the threshold. Only then do I realize that I'm just staring at him, my future father-in-law, not saying a freaking thing. "Can I come in or not?" he finally asks, laughing in a way that reminds me a little of Maxwell, oddly enough.

"Yeah, yeah, of course. Come on in, sir," I say as if this is perfectly normal, him showing up on our wedding day. "Just, uh, finishing up here." I give my shirt hem a tug to emphasize my point.

"Looks like you've still got a way to go, son." There's warmth in his eyes and voice, so maybe this is a friendly visit

231

after all. Maybe he's even here to take his place in the front row, my wedding wish for Maxwell come true today.

"Why're you here, sir?" I can't hold my peace, not when I need to know if he's here to hurt my baby or celebrate our event. "Really, why?"

"Hunter, we need to talk," he says, perching on the edge of some absent inn administrator's desk. "We've needed to for a while now."

"Phillip, if you're here to try and convince me not to do this, well then I'll have to ask you to leave, especially since—"

He cuts me off, lifting his hand. "Can I share something with you or not, son?"

I tilt my chin upward, meeting his sharp gaze. "I'm listening." My tone is far cooler than I intended it to be, but I've got to deal with him, man to man. No way I'm about to back down at this late date.

But something has changed in Phillip Daniels's tired expression since Christmas; I see a spark of life that's been missing in our previous interchanges. Or maybe it's just a spark of reaction to me because he's not guarding himself so closely today.

He reaches inside his suit jacket and I pray he's not going for that gun. Instead, he removes a small brown package. "We need to talk about this," he says, his face inscrutable as he hands the parcel to me. Doesn't feel like a bomb, so slowly I work the paper loose until I'm left holding a small, framed picture.

It's the one Max was going to give them for Christmas, of the two of us at Long Beach, lost in each other's arms. Shit, I'd forgotten just how hot we look for one another in that photo, how freaking close I was holding him in the crook of my arm. My face burns beneath Phillip's gaze. I feel it on me, even as I stare at the small picture in my hands.

"What about it?" I mumble, refusing to look up. I feel heat creep into my neck, because it's as if I'm facing my dead father after all these years. I don't know what my dad would have said about this union, and I'm not sure I should hear what Phillip Daniels has to say today either.

"Max sent the picture to me this week. With a letter." I nod, staring at my lover in the picture. He's such a beautiful, gentle man. He's all I've wanted, all my life, just a soul mate to spend the years with. "Hunter?"

"Yes, sir?" I don't look up, just stare into the captured moment held within my hands.

"I'd like to read part of what Max said in his letter. If that's okay with you?"

"All right," I say, swallowing hard, and turn away from him. I walk to the window and gaze down at the flowers and the possibility of joy. Our special day, spread all below me in a happy dazzle of ribbons and flowers and music.

Phillip clears his throat and begins. "'I didn't want to be gay. Maybe you and Mom never understood that,'" he reads, and I'll be damned if tears don't well right within my eyes already. "'I fought this thing inside of me, fought it as hard as I could, for as long as I could. But that never offered me any peace. I never knew peace, Dad. Not until Hunter. He answers something in me, some long-asked question that's haunted me all my life. And the thing is, if I'd known he was waiting in my future, I never would have fought what I am. I would have run for it, with all that's inside me, Dad. I would have run toward Hunter.'"

Phillip pauses, clearing his throat with a cough and I can tell he's close to tears himself. "'All I want is for you to know him. To understand why I love him so much. For you to let him

233

be part of our family, not just for me, but for him, too. And for all of you.'"

Phillip stops reading, and I hear the echo of his steps on the stone floor behind me, though he says nothing. Still, I won't turn, and just stare down into the garden until I feel him clasp my shoulder as he finishes, "'I'm asking you to be there on my wedding day, because just like I love Hunter, I love both of you, too.'"

Phillip continues to stand with his hand on my shoulder, and I hear the sound of folding paper. I bite my lip until it nearly bleeds, anything so I won't cry in front of this man. A man who could be the father I never really had.

"Hunter, I remember last fall, you told me you didn't think I understood how much you loved my son. At the time, I thought I did."

"And now?" I croak, glancing over my shoulder at him.

"I realize there's a lot I still have to learn about love," he says and tears fill his own eyes. Eyes that look so much like my baby's. "Maybe you and my son can teach me."

"That why you came?"

"I came to bless this marriage. To be part of it," he says and I turn to face him. "To be here if it's not too late."

"It's never too late to be a family," I say.

"That's what I wanted to believe. That's what this letter made me believe."

"You have an amazing son."

The tears that have been threatening to fill his eyes do so in earnest with that statement. He swallows, wiping at the dampness. "Want this?" I extend Max's handkerchief with a nervous laugh and he stares down at it. "Maxwell's. It's clean enough."

He gives me a grateful smile, then hands it back to me. "You keep it for later. If it's anything like my wedding day, you're going to need it."

I'm preparing a snappy reply, the kind that will get the old guy laughing, when a loud rapping sound on the door ruptures the palpable nervousness between us.

"And that would be Veronica," I say, stepping past him. "Apparently it's her job to keep me together. Although it's a little late for that," I say, with a laugh, opening the door.

Only it's still not Veronica. Instead it's Max, and he's just standing there, shattering every wedding day superstition I might have been clinging to.

"Veronica said you needed to see me," he says, beaming at me. He's only got his dress pants and shirt on, but he looks stunning already. He's equally busy assessing my appearance, because he gives a low, appreciative whistle. "Wow, you look..."

"Maxwell," I cut him off, stepping aside to reveal his father standing there by the window.

"Dad!" he cries, his eyes growing huge. "Wh-what are you..."

"He's here for the wedding," I answer, before his old man can even explain himself. "Your folks came to support us."

"You got the letter," Max says simply, kind of shaking his head in disbelief.

"Yes, son. I got the letter." Phillip's admission is quiet, chastened even, as he stares across the room into his son's eager eyes. As he confronts all the things that have stood between them for so long.

Max rakes a hand through his hair, disheveling it as he steps into the room. But his mind's not on appearances at the moment, not even on our wedding. All his attention is trained right on his father. "When you didn't call, well, I just

235

assumed—"

"That I wasn't coming, yes, I'm sure that you did."

"Must've been a close call," I add, thinking how he's only here just now. "Or you'd have been here sooner."

Phillip gives a heavy sigh, as Max steps closer to him. "What finally changed your mind?" Max asks, folding his arms protectively across his chest.

Phillip stares at the floor a moment, gathering his thoughts, maybe even his nerve, then says, "Because years from now, I didn't want today to be something I couldn't remember. Something I couldn't relive with my son whenever he talked about the most perfect day of his life."

"Your coming is what makes it perfect," Max says, tears shimmering in his eyes now. Hell, at least he's joining the club. I step close, offering the faithful handkerchief again, just pressing it into his hand, as he adds, "You have no idea what it means to me that you're here."

"I wish we'd made it for dinner last night."

"That doesn't matter, Dad. Not at all," he says as his father opens his arms and draws him close for a tight embrace.

Phillip holds Max for a long moment, not letting him go, and even gives his head a tender stroke. The kind that might have been natural when Max was still just a small boy. "I remember how terrified I felt when we found out we were expecting twins," he says quietly. "So excited, but frightened that I could never be enough father for you both."

"I can imagine," Max says, as they step apart.

"The thing is, Max, I felt scared like that again the day I realized the truth about you. Terrified that I wasn't able to give you what you needed."

"The truth?" Max asks, his whole body growing visibly

tense. For a brief moment, I fear that this peace summit is about to tank in the worst possible way. Until his dad gazes nakedly at his son, and says, "I knew you were gay when you were seventeen, son. It was obvious. You and I both knew it then."

For a moment, nobody speaks and I hold my breath. Literally. Because I can't believe his dad's just alluded to the whole cross-dressing fiasco, not now of all times. I think Phillip might be holding his breath, too, until Max almost whispers, "Dad, I tried to be straight for so long because I wanted you to love me."

"But I always loved you, son. Always. I just failed you, that's all."

Neither of them says a word for a long moment; they just kind of eye one another cautiously, emotion running between the three of us at a fever pitch. "But I never gave up on you, Dad," Max says. "And you're here now."

"Yes, I'm here now."

"And that means we need to figure out where you're going to sit!" Max suddenly cries, walking toward the window. "Nobody even knows you're here. Where's Mom? We need to talk to Leah." I can tell that a critical gear has shifted in my lover's mind, and ever his sister's twin, he's launching into mini-wedding nazi mode.

"Actually, they do know we're here. Veronica's the one who told me where to go," Phillip says.

"Which would explain why she sent me up here, too," Max finishes, as realization dawns for all three of us.

"Yeah, well she's a sneaky-assed devil, always has been," I laugh. "Which makes her the perfect 'best person' for me."

With that pronouncement, the three of us arrive at a plan, one that will restructure the seating arrangements and even the service itself.

Blessed wedding day, coming off just like the dream I've always imagined. Funny, but watching Maxwell laugh with his father there by the window, glowing beneath his father's approval and acceptance, I realize that this reality is even better than the dreams I've held all these months.

Maybe dreams are just like that sometimes; fantastic, but a dim reflection of true possibility.

Chapter Nineteen

Of course the music Max chose for this processional is the total bomb, some Mendelssohn piece he played at least a dozen times around our apartment. Yeah, so I'll focus on that random fact in an effort to keep myself together because so far I'm on shaky ground here. Especially since right before Veronica and I started this long march down the gauntlet, she whispered in my ear, "I love you, Hunter. You're such a good man, and I can't think of anyone I'd rather see Max spend his life with than you."

Great, she said that and of course I couldn't even talk, the emotions were that intense. Instead, I just mumbled something incoherent, staring down the flower-lined garden path at my fiancé, and Veronica laughed as we took our first steps together. Talk about good men, there's one staring right at me now from that gazebo. For months neither of us could decide who should go first, so finally I told Max that I'd take the usual bridal position, just to shake things up.

Our friends and families line both sides of the aisle, not too many people, but definitely the critical ones. From the periphery of my vision I see Aunt Edna, her hands clutched expectantly at her throat, beaming like a mother. On the other side, Phillip and Diane watch our procession with obvious pride. But even though I'm aware of them, along with Leah and John, the Carters, Ben and his parents, and everyone else gathered here today, I don't look. I don't even glance sideways at Louisa, standing there right beside my gorgeous groom.

I only have eyes for one person in this garden, and he's gazing right back at me.

Across this small distance, our eyes are locked in a lovers' dance. Nothing has prepared me for how breathtakingly handsome he is, not even my sneak peek at his full ensemble from the window up above. There's a smile spread across his face that makes my heart turn crazy back flips, as finally I reach his side. Veronica pats my arm, stepping apart from me, and taking her position to my left. Max and I stand together, staring up into Reverend Donnelly's kind eyes.

Then quiet, so nobody can hear, Max murmurs, "I love you, Hunter."

"Me, too," I whisper under my breath, as the reverend begins the show.

We've made it through the spiritual side of things, the reflections on the mystery of joining like we are. We've heard the word of God, that "there is nothing love cannot face; there is no limit to its faith, its hope, and its endurance". A scripture that seems particularly apt today, as we embark on this unusual marriage of ours—especially since Phillip Daniels was the one who read it.

We've even made it through Veronica's song, the old Fleetwood Mac tune, Landslide, which Max asked her to sing as a surprise for me. Yeah, boy, I was surprised all right, when Ben stepped up and grasped his guitar, and Veronica took her place beside him. Thank God for that damned hanky—no wonder Max thought I'd need it. As if the event itself didn't unravel me enough. That line about being afraid of changing was the one that really did me in. Listening, I couldn't help but think of how afraid I was of Max, and for so damned long. What a waste of precious time, when he stood there on the mountain extending his love to me with both of his generous hands.

The hands I'm taking within my own now, as we face one another for these vows.

"Hunter, repeat after me, please," Reverend Donnelly instructs, and we begin to pledge our hearts, our love. Our very lives to one another.

I take you as my husband...

As I look into Maxwell's eyes, I find I'm staring into the face of a younger man, one watching my approach across a crowded, smoky bar. He's not dressed in a tux; he's wearing a red polo shirt and smiling up at me, innocent, perfect. The most beautiful man I've probably ever seen in my life, just sitting there with my girlfriend.

For richer and for poorer...

I'm not only staring into the eyes of my lover, of the man who's becoming my husband at this very moment, but into the eyes of my companion. A twin of my own, to mirror my heart and soul; a whole family for me in the form of one person.

In sickness and in health...

Now I'm looking into aged eyes, the eyes of a man I've spent a lifetime with, still bright and filled with life, despite the many years etched between us.

Until death do us part...

I'm gazing into the rest of my life, right as I stare into those familiar dark eyes, flecked with strange, mercurial gold. Eyes that promise countless hidden mysteries of love and worship and eternity with him. Eyes that already own the complexities of my very soul.

With this ring...

My damned hands are shaking so badly, Maxwell's having

a hard time working the simple band onto my finger. So he steadies my palm between both of his, telling me that he's got it under control with the flash of a simple smile and a tender squeeze of his hands. Then just like that, I'm marked as his, forever, as the reverend pronounces us civilly joined. Husband and husband, for all the crowd to see.

"Gentlemen, you may share a celebratory kiss," he tells us with a conspiratorial grin. I even chuckle to myself, wishing he'd said, "You may kiss the bride", just for the hell of it.

Slowly, I turn to face my groom, my face burning beneath this collective group's gaze. It's one thing to profess my undying love to Maxwell in front of them all, but quite another to lay a big sloppy one on him like I'm about to do. In front of his dad and mom, my own sweet aunt. Right beside Veronica, the last girl I ever made love to before I got with him. And with Louisa watching, a woman who could have easily been his wife in some alter-universe.

So I cup his face within my trembling hands, close my eyes and allow everything else to fade away except our moment. I focus on the scent of him, that delicious aftershave that always makes me kind of crazy with desire, and draw his mouth to my own. Slow, tender; I want this kiss to last forever. Our lips meet and brush together, then I kiss him as hungrily as I ever have, right for the whole world to see. For his old man to understand just how deep our passion really runs.

And then, as we break apart, there's a roar of applause and even happy shouts from Brian and Ben and John and who knows who else, as Reverend Donnelly asks all of our guests to welcome the newly joined couple.

Then like a blurry vision, next thing I know, Maxwell and I are practically sprinting down that aisle, a shower of cherry blossoms lighting our joyous way.

The sun has dipped low, filtering golden orange along the tree-lined horizon, a romantic mirror on the lake at the bottom of the hill. The music has kicked into overdrive, just like the champagne. In fact, I think my party train might've left giddy somewhere back down the track a while ago. Max and I haven't stopped dancing, not for the past two hours, just switching off to spin turns with all the people we love, gathered here beneath the wedding tent. At the moment, I've got Veronica's hand in mine, kind of leading her in a wild, semi-drunken twirl.

"Woooooo," she laughs, reaching out to steady herself. "Watch it, there." The band is belting out that old Santana tune, the one with "little bit of this, little bit of that" in the chorus, so I sing it back to her and she gives me a gorgeous smile. "Ah, Willis, you make one hell of a handsome groom," she says, leaning up to kiss my cheek. "Not my groom, thank God, but a great looking one."

From the corner of my eye, I see that Max has Aunt Edna bobbing along with him to the music. I have to smirk thinking back on the bachelor party. Wonder what Ed would do if lover boy stripped down to his tux pants. She'd probably still worship my new husband, which is fine by me. Apparently, bonding over Hermes and Rodeo Drive can be a powerful thing. But I know it's far more than that—Edna loves the ones I love, always has.

I also see that Louisa is standing alone by the punch bowl and that gets me inspired. After kissing Veronica on the cheek for about the tenth time today, I head over to my husband's best friend. It's time the two of us shared a wedding dance together, and I sure don't like the image of her standing by herself, especially not today of all days.

"May I?" I ask, extending my hand with a dramatic, gallant sweep. For a moment, I swear Louisa seems surprised that it's me, almost like she'd been expecting someone else.

243

"Of course! I'd love to dance with you, Hunter." She extends her hand, and I lead her out onto the floor, finding us a good, spacious spot.

From the get go, it's different than with Veronica, not so relaxed and easy. For one thing, I've never had a physical relationship with Louisa before. But it's more than that; I'm always shocked by how graceful Louisa Carter really is. Just small, delicate like a little bird or something whenever I hug her. So now, slipping my palm around her waist, the contrast between her feminine body and the very masculine one that I've grown accustomed to holding all the time, well it kind of shocks me.

She looks up at me, laughing self-consciously, almost as if she reads my thoughts. "What's wrong, Hunter?"

"It's not you," I rush to assure her, shaking my head. "Was just thinking that I'm pretty much a boy's boy now."

"You're more comfortable dancing with Max," she interprets, her expression intent and thoughtful. "With being gay." Somehow I feel a little like I've just been caught with my hand in the proverbial cookie jar.

"Guess I'm not so used to women anymore," I clarify, feeling oddly shy with her. As if the truth of my sexual existence hasn't been on display all day long. As if she hasn't seen me holding Max in my arms on plenty of other occasions. Or maybe it's that my lover once held her this way, and that thought's just kind of weird to me.

But Louisa seems to get my discomfort, and blesses me with a huge smile, a generous one and says, "Hunter, you make him so happy. I've never seen him as happy as he's been in the past year."

My chest swells with a strange kind of pride at her assessment; that of all the people in the universe—even her—

I'm the one who held the keys to his happiness. But then guilt chases hard on the heels of that thought, as she stares up at me with such sweet, honest eyes. Eyes that I know looked up into Maxwell's once upon a time and believed in the possibility of true love.

"Louisa, look," I say, drawing in a steadying breath. "I don't want you to feel like, well, that I took him from you or—"

"Hunter!" she cries, stopping right where we are on the dance floor. "You've got to be kidding me." We stand locked together, not dancing, just still in one another's arms.

"Uh, well, not really." What was I thinking? Suddenly, I'm not so sure, except that I wanted her to know that she means the world to me too. That she's my good friend and I never want her to think of me as someone who stole Maxwell away from her. Not as a lover, or even as a best friend.

She slips a reassuring hand around my neck, pulling me low so she can whisper in my ear. It's not like anyone around us can hear, but still, that's what she does. "Hunter, he and I'd been broken up a long time before you got with him."

"I know."

"No, Hunter, I don't really think you do. Deep down, I always knew he was gay."

"But you were together," I begin to argue, until she closes her eyes. It's a weary, unexpected kind of expression that shuts me up completely. Maybe because of all it says about their two-year romantic relationship, in just that one snapshot of a moment.

Finally the dark eyes open again, searching my face as she whispers against my cheek, "I did love him, Hunter. But he was gay, and I knew it going in, okay?"

For endless dance beats we sway together, silent. Safe as best friends, chaste as brother and sister, then I murmur back into her ear, "Then what changed?"

"I wanted him to be happy, Hunter. And I knew he would never let go of me. He was just holding on too hard."

"So you broke it off," I finish and she nods, a melancholy expression shadowing her eyes momentarily. But then it's gone, replaced with the smile again, as she returns to this moment.

"And now?"

She grows quiet a moment, reflective, holding on to my shoulder; I feel her inner strength beneath my palms. "I still love him. He's my best friend in all the world, so don't forget that, okay?" I give her a slightly dazed nod, just listening to these revelations. "But it's really different now and not just because he's with you. Now I want more. I want to be happy, too."

Way to go, sweetheart. That's what I want to say, but instead I pull her closer and hold her for a long moment, feeling her strong heartbeat against my chest. I thank God that Maxwell Daniels is queer and mine and that Louisa is on her way to finding true bliss with someone of her own. That she's found release, just like Max and me. In her own strange way, Louisa is coming out of the closet, too.

I'm lost in those thoughts, feeling really good about all of our futures, when suddenly she says, "You know, when Max first got with you, I used to worry that you'd hurt him. I was so petrified you'd break his heart."

"Why?"

"Because I could see how desperately he loved you." I swear the floor grows a little unsteady at her easy observation. I can't believe it was so obvious, though of course it would have been to her.

"What changed?"

"Well, as time went on, I saw how much you loved him,

246

too," she says with a tender smile. "I knew you weren't capable of hurting anyone you cared for like that."

"So you stopped worrying?"

"A long time ago. Now I just feel lucky that I'm gaining another best friend."

All right, where'd that goddamned hanky go? Because I swear, I'm about to fall apart all over again, right in the arms of one Louisa Carter. So I reach into my jacket for the thing; I'm patting down my pocket when I feel a familiar hand touch my arm. "Mind if I cut in?" Max asks sweetly. "I miss my husband."

"Oh, please," Louisa says, as she releases me with a throaty laugh. "As if Hunter Willis has eyes for anyone else here tonight."

"Well he wasn't looking at anyone but you just then, sweetheart." Max kisses her on the lips with a quiet laugh. "And no wonder. You're absolutely beautiful today. That dress makes you shine like ten million bucks."

She makes a feeble attempt at waving off his compliment, but he only groans, wrapping both his arms around her. "Come on, you know it, girl! Come on!" She begins to laugh, resting her cheek on his shoulder for a moment.

"Girl, you're beautiful and we all know it," she teases him saucily, kissing him in return. For a moment, they kind of linger close like that, clinched in each other's arms. How much they still love one another is undeniable; it shows in every gesture that passes so easily between the two of them. They just weren't destined to be lovers, that's all.

"Speaking of looking," Max says pointedly, gazing past her toward a guy I hadn't noticed before that moment. "I see you met Mr. Edwards."

As if on cue, Louisa's entire expression changes, a kind of demure look coming over her that I swear I've never seen before.

"Max Daniels, don't you dare say a word," she cautions, dropping her head shyly, and I'm still wondering what the hell they're even talking about. That is until the strapping, handsome guy tracks right her way, a disarming smile on his face.

"Inbound!" Max laughs giddily, watching Mr. Blond and Beautiful head right for her. "And I think he's got missile lock."

"Stop it, DeLuca in training," Louisa quips, swatting at Max's arm as she leaves us to dance.

"So who's the guy?" I ask, feeling curious about this stranger. Something about him is weirdly familiar, and besides, he's at my wedding. Shouldn't I know who the hell he is?

Max stands with me for a moment, watching the two of them laugh together. "Darcy. Darcy Edwards," he explains, and at that precise moment I make the connection.

"Brian's brother?"

"Bingo. In from Manhattan for a whirlwind weekend of fun." I'm beginning to get a very clear picture of just how this "stranger" wound up at our wedding. The thirty-sixth guest on the list if you will; I'm telling you, Maxwell Daniels can be a devious fellow if you give him free reign over an event.

"Uh, huh," I say, giving him my most dubious expression. "Too bad Louisa lives in Los Angeles."

Max reaches for my hand, drawing it to his lips. "Oh, didn't I tell you?" he asks, showering my palm with tender kisses. "Darcy's starting with our firm out in L.A. next month. Going to room with Brian and Peter until he finds a place of his own."

"How convenient."

He flashes me an innocent smile, but I know he's just a sexy wolf in sheep's clothing. I also have a sneaking suspicion that Max has great instincts when it comes to his best friend's happiness, especially when I spy her twirling in Darcy's manly arms, an Audrey Hepburn smile shining on her face.

One word pops into my mind, one word that will forever frame the way the two of them look together at that moment. Smitten. Definitely smitten.

Max folds me close within his arms, and this time we're a lot more certain than with our first dance in front of everyone today. We've been at this for hours now; on and off we've shared a dozen of them. The music's taken a decidedly sexy turn with another Santana song, so no wonder he needed to nuzzle close, and he wastes no time slipping a cozy arm right around me.

"Hey," he murmurs against my ear and the hair on my nape stands on end. Something about how husky and filled with desire his voice sounds.

"Hey, yourself." He pushes in closer, gets a little daring with the way he urges his hips against mine. "Watch it," I caution him, but he'll have none of it. In fact, he moves even nearer.

"Watch what?" he asks, staring up at me through dusky lashes and my heart does a two-step of its own.

I nuzzle his cheek with my mouth, kissing him on the jaw. "That hip action," I explain, pulling him closer to illustrate. "You're gonna give me a massive hard-on if you're not careful."

"And that's a bad thing?" comes the reply, a breathy sigh against my ear.

"It is with your old man watching this dance."

"Um, so that's the objection?" he teases as the music changes into some kind of samba-influenced gyration that gets everyone throwing their hands into the air. Max begins moving his hips faster to the rhythm, and I have a sudden flash that I'm spending my wedding night with Ricky Martin.

"Too late for objections now, Maxwell." I close my eyes, like that night at the club, and just lose myself in the motion, in the

249

sensation of him holding me this close. I lose myself in the rhythm of our love and it's a beautiful, perfect thing.

Somewhere in the wings, I feel the gaze of our families on us, but I can only smile. Let them watch because I don't get any happier than this, and I want them to see that. Just like our kiss; they need to know what Max Daniels does to me. What my husband does to me.

My eyes open and I find him smiling at me with a satisfied expression. "You're so beautiful," he reflects quietly. "You always are, Hunter, but you've never been more gorgeous to me than today."

For crying out loud, the boy makes me blush like a madman. How is it he can still undress me like that, with just one easy compliment? I wave him off with a flustered grin. "Oh, baby, you're it, and you know it."

"It?"

"The beautiful, seductive, gorgeous one here tonight." I'm babbling at him, but I can't possibly help myself, not today.

"You saying you'll spend forever with me?" he whispers in my ear and I feel his warm fingers slip beneath my jacket. At that precise moment, I spy his dad across the dance floor, Leah in his arms. He doesn't give a shit about what I'm doing with his son, not anymore.

I press my lips against Max's jaw, feeling the soft bristle of his cheek. "I knew it was forever a week after you'd kissed me." He pulls back, staring at me in surprise, kind of blinking. "Don't look so shocked." I brush my hand across his cheek where a little bit of glitter sparkles beneath the light. Must have come off one of the tables, since they're dusted with the stuff.

"It's just, well, I fell so hard for you, Hunter. It seemed to take you a lot longer."

"Nah," I say, spinning him in a dramatic turn. "I was just

lost in hetero land for a while there. You had to do a recon mission to find my queer ass." He bursts out laughing at that one, the kind of belly laugh I've always been able to work right out of him. I think it might even be one reason why he fell in love with me.

"Queer ass just invokes all kinds of vivid imagery, Hunter," he admits, giving me a demure smile.

I shrug like it's no big thing. "You said it, baby. Not me."

For a moment, he studies me, blushing a little bit. He's happy drunk too. I can tell by the way his pupils have grown large, and by how he's laughing too loudly.

Then just like that, he kind of cries, "You know what? I'm ready to get to New York City. Now." With that eager and none-too-subtle pronouncement about our honeymoon destination, he takes my hand and leads me toward his parents, who are now talking with Edna on the other side of the tent. Phillip and Leah have just finished their dance, so she stands right with them. Good time to make our goodbyes and cut out of this wedding joint.

Phillip laughs heartily over something Edna's told them, smiling and nodding at whatever joke she's made. Edna has that gift, the rare ability to open people up despite themselves. "Somebody's glad they came," Max observes, nodding toward his dad. "I think he's had a blast today."

"Yeah, he's definitely happy, Maxwell," I say. "Took him a while to come along, that's all. Kind of like another guy we both know."

For a moment, he stops right there on the floor, staring at me. "What do you mean?" he asks, looking a little confused and kissable all at once.

"Just that in a lot of ways, he's no different than me," I say with a smug grin. "You know, stubborn as hell, and trying to deny the obvious facts."

"Oh, that guy." He gives a knowing laugh, tugging me toward the punchbowl where our families stand.

I lean close, brushing my lips against his cheek as I whisper in his ear, "Yeah, that guy. Took him a while, just like your old man, but he figured out the score. Nobody can deny that you're the love of my life. Not even me, sweetheart."

Not even me, or every macho vibe in my body can deny the facts anymore. After all, Maxwell Daniels is the husband of my dreams. I just didn't know I needed to adjust my dreams a little, not until I met him. Now I can't imagine spending forever with anybody else in the world. Not boy or girl, or anything in between.

All my dreams have come true with him today, even the ones I never knew I had.

Chapter Twenty

The last moments of daylight fill the Vermont sky, brilliant pinks and oranges streaking the horizon. Max holds my hand as we wait just inside the arched doorway of the inn for the limo to pull up. Our guests are on the curb with rose petals in hand; ready to shower us as we make our break for it. It's kind of like we're offstage, waiting in the wings for the spotlight to illuminate our big moment.

Max gives my boutonniere an adjustment. "Perfect now," he assesses with a tender smile. I lean in to steal a kiss, closing my eyes as our lips meet, right when I hear Leah say, "You two weren't going to leave without telling me goodbye, were you?" We snap apart like a pair of naughty soldiers, and find that she has an angry hand on her hip. It's trouble, too, because my sister-in-law looks genuinely miffed.

"Oh, Leah, I couldn't find you," Max explains, rushing to kiss her on the cheek. "We asked John to tell you thanks for doing such a marvelous job on everything. I looked all over the place for you."

"It's been amazing, Leah," I chime in, nodding my head in vigorous agreement, but she still looks a little peevish. "We appreciate everything. Really."

"You've thanked me like a dozen times, guys," she admits, rolling her eyes. "That's not it. I just wanted to talk to you both for a minute. Alone." Out of nowhere, a weepy expression comes over her features and she drops her head quickly so we won't see.

But of course Max notices, since after all they share the spooky super twin thing. "What's wrong, Leah?" he asks, his dark brows drawing into a tight line of concern.

Leah wipes at her brow with the back of her hand, breaking into a bright smile. Only then do I notice a thin sheen of perspiration along her hairline despite the late spring chill that's in the air. "Nothing's wrong, Max. Nothing at all. But there was a reason you two couldn't find me."

"Okay." Max gives an encouraging nod, but he still looks worried.

"I was in the ladies room because I wasn't feeling well."

"All right, so what's the matter, then?" I bark, worried as hell all of a sudden. 'Cause she's pale, I realize now. Very pale and looking like there's a definite problem. "What are you trying to tell us here?"

She shakes her head, kind of laughing and crying all at once. "I'm absolutely fine, guys! Fine. But I am pregnant. Almost twelve weeks to the day."

"What?" Max squeals, grabbing hold of his twin with both hands. "You're kidding? You've got to be kidding! No, no, you're not kidding," he stammers. "You're serious, aren't you?"

She bobs her head, her large eyes brimming with happy tears as Max clings to her, bouncing on his toes in tipsy enthusiasm. "Why didn't you tell me?" he insists, pulling back to study the length of her. She doesn't seem different yet—well, maybe just a tad fuller in her figure, now that I really give her a careful look.

"Max, this was your special day. Your time with Hunter." She glances at me, smiling in approval. "Nothing should have taken a moment from your celebration."

"Do Mom and Dad know yet?"

"Yes, but I asked them to keep it a secret until after the wedding. Otherwise, you're the first ones I've told," she says, and I slip my arm around her, giving her a gentle hug. "Well, apart from John, obviously."

"Yeah, good thing he's been brought in on the deal," I say. "Key players and all that."

"I wanted to tell you both today so it would always be something we'd remember on your anniversary. Especially since I have something important to ask you."

"Okay," Max says, nodding encouragingly.

"John and I want you to be the godparents."

For a mini-eternity, neither Max nor I speak, just kind of nod, staring at one another, until Leah adds a little nervously, "Well, if you want to be, that is."

"Leah, trust me, we want to be," I blurt, answering for us both. One look at my husband tells me I'm right on track, so I continue, "It's just, well, I mean you must really believe in our union to ask that. To want us to be part of your baby's life that way."

"Hunter, don't you see by now that I think this marriage is a beautiful thing?" she asks, staring openly into my eyes. "That you're the best guy in the world for my brother?"

"I know, Leah, but—"

"Hunter, I love you, okay? I feel so thankful that you're a part of my family now."

She reaches upward onto her toes, and pulls me into the warmest hug she's ever granted me. We're talking the holding tight and snuggling close kind. "Besides, I'm on to you," she says with a laugh. "You're nothing but a big softy, so you'll make a great godfather."

Wow, so I've been married about four hours or so, and I've already managed to finagle my way into a kind of surrogate fatherhood. Pretty damn cool, I tell you. My new family just keeps on growing.

The limo pulls down the long, tree-lined drive, circling back past the inn with a chorus of blasting horns as Max and I lean out the window, waving goodbye to everyone. Finally, when our family and friends disappear from view, Max raises the window again, settling beside me in the plush, leather seat.

Hard to believe, but it's finally just us. Two grooms left to their own wicked devices, on the way to the Big Apple. The driver is separated by a discreet, darkened privacy window, which means that whatever we do or say is only between us. I lean back in the seat and kick off both my shoes. Maxwell reaches for the remote control for the CD player, just beside him in the door and hits play.

The first notes of No Doubt's "Hellagood" blast pretty loudly and he gives me a seductive wink. "Oh, Maxwell," I sigh, because this is sex music, all the way. We've made love to this CD dozens of times. "You didn't."

"Oh, but I did. Planned ahead," he explains, dipping into a champagne bucket for another bottle of the stuff, already uncorked with two lovely flutes right beside it. There's even an oriental rug beneath my socked feet. Sinful pleasure palace on wheels, designed by one Maxwell Daniels.

"Max, I'm not making love in a moving vehicle," I argue, a little lamely as he hands me a foamy glass of champagne. "Not with a stranger five feet away."

"Who said anything about making love?" He lifts his glass, clinking it against mine. "This is a pure seduction scene, my love."

"I'm getting that general idea," I say as he nudges the volume upward on Gwen Stefani's sultry voice.

"Don't worry, Hunter, I won't make you do anything you feel uncomfortable about." He gives me a disarming smile, sliding out of his own shoes, and rubbing his toes against mine. Damn, how can something so mundane seem so sensual and erotic? Those ticklish toes of his are managing to give me a serious hard-on.

"Four hours to New York," I remind him, my voice cracking over the words. I sound like I've just hit puberty. Yeah, well I feel like I'm thirteen and discovering the joys of the human body for the very first time, as he folds himself right within the crook of my arm.

"That's four hours to have fun," he explains, cupping my jaw and pulling me close for a kiss. "Four hours of kissing and touching and loving you, my husband."

"For crying out loud, Maxwell! You're a terrible cock tease."

"I'm in love with you. Is that so bad?"

That backbeat pounds through my body, my head, as he slips a sweet palm onto my thigh. My erection juts upward, making a lovely bulge in the tuxedo pants, and he strokes it softly with his fingertips. "That's just beautiful," he says with a throaty laugh. "Can't wait to get a better look."

"Yeah, well maybe I'll get drunk enough to withstand all this temptation, Daniels."

He sets the champagne flute beside his seat, then takes mine from my hand. Curling his fingers around my neck, he pulls me close for a kiss and I find myself lowering atop him on that leather seat. I hardly care that some stranger is driving this vehicle; after all, he can't see a goddamned thing. I just want to make out with my husband for all I'm worth.

I just want to spend these hours anticipating my wedding night.

We pause at the door to our corner suite and I see an adorable uncertainty shadow Max's eyes. I mean this is it. The threshold, our wedding night. The awkward thing is that never once in all our planning did we discuss this moment. We've been traditional as hell in our very non-traditional wedding, yet here it is—something that flat doesn't translate, no matter how many ways you try to spin it in a gay context.

I give a strained laugh. "Sorry, baby, I'm not carrying you over the threshold, no matter how much I love you."

"Who says you'd be doing the carrying, Willis?"

Not much I can say to that, so I give him a flirty look, the kind that tells him what I want to do on the other side of the doorway. Even though we never talked about it, I do have a definite plan in mind, a way that I want this moment to go. I just wasn't going to tell him until we got here.

But Max obviously didn't anticipate it, because he just kind of grins, inserting the card key, his hand shaking so badly that the damned thing won't even go in.

Ever his white knight, I shift the champagne bottle we brought up from the hotel bar to the crook of my arm, and deftly slip the card into the slot for him.

"Good work," he laughs, sounding self-conscious.

"Practice makes perfect."

"Oh, what, you're in the regular habit of taking a penthouse suite?"

I shoulder the door open, and a cool blast of air conditioning moves over my skin from within the darkened room. "Nah, I've just fantasized about this moment like a million times."

And with those words, meant to woo him and romance him for all he's worth, I step gallantly through the doorway and reach for his hand. This will be me leading him into our future, the two of us stepping together, equal partners sharing in union.

This is the way I've imagined taking him over the threshold on our wedding night nearly every day for the past nine months. Simply, purposefully, like the two strong men we are in this relationship.

I have to squint, staring back into the bright hallway, and for a moment Max seems to just gaze at my hand, almost like it's some foreign thing he's never seen before.

"Baby?" I ask, a little uncertain. "You coming or what?"

At last with a gentle smile, he slips his hand into mine, and follows me over that threshold. But when he closes the door behind him, and leans against it, watching me with hushed anticipation, something changes in his demeanor.

I flick on the dim lights that line the entryway, and within the space of a moment, those lovely eyes grow sultry, as he transforms from my sweet love into my wily lover.

I'm no longer staring at the debonair guy who held court down in the hotel bar, wooing me with fine cigars and champagne; the one who managed to both seduce me and remain discreet in his attentions all at once.

That man's vanished, replaced instead by this Armani-clad and stormy eyed version of Maxwell Daniels; my pure fantasy come true tonight.

The champagne bottle's been discarded on the bed, and in the frenzy of kissing and touching that immediately ensued, I think I've lost half of my tuxedo. I'm stripped down to my

259

undershirt and dress pants now. Well, and the silky little boxers Maxwell's about to discover underneath.

I've endured this day, just staring at him like some infatuated teenager. Hell, I am desperately infatuated, there's no kidding about that. Trouble is, I never should have let him grace the doors of Armani, because that tux nearly cost me my composure long before our limo ever hit New York City. Especially with the romantic scene my lover created for the two of us in that back seat.

Then again, I'm pretty damn thankful to Mr. Armani right about now, because I've hit payday, here in this thousand-dollar-a-night bridal suite of ours.

I've got my baby right where I want him. He's pressed back against the glass windows overlooking Broadway and Times Square, the neon flashing behind him like heat lightning, and my hands are splayed against the glass.

Yes, I definitely have Maxwell right where I want him tonight. A little helpless and a whole lot aroused. Only problem is that I can't seem to strip him out of the freaking tuxedo.

"Need you," I finally growl in frustration, giving his shirt hem an urgent tug of explanation. "Out of this."

But he doesn't stop working at my own clothes. In fact, he's just no help at all, as I pull and jerk at the buttons of his crisp white shirt. "Baby, please help." I whine plaintively and he shivers with pure pleasure.

"Oh, I love it when you beg."

"I can't take this," I complain, taking a step apart from him.

He leans against the glass, lolling his head back with a lazy gesture as he studies me. "No, Hunter? Not take me in this tux? Or not take what I'm doing to you?"

When did he get so damned proud of himself, I wonder, feeling a little frustrated with how gorgeous he is, just leaning there against the floor-length window in his dress pants and disheveled shirt. The bow tie hangs askew and his lips are swollen, ripe from my needy kisses.

"Take it off," I command throatily.

This earns me a coquettish smile. "No, baby."

I cross my arms over my chest, narrowing my gaze into something threatening, primitive.

"Take it off, or there's hell to pay."

He shrugs, running his fingers through his hair as he watches me, his lips parted to kissable perfection. It's a goddamned feminine gesture that makes me quake with desire. "I'll pay it," he promises softly, and for a moment I wonder if Maxine's joining us, too.

"That's it, Daniels," I say, and then I'm all over him, pinning him against the broad expanse of windows. He staggers slightly, as I push against him hard, taking his mouth in a crushing kiss. A soft sound escapes his lips, a half-cry coupled with a groan of pleasure. No, Maxine's nowhere in sight; he's pure male tonight.

And then he starts with his hands again, working them between where our hips are pressed so tight together. With his palm, he spreads me wide, urging my legs apart and I can't resist.

It's all a blur, but suddenly he's spun me around until I face the window. I'm just standing there, legs open wide, hands splayed desperately against the cool glass. My unfocused gaze takes in taxis, lights, throngs of people, but I've never been more unmoved by such an impressive sight.

Because my only center is Max, who's working my pants off my hips, tugging at them until I hear a soft gasp when he discovers my satin boxers. My fingers curl in pleasure when I feel the first caress of his hand over my cock. My whole body

261

arches and tenses when he uses that silken material to begin pleasuring me, bunching it over my erection until I'm writhing in ecstasy.

There's a muffled sound, like maybe he's undressing, and that's the moment when he presses his graceful body right behind mine.

"Maxwell, wh-what do you want?" I ask, feeling vulnerable, especially because he doesn't stop with his hands. He keeps at me, rubbing and stroking my swollen length until the aching sensation is about to break me.

"You. That's what I want," he insists, his voice deep and sexy.

"Oh, oh okay," I whisper, swallowing hard. It's a stupid thing to say, but it's all I can manage at the moment. Slowly, he trails his fingers over my hips, over those satin boxers, so appreciative.

"Love the boxers," he purrs against my shoulder, tugging the undershirt over my head. I crane my neck, needing to see him, but he just nuzzles my nape with his mouth, his soft chest brushing against my bare back. "Don't look, Hunter. Just feel me."

I nod wordlessly, as the strong hands strip the boxers off my hips, and I feel him drop to the ground behind me. Then sweet lips begin to kiss me in the small of my back, the place I've always adored on his body. My hands slap against the glass pane, seeking some kind of security that I just don't feel, not with him tantalizing me this way.

"Don't fight it," he urges. "Let me do this for you, Hunter."

"Do...what?" I manage, aching for him until I'm blind with it.

"This," he whispers, and that's when his tongue dips lower, right as his hand takes me from the front. But that's not all, because then there's the cool sensation of his fingers working into me from behind with his other hand, so slippery and wild that I begin to shake uncontrollably.

He's destroying me, and seizing me all at once. I'm being branded by him tonight, and I understand it when suddenly I feel him rise to his feet again, urging my legs even further apart.

"I'm going to take you," he breathes against my ear. "Have all of me, Hunter. Relax, and have it all, love."

With those words, and my stumbling murmurs of ascent, he thrusts into me so hard I can't even breathe. There's not a damn tender thing about it, and I know he's forceful on purpose, especially since he's the gentlest lover I've ever been with.

He's taking me completely, even as he's giving his body completely in pledge.

With his furious thrusting and our mingled howls of painful pleasure, he's sealing our marriage.

When Maxwell finishes, I collapse against the window, feeling the cool pane press against my cheek. For what seems forever, he leans against me, kissing my shoulders, suddenly as soft as a whisper in the way that he touches me. He's so attentive and loving, and doesn't know that tears burn my eyes from the intensity of what he just did to me.

"You worn out?" he laughs, kissing my jaw. He gives it a sweet little lick that makes me smile.

"Kind of," I agree with a groan, closing my eyes, as he slips out of me. I'm aching deep inside, and can't help but wonder how I can possibly take more, not with the burning sensation he's left all within me.

"What if we, well, part ways for a few minutes," he asks, stroking the planes of my back with his fingertips. "I want to shower, and then, well we could meet up again."

All right, I know this boy. He's got something serious in mind. I know it like I know my own heartbeat, like I know the erection threatening to form again just from imagining what he might have planned.

"What are you up to?" I ask, slowly turning, until our chests push close together. I wrap him in my arms, holding him tight against me, and that's when I see how flushed his face has become from our exertions. "Look at you," I tease softly, lifting my hand to touch his warm cheek. "You're all hot and bothered."

"I just want a shower," he says again, but he's beaming and giddy.

"Yeah, right, Daniels. You go take that shower, and I'll be waiting when you get back out."

He nods, pleased, then says in a shy, quiet voice, "Just, uh, turn around for a moment, will you?"

I lift my eyebrow in serious question, as he kind of urges me to look away. I turn, focusing on Broadway and Seventh, on the Panasonic sign down in the middle of Times Square. But my heart is fixed squarely on him.

"There's something I need to get," he explains and I hear how he's grinning as he says it. Yeah, baby, you're up to something good.

"Uh, huh. Something for that shower."

"Exactly," comes his soft-voiced answer, as I hear him unzipping the suitcase. I wonder what he's got in mind?

He's going to be damned lucky if I don't go join him in that shower. Funny, but secrets are a fucking turn on sometimes; at least when they're the good kind that he's obviously keeping.

It seems he really did take a shower, although apparently that was only part of the plan. Someone should have seriously warned me about this, because when I get my first look at him, framed in that bathroom doorway, my heart nearly slams its way right out of my chest.

Truth is, I've never seen Max in anything quite like this before. Instead of his usual loose cotton boxers, he's dressed out in skin-tight boxer briefs. Calvins, I think with an admiring glance, my gaze roving hungrily over the length of him.

The white cotton material covers him halfway down his thighs, and fits with the clingy perfection of a glove. In fact the underwear is molded so perfectly over his body, that every nuance is emphasized with maddening detail. His hard cock, the bulge of his balls, his rippling thigh muscles.

Damn, he's never affected me this strongly before, and I know it's not just because it's our wedding night, either. I mean, here I was in my dainty satin boxers, feeling like the shit. When all along he had this moment planned for me? I swear he's bound tight in something so masculine, it nearly brings me to my knees.

"Baby," I moan, as he urges me down onto the bed, onto my back. He's wearing a tank T-shirt that bunches within my hands, as he mounts me like a quick wildcat. Then I'm just lying beneath him, shaking a little, as I gaze up into his lovely eyes. Moody, quicksilver eyes.

"Don't fight it," he breathes against my cheek, lifting his hips, adjusting so that now I feel the decided ridge of his erection jutting right against my own.

My hands wander all over his body, but what I can't fight is my fascination with those damn briefs. Snug is an understatement; they fit him like a second skin, stretched tight over his hard ass, his thighs. They cling to him like he's some modern day Adonis; solid steel sheathed in velvet softness.

And to top it all off, the feisty devil worked double time in the weight room these past weeks, I'm sure of it now. I feel the evidence every place that I touch him.

"Gorgeous." I can't say another damn thing, as I stare into his eyes with a helpless sigh. "Mine." Well, apparently I can.

He leans up on his elbows, and brushes his thumb across my lower lip. "Yours," he whispers with a soft smile. "Definitely all yours, Hunter."

I've gone to bed with a man, of that there is no doubt; Maxwell Daniels is the one with the power in this room tonight. I'm with my husband, my partner. My love.

"These...these boxers," I stammer, tugging on his elastic waistband with my fingers.

"Wedding gift to you from Louisa and Veronica." I'll be damned. With studied grace, he moves his hips against mine, so that we're just nestled together. "You like them?" Somehow, the question is genuine and innocent. Doesn't he know his own beauty?

"Oh, yeah." I nod, swallowing hard, still just caressing his thighs and cupping him from behind. "I never knew you could look this hot."

The little hip movement intensifies at my words, and he leans low to kiss me. He's the one doing all the leading tonight, he's determined to take me completely.

"I wanted to turn you on. To look perfect for this night."

"Oh," I manage, a soft little sighing sound. Far more helpless than I meant, and he giggles sweetly in my ear. "You do," I gulp. "Look perfect, I mean."

"So do you," he promises, slipping one hand beneath my thigh, and drawing it up around him. "And feel perfect, too." He runs his palm along my bare leg, a strong caress that makes me feel unbelievably masculine and desirable. Especially the way his eyes never leave me as he does it.

"You have a body that just won't quit," he says, palming my chest with a hungry gesture. "Suppose I should thank Universal for that."

I laugh, and the sound comes out all gravelly and alpha male when I say, "Swing gang."

He narrows his eyes predatorily, and then our talking just ends, as he leans low and suddenly presses his lips to mine with one of his soul-slaying, unraveling kind of kisses. I'm all over, from that moment on. I'm lost thinking of him taking me again, this time in the soft confines of our bed.

But I need to do a little taking, too, I realize, as I feel him rocking against me with a furious motion. Maybe it's the rhythm, or maybe the taut material of his underwear, smooth beneath my fingertips, I don't know for sure.

But next thing I know, I've rolled him right off of me, and I've pinned him against the mattress, hard. I need to be back in charge here, I need to be the one with the power. But then I sit up, kneeling there between his legs, and he stares at me, panting softly.

"These are coming off," I growl, and I tear at the boxers, rolling them low down his hips. Damn, they don't even want to give an inch, and so my tugging gets really intense for a moment. His eyes drift shut, and he leans back into the pillow, and then I just peel them off of him.

Now he's staring at me again, through thick lashes, with wild, smoldering eyes. His smooth chest rises and falls with quick breaths, and I caress it with my palms. There's not a hair on that chest, and I realize that he waxed it just for me. And with that thought, I've just got to have my sweet little vixen.

I drape my body over his and we begin rocking frantically, our hard cocks pushing and warring against one another. I slip between his legs, and thrust hard.

Where's the goddamned lubricant? I don't even have time to think about it, I want him that bad. We can't stop moving, can't stop this fevered bucking, and for only a brief moment, I manage to break the kissing. I look around for the tube, but when I don't see it there on the bedside, I begin working at him again.

"Get me off," he whispers in my ear.

"Wh-what?" I ask, surprised as hell.

"Get me off and use that."

Holy shit, he's got to be kidding me. "It's what I want, Hunter." His voice is intense, focused.

"Maxwell, that might...hurt or..."

"It's what I've fantasized about. For tonight." He cups my face within his palm. "I wanted to take you first. Like I did. But then I wanted you to take me that way. Besides, I'm relaxed enough."

I bury my face against his shoulder, nodding, and wind my fingers between our abdomens. I feel the perfect length of him, and while working my hips, I begin to stroke him into a heated desperation.

Then I ease up, kneeling between his legs, and I can't deny that he's lovely, squirming beneath me in pleasure that way.

His eyes are closed, his mouth open with quiet pleas and words of pleasure. Talking nonstop, my sweet Maxwell. Talking and heading straight to heaven, thanks to my strong fingers.

His dusky eyes fly open, as his lips part. "Now!" he barks, a harsh sound, and I cover him with both hands.

"Oh, oh," he moans. He arches up against me, lifting his

hips, and the warmth of him spurts over my fingers.

I don't waste a moment, because I know that I can't, and I slather his warm seed all over my own erection, coating it completely. The sated, dreamy look in his eyes almost causes me to lose it then and there. Instead, with loving gentleness, I draw the muscled thighs up around my hips and push against his opening. Hard. Because the slippery warmth of him is drying against my skin already, and we don't have a moment to waste.

It feels different going in, not so smooth and easy as it normally does. But I'm mad with desire, knowing that it's his stuff that's made me wet this way.

For a moment, I wish I'd feel him harden against me again. But I don't, because he's just spent. Now he's helping me find my own way home right within his warm, tight walls.

His sweet hands knead my lower back, then cup me from behind, urging me onward as I give tender little thrusts. God, I don't want this to hurt him. Not tonight of all times.

"Feels...perfect," he whispers, nodding in encouragement and all my inhibitions vanish as he locks his hard calves around me.

His lovely eyes flutter open, and for a long moment I grow still within him. We just look at one another, and I stroke the damp hair along his nape.

It's one of those strangely hushed moments; I'm wedged tight inside of him, he's burning beneath me. But somehow, everything just fades other than the knowledge that we're joined as one.

I brush his bangs away from his forehead, and press a loving kiss there. Then, as gentle as I can be, I begin rocking against him. He works to meet my thrusts, giving urgent little lifts with his hips.

My husband, my lover, I think again with a shiver of pleasure. Mine, all mine.

Then it's just unstoppable, the tidal wave of release spiraling through my body. I'm shaking and dying a little, because I need him that bad.

When we're done, I know the truth. Max Daniels owns me now; he's seized my heart, my soul, my very body this night.

Like that minister said, it's a mystery when two become one this way.

It's just a mystery to me that I ever could have fought this. Thank God I finally stopped trying.

And thank God I knew my way home once I finally found it.

About the Author

To learn more about Cooper Davis, please visit www.CooperDavisbooks.com. Send an email to Cooper at Cooper@CooperDavisbooks.com or join her Yahoo! group to join in the fun with other readers as well as Cooper! http://groups.yahoo.com/group/CooperDavisBooksNewsletter/

GREAT CHEAP FUN

Discover eBooks!

THE FASTEST WAY TO GET THE HOTTEST NAMES

Get your favorite authors on your favorite reader, long before they're out in print! Ebooks from Samhain go wherever you go, and work with whatever you carry—Palm, PDF, Mobi, Kindle, nook, and more.

SAMHAIN
PUBLISHING

WWW.SAMHAINPUBLISHING.COM